2078: THE FALL

STHENOTYPE

Editing by Rose Allen
Cover art by Michael Allen

Special Edition 2025

ISBN 979-8-9923513-5-4

Published by SthenoType
Medford, NJ 08055
www.SthenoType.com

This book is dedicated to my family. We are always there for each other even when we don't agree. I couldn't ask for a better group of people to make a trip around the sun with every year.

Lima
Kokomo
Muncie
Ohio
Columbus
Fairmont
Morgantown
Dayton
Lancaster
Kettering
Washington
Cincinnati
Harrisonburg
Bloomington
Huntington
Charleston
West Virginia
Frankfort
Winchester
Lynchburg
Beckley
Kentucky
Lexington
Berea
Roanoke
Campbellsville
Somerset
Eden
Glasgow
Middlesborough
Winston Salem
Nashville
High Point
Cary
Tennessee
Asheville
Murfreesboro
Gastonia
Monroe
Chattanooga
Spartanburg
Dalton
Clemson
Greenville
Columbia
Huntsville
Gainesville
Athens
Marietta
Aiken
Orangeburg
Monroe
Oxford
Atlanta
Augusta
Leeds
Hoover
Macon
Opelika
Dublin
Statesboro
Vidalia
Columbus
Savannah
Hinesville
Troy
Albany
Douglas
Ozark
Moultrie
Brunswick
Enterprise
Valdosta
Kingsland
Crestview
Destin
Tallahassee
Pensacola
Palatka
Gainesville

Prologue

It had been nearly 35 years since CNAW, Conserving North America's Wildlife Act, became law in 2044. Conspiracy theorists now think it was the most brilliant political move in history. They believe CNAW was a CIA project that used intense research and social science modeling. Supposedly, the CIA bolstered the research with data collected through the social media giant Picture Page. Regardless of who designed it, the law began a cascade of events that were an unmitigated disaster.

Perceived threats to wildlife became inflamed on social media leading to a call for government action. Congress responded with CNAW. The federal government designated National Forests and undeveloped federal lands as Wilderness Areas. As hunting is illegal in Wilderness Areas, it became illegal in all National Forests. Congress then used huge monetary incentives to encourage states to convert their lands to wilderness areas too. Most states complied. Large game Wildlife populations responded, explosively.

With no hunting allowed on federal and most state-owned lands, a majority of the public continued to push for a ban on all guns. Three years later, they succeeded.

Within 10 years of CNAW becoming law, human-wildlife interactions became common. Within 20 years, the majority of those interactions were termed conflicts. This was due to the negative outcomes for the humans. As the third decade of CNAW came to a close, most citizens in the suburbs had moved to cities where they felt safe. The towers of Judge Dredd were becoming a reality.

Social media continued to play a major role in society. There was a call for the government to "do something" about the wildlife problem. The enlightened society was against killing for any reason. The only answer was to fence in the cities. The government built walls around all major cities and the citizens rejoiced.

The Silent Coup of the United States of America occurred only 34 years after CNAW became law in 2076. The coup led to the formation of the Social States of America (SSA). The SSA was the latest advancement in the new socialist world order. Imagine the citizens' surprise as social media was immediately regulated. Censors redacted all anti-government sentiment and shock troopers imprisoned the violators. True socialism had finally come to North America.

The People's Republic of China (PRC) helped establish the SSA. Despite that, they soon found their client state was not as well-behaved as planned. With the help of the PRC, it only took 6 months for the SSA to solidify its hold on the country. It was at that point that our new government showed its true colors. The government of the SSA began to threaten every other nation with nuclear strikes. Like other power-hungry governments before them, they demanded recognition and respect. The "arrogant dog" liked its new power and wanted more. The tariffs and economic sanctions that followed were "a strike at the sovereignty of our great nation" that "could not be tolerated".

A year later, in 2077 the world finally had the excuse to put Americans in their rightful place. Fortunately, they still lacked the will to do so. China did not lack such willpower. The only warning of the end came in a news conference stating the SSA's demands were "that of a petulant child". The PRC stated they "would no longer tolerate the primitive Americans' behavior in our civilized society". The bombs fell within the hour.

To show their humanitarian side, the PRC used high-altitude air burst nukes. Converted commercial airliners delivered the bombs, hiding in plain sight. The EMPs destroyed 97% of the SSA's power grid and 95% of all motor vehicles. The EMPs affected parts of Mexico and Canada, with sincere apologies from the PRC. Rumors flew about backroom payments from the PRC to Canada. Complaints from Mexico were ignored.

A week after the EMP attacks, the "petulant" SSA government attempted to retaliate. The PRC shot down the few planes in the attack and sent the plague. After the war between Russia and Ukraine, the world's industrialized nations lost their feeling of safety. They all began putting more effort into hardening their infrastructure. The rumors claim this to be the reason for the plague. It seems the PRC must have brought it into the SSA as a failsafe when they sent troops to help their new client state. No one is sure which was more devastating, the bombs or the plague. However, we're all sure of the result. North America became the land of nightmares.

Chapter 1 – Evasion (JC)

What the hell? I can't see. Those were my first thoughts when I woke up. I was seriously on the verge of panic! *Come on James, CALM DOWN*, I told myself. I wasn't sure how but I managed it, and when I did, it all came flooding back. I was in a road culvert, a freakin' culvert. WTF! How did my life get so screwed up? Oh yeah, greedy asshats in the government. Who'd a thunk?

Those dang Murdochs had been chasing me and I wasn't going to make it. I saw the pipe and had to take my chances. Those things are big and this pipe, well, not so much. In fact, I knew I was gonna get claustrophobic if I kept thinking about it, time to start working the problem. Dang if that wasn't a long culvert.

I thought it must be night for it to be that dark. Dear lord, how long had I been out? I knew how tired I was, and there was nothing to do but wait. I didn't really think I could have slept, not with all that scratching and grunting from the Murdochs. Just goes to show. Ya know I'm not really sure what it shows. I've always wondered about that saying. NOT NOW, brain. Damn, that thing likes to get off-topic. I needed to get this figured out and start moving.

Speaking of off-topic, I had no idea what happened to Mom and Jules. Mom had named her July. Let's be real though, no self-respecting teenage girl was going to put up with that nonsense. I smiled. She really did hate being called July. And there I go drifting off topic again. It was time to get to work!

Light wasn't an option until I could be sure I was alone. Dad always said you were a fool to jump before knowing what was below. He had a lot of jewels like that and loved to share them, with me, all the time.

I started to crawl forward, trying to be as quiet as I could. That was harder than you might think, with sand and rock scattered across the bottom of the steel culvert. It was pretty hard on me too, for that matter.

I was nearing the end of the culvert and I could have sworn I heard something. Naturally this is the point that I realize, you can't reach down and just grab a weapon when you're in a 20-inch pipe. So there I was, crawling headfirst towards God knows what and not even a toothpick to defend my honor. I felt like a push-pop just waiting to see what wanted to take a lick.

I crawled, well OK, fell out of the pipe onto rocks a few feet below. Not exactly graceful, but I made it without anything trying to bite my head off. I decided to consider that a win.

Sure enough, it was night, and a dark one at that. No moon, just starlight to see by. At least I could tell there was nothing within 15 or 20 feet. I could tell the Murdochs had given up and left, mostly because they weren't currently eating my spleen.

Damn, those things are vicious. I wasn't too worried at this point because they would have heard me crawling around, and since I'm not dead, well, once again, it was time to move. That seemed like all I did these days. Assess the surroundings and move my ass.

I found my pack on the other side of the road. Since I didn't have any food, the Murdochs ignored it. Thankfully, that meant it only looked like it belonged to a homeless beggar (instead of a dead homeless beggar). I even managed to backtrack and find where I dropped my M1 while trying to reload. I sure love that gun but damn I hate stripper clips! What I wouldn't have given for a good ole AK-47.

With my kit back together and me mostly in one piece, it was time to find a better place to rest.

Yeah, I know. I had just woken up. The problem is you don't travel at night if you don't have to. There are way too many things to stumble into in the dark, and none of them are good for your health.

Normally, I avoided roads. In this case, dark as it was, the road seemed like the best option. The one good thing about the EMPs was the stranded cars. They make pretty good shelters in a pinch and are usually unlocked. Few people bothered locking them once they realized they were dead.

I found an old Toyota Camry and climbed into the back to wait for daylight. It seemed to be getting colder, so it had to be late, maybe 3 or 4 AM. I knew it shouldn't be too long before first light. I should have just enough time for a quick nap.

Screeeeech.

"What the -" I mumbled before my brain could get control of my mouth. Stupid, stupid, stupid; that, my friend, is a good way to get killed. And what was that awful smell?

God, I must be tired. Only one thing smells that bad, Murdochs.

What is a Murdoch you ask? Well, that nasty little plague that hit us was a real bastard. It killed 37% of the US population in the first month. That was over 100 million people. That was a huge problem all by itself. Only about 10% of us were immune, say 30 million or thereabout.

Everyone else, well, it changed them. The flyers that dropped from the few working government aircraft said the virus was increasing metabolism, appetite, and aggression. At the same time, it lowered inhibitions to the point of a primitive ape. Couple this with all the instinctive traits of a threatened animal population, to feed and reproduce. These are what my family calls Murdochs.

Essentially, Murdochs are like pissed-off bodybuilders on extreme amounts of steroids. They're not real bright, they're super aggressive and most of them are pretty damn strong. There were definitely a few runts in the litter. Some people just don't have the genetics for even viral steroids to make much difference.

The one thing I didn't mention is an increased sense of smell or hearing. That's because they don't have one. Thank God. They may be strong as hell, fast, and want to kill everything that crosses their path, but they're not superhuman. No super smell. No super hearing. Just normal, everyday wild man cave dweller kind of primitive killing machines.

So there I was, laying in a damned Camry trying to stay still and not make a sound. My breath sounded like an industrial fan to me. The only saving grace was that the car still had all its windows, its closed windows. I thanked all that was holy that it was still dark.

The Murdochs use their long, thick nails like claws, and that one seemed to delight in scraping them along the car. I bet it worked great to scare prey from hiding. It definitely had me scared! As if that's not enough, he also had a club. Yep, they could still use primitive tools. Yippee.

I was lying on my back and could see the beast turn towards the back door. I gently slid my pistol from its holster and eased it into line with the window. With the safety off, I began to slowly squeeze the trigger.

A sudden wail from a little way off nearly caused me to fire. It seemed to startle the Murdoch too. It snorted loudly, almost in disgust, as it turned towards its companion's call and began to jog away.

I let out a long breath I hadn't even realized I'd been holding. Putting the gun back in its holster, I slowly sat up to be sure the Murdoch was gone.

Two encounters in one night? I couldn't decide if I'd angered the gods or had a guardian angel. Either way, that luck surely wouldn't hold.

After some consideration, I decided to stay put. Blundering around in the dark with roaming Murdochs is no bueno.

I didn't think I could sleep with everything that had happened, but sure enough, I drifted off. When my eyes opened this time, I saw the muted rays of first light.

"Now that's what I'm talking about!" I said it and immediately regretted the outburst. I have got to get control of that blunderbuss mouth of mine.

I raised my head slowly. Thankfully, there was no sign of movement. I decided to wait a little longer, then get a move on. I had a long hike ahead in enemy territory.

Every morning before we'd break camp, my mother picked a distant landmark where we could meet if we got separated. The current landmark was an old cell tower. It didn't seem far when we picked it. Now I swear I'd be lucky if I could get there before sunset. It was amazing how much further a few miles seemed when you didn't have a car.

Chapter 2 – June

I began my morning repack and started thinking about the raiders that caused us to separate. I had been scouting around a strip mall when I heard them coming. It was the biggest group I'd seen yet. Most are only 10 or 15 strong at best, but I bet there were at least 30 or more in that group. They seemed to have rigged up an old school bus and chopped the top down, so it resembled something more like a parade float. It looked like they could come off that thing like rats off a sinking ship. There was just no good way for me to get back to our old farm truck.

As they approached, I could faintly hear Mom start the truck and ease away. I was glad that Mom was always decisive and that we added the extra mufflers to the old beast. Dad used to always joke that it was his apocalypse truck. He never knew how right he was.

I had everything packed up. Now I just needed to find a spot for a PAPSMEAR, and I'd be on the move. Yes, I said PAPSMEAR. Don't blame me. It's Mom's acronym. Stands for Post Apocalyptic Poop – Scout, Mind your back, Excavate a hole, Annihilate the evidence, Recon the area. What can I say; she was a major in the Marines and left any self-consciousness behind decades ago. Besides, it was a handy reminder, and we quickly shortened it to P.A.P.S, at least among ourselves. Murdochs may not have superhuman noses, but they can smell, and so can other predators. We developed a good routine and to be honest, traveling with 3 girls, I was getting over the bashful shit pretty damn quick myself. We all were.

I hit the road a bit lighter and started looking for a good cross-country path towards the tower. I was ready for some food and didn't want to hit my only reserve granola bar if I could avoid it. Yeah, I know I said I didn't have food, but the bar doesn't count. It's a sealed backup bar that we kept for emergencies. I did not, in fact, have my food pack with me. I had dropped it per our standing operating procedure, as commanded by Major Mom. We left our food packs tied to the bottom of our ruck with a quick release to drop them as a distraction for Murdochs if we had to. It had worked yesterday, just not well enough. You can only distract a few Murdochs with a small food pack.

Pushing through a hedge, it looked like I'd entered a widely spaced housing development. It almost sounded like... shiiit, voices. In general, voices are bad. I stopped walking and eased over into the shadows of a holly bush. It seemed like someone must be a couple houses over. That really sucked. I wanted to skirt around it. To do that I had to know how many and where they were.

I stayed still for another 5 minutes, giving the birds time to resume chirping and me time to pinpoint the voices. They were definitely a few houses down from my bush.

I moved slowly through a shadowed drainage along the back of the houses. As I got closer, I saw several men crowded around something on the ground. One of them began to laugh as another bent down & I heard a high-pitched blood-curdling scream.

Now, I'm as brave as the next guy my age, and probably a little more so. Modest too, did I mention modest? Anyhow, I may be brave, but my mama didn't raise no fool. Running in to save the day sure would feel good. Unfortunately, it would probably get me and that girl dead. Great, another girl, that's all I needed.

Then my brain caught up and thought, oh crap, that better not be one of our girls! Damn, my brain was slow on the uptake sometimes. I had to get the show on the road.

They seemed to have nothing but eyes for that girl, so I picked up the pace just a bit. I still needed to scout around. If video games have taught me nothing else, it's that there is always another one waiting to shoot you in the back as soon as you rush in.

I made a full circuit and didn't see anyone in the shadows. Meanwhile, those screams had turned into the most pitiful whimpers. While I scouted, I'd been working on a plan, and I thought I had it figured about as well as I could.

I eased back around to a house behind and over one from that group of men. The garage was open and the door inside was unlocked. I eased upstairs, checking the house as I went. The last thing I wanted to do was get my throat ripped out by a Murdoch while trying to shoot a raider. Once I was upstairs, I found the open window I'd seen and used the sill for my gun rest. Then it was time to wait.

The tall goofy one with the big ears, I'll call him Dumbo, kept looking at the bald one (Curly) like Christmas had come and then he'd giggle. That goofy bastard was honestly giggling every time the third greasy little fucker would bend down and make that girl scream. When he stood back up, I saw the lighter in his hand. I damn near lost it then and there. Lucky for me, the major's voice was in my head saying "There's a time for everything JC and his time is coming. Just make it on your terms!" A bit calmer now, I waited.

Just as I'd seen 'em do several times before, Dumbo walked back to grin at Curly again. Dumbo lined himself up perfectly with that bald-domed bastard and I squeeze the trigger. That bullet took Dumbo through the right side of the chest and spun him away. Fortunately, that beautiful M1 packed enough punch to take Curly down behind him.

Shemp, because what else do you call a slime ball like that, dropped to the ground. Too bad for him, I was in an elevated position. With Dumbo's turn, Shemp probably thought I was in the house next door. There was a small shed in the back, and it would make the best place for cover from that direction. I steadied my gun and took several deep breaths. Just as he popped up to run, I squeezed the trigger for a second time. Only, he never even missed a step. I'd missed my damn shot!

Damn, damn, damn it, damn! Now that slick-haired bastard knew right where I was. He raised his rifle and fired two quick shots toward the house. Both missed by a mile, but instincts had me kissin' the floor and it gave him the time he needed.

I wasn't sure what his next move would be until I heard the kid scream. As I looked back through the window, he had her by the hair and was dragging her around the corner of the house. I heard a car door slam and a big engine turn over.

There was no way I could make it. By the time I got down the steps, he'd be long gone. I did the only thing I could. Praying that girl was on the floor, I started looking for my shot. I'd seen that car in the street when I was scouting, so I knew which way he should go if he drove straight away. I lined up

13

the space between the houses in my sights, right about where he should pass as he fled. When I heard him hit the gas, I began to squeeze.

That big old sedan began sliding past the gap between the houses. I lined up, finished squeezing the trigger, feeling the M1 buck in my hands.

I swung over to the next gap. I knew if I'd missed the first time, I would have a helluva time getting a second shot. Just as I thought he'd made it, I heard a huge crash. I jumped up and started running for the stairs.

When I rounded the houses into the street, I saw the car wedged into the back of a delivery truck. Slinging the rifle, I pulled my pistol. As I got closer, I didn't see any movement. The driver was still there, and there was blood running down his face. When I got up to the door, I heard him groan. That bastard was still alive. I missed again? Well, sorta. I'd grazed him. He must have had the luck of the Irish.

When I saw that girl crumpled in the floorboard, his luck ran out. I flipped into a rage and before I could stop, I'd shot him at least three times in the chest. He wouldn't be doing that shit to anyone again, much less a defenseless little girl. Even with the Murdochs out there everywhere, bastards like these were still the greatest threat to survivors.

I walked around the car and carefully pulled the kid out. I laid her on the sidewalk just a few feet away. She was covered in blood and dirt but still alive. I started with her head and began a full evaluation, just like Mom taught us. I looked for signs of head trauma, major cuts and broken bones. I felt down each arm and across her back and stomach. Despite how she looked, I couldn't find any obvious breaks or large cuts. She was still unconscious though, so I picked her up and began carrying her into the house they seemed to have been using.

After finding an old bed to lay the girl down on, I searched all 3 bodies for anything useful. The rifle Shemp had been carrying was an old Savage 270. It amazed me that the thing hadn't blown up in his face when he'd tried to shoot me. It looked like nobody had cleaned it since it was new, not that cleaning would have improved it much, it would still be a Wally World special. I did find a decent S&W .38 and ammunition for both guns. There were a few knives, all were junk. Probably came out of the same display case as the Savage.

The real find was the food. They had several boxes of canned goods and four of the newer MREs. It was a good thing I had packed light for scouting because I was surely gonna need that space for food. I packed up everything I could carry and went to check on my patient. She was still out so I resigned myself to carrying the damn girl. There was no way that car was going to be of any use after a crash like that.

I'm a tall rangy farm boy, but all that work throwin' hay, feed, fertilize, and the like had left me plenty strong. We'd been walking a couple of hours when I set the girl down for a rest. She stirred then, and when her eyes opened, I thought she was gonna try to rabbit. I held her ankle firmly and talked nice and calm, like I would to a wounded calf.

"You're safe. I'm not going to hurt you. Those men are not going to hurt you. We are far from them and they can't ever find you again. Now, I'm going to let go so that I can give you some water. Don't run. I have food and water. OK?"

15

She nodded and as soon as I let go, she jerked her leg away. Truth be told, she tried to bolt. It was just her body wasn't in on the plan. She fell facefirst, about two feet from where she started. I left her there and went over to the pack to get some water and the saltines from one of the MREs.

By the time I got back, she had turned over and warily took the food. I let her have a few sips of water and only a few crackers at first. I told her there would be more; we just needed to take it slow until I saw how she was doing.

"What's your name?" I asked. No response. "My name is James, but most people call me JC and some call me Jimmy. I wouldn't call them friends. You can call me JC." I said. "I'm going to put this pack back on and we'll head out. We're going to meet up with my family. Luckily for you, we got separated. I just happened to be strolling through when I heard you scream. Don't worry. We're good people and you'll be safe with us. Now, any chance you're gonna give me that name?"

She just shook her head. Well, that's progress, I thought. At least I know she understands me.

"Now, since you can't walk, I'm going to carry you. I'll be careful and I'm not going to hurt you, OK?"

I got the pack on and walked back over. She leaned away from me so I knelt down. Speaking soft and smooth I said, "Now, I've got to carry you. I'd let you walk but we've both seen that ain't gonna happen. Let me pick you up, OK? You can let me know when you need to get down or want to try walking. Until then, I've gotta carry you. Got it?"

She stiffened when I picked her up. After a few minutes of

16

walking, I felt her relax. We were making good time and I was glad of it because the sunset wasn't too far off. It must've been rolling on close to around 16:00 (that's 4 p.m. for you civilians). I needed to get up high and see if I could spy that tower again. My compass works great for direction, but I had no idea how far I'd come, especially carrying all that extra weight.

My little companion had fallen asleep as I walked. When I found a place to stop and get a good look around I woke her up.

"I'm going to climb up on the roof of that old house yonder and check our progress. You should be fine here and I'll be back in just a few minutes. You can yell if you need me." I told her.

I put her down at the base of a tree where she could see the house. As I walked away I heard a noise behind me. When I turned around she was gone. She couldn't have gone far and when I looked closer I could see a pair of eyes peeking out of the bushes next to the tree.

"Alright, that's probably a good idea. You stay hidden there and I'll be right back." I said.

I did a quick recon around the house. It looked like it had been abandoned for years. That wasn't too unusual for a remote house like this one. That in mind, I didn't spend too much time on it. The front porch had a small roof and I was able to scale the outside. Once on top, I made my way over to the chimney to help me blend in while I looked around. What I saw astounded me. We couldn't be more than a quarter mile from the tower.

It scared me to think of how fast I must have been moving over the last few hours. Fast is sloppy and noisy. Fast leaves big tracks. Fast is a good way to end up dead. Mom would be pissed if she found out! Best to just be sure she didn't then, right?

I had a slow look around before getting down. I broke the horizon into 8 sections and scanned each one for movement. When I saw nothing, I climbed down to go back and get June. June? Now where in Grandpa's left testicle did that come from? Dad was a bad influence, don't ask, I'm not really sure myself. My family must have a real hang-up on names beginning with J, and names of months for that matter. Anyhow, I found her right where I left her, glaring at me like I'd broken some solemn vow.

"Whaaat?" I ask innocently. She just glared.

"OK, so that took a little longer than expected but you could see me the whole time." As I said that, I looked up and saw that no, in fact, she could not see that side of the roof from her hiding spot.

"Oops." Now, I'm not sure how many of you have been the victim of a stare from a rabid badger with hemorrhoids, but that's the kind of vibe I was getting out of little June there.

"Damn, I'm sorry little one. I didn't realize you couldn't see me." OK, the "little one" comment probably didn't help based on the deepening of the scowl.

"Well, shit. I just can't get it right today. Look, I'm sorry. It's been a long day that started well before I was ready. Let's just chalk that one up to stupid James being, well, stupid, and go find the family. How 'bout it?"

The scowl seemed to; well not soften so much as relent to a steady glare. Good enough.

I shouldered my pack and reached over to June with an open hand. "It's about a ¼ mile to the meetin' spot. Feel like trying to walk or should I carry you the rest of the way." She gave me the universal two-handed "up" sign and I hauled her up. We started on again, slowly this time.

I picked my way carefully over to the tower. We'd been there nearly 20 minutes just scouting the place out and couldn't find any sign of the family. I had to admit that I was getting a little worried. I wouldn't be too surprised to not find anyone but we always leave a sign. We've done our best to disguise our marks as graffiti, like simple childish stuff that wouldn't stand out. A short message followed by the initials of who left it, the date with the year 77 (that way it would appear to be pre-war even though it looked new). Just a short tag that you'd see anywhere, something like this:

AHE16 JM 10-7-77

A simple message meaning James McKinney was here on October 7th Alone & Healthy. I will check back Every day at 16:00 (4 p.m.). FIO would mean Followed Injured will return every Other day. The first letter is your status: Alone, Followed, Hunted. Next is health: Healthy, Injured, Mortal wounds. The last letter is when you will return: Every day, every Other day, Weekly. We've never used that last one. If someone were on the run though, we might need it to avoid leading a hunter back to the group. Mom kept the system simple to remember and hard to figure out. It was just one more graffiti tag, nothing special.

But that's just it. There was nothing there and no tracks since the last rain. That was four days ago. It was a good thing I had little June over there to worry about or I'd be freakin' out. I usually don't stay near our meeting spots because they're obvious and easy to find. After carrying a full pack and June though, I was done in. I didn't have the energy to go farther. Besides, who the hell would bother going to a cell tower during the apocalypse? It would be pointless, right? They're everywhere and just another part of the landscape.

June and I, she still wouldn't tell me her name, did have enough sense to ease back into the bushes along the tower clearing. I opened up 2 cans of peaches I'd found in the stash from the men who were holding her. They were the best thing I've tasted all day! Don't know what it is about Georgia but we do love our peaches. I was damn glad too or those asshats might not have had any, and wouldn't that have been a travesty. We shared a canteen of water between us. I could barely keep my eyes open, though maybe I could make it 'til dark.

I woke with a small cold hand shaking my face. Yep, she grabbed my nose to shake me awake. I must not have been asleep long because the sun was starting to set. It couldn't have been later than 20:30. June's hand moved from my cheek to my lips and squeezed them shut. OK, something was close and she didn't want my loud mouth making any noise, got it.

I nodded slowly so she could tell I understood. I reached down to get my pistol and felt an empty holster. I was about to get real excited when I saw a small hand wrapped tightly around the butt of that big ole 1911. I used both hands to gently pry it away. Apparently, whatever was out there was very scary and June was taking no chances. June pointed toward the road and I heard what sounded like a heavy gate swinging open. It's then that the motor coughed to life.

At first, I thought of the family but the sound was all wrong. Well damn, me and my big mouth. Who would bother coming to a cell tower anyway? I'm beginning to think my sister Jules is right, big stupid jinx. I grabbed June's hand and we quietly moved farther back into the brush. Slow and smooth. We just needed to melt away. Even with the pack we made it into the deep shadows before they made it to the tower and found a nice little dip where we disappeared.

The racket those yahoos made went on for hours! I swear, it was a wonder they didn't attract every Murdoch in a 10-mile radius. Most of the noise died down around midnight and I could tell they'd got 'em a little hooch. There couldn't be more than half a dozen boys down there. You wouldn't know it since the noise level cranked up again as they drank more. Then they started into fightin'. I was really starting to wonder if I was ever gonna get another good night's sleep. Little June, on the other hand, had passed slam out again leaving me to wallow in my misery alone.

After a few hours, they too seemed to pass out and leave the rest of the world in peace. Amazingly, I still couldn't sleep. I was scared one of them might wake up and wander into us in the dark. That night crept by like a snail stalking his next meal. I'd jerk awake every time I was about to nod off, and twice I thought I heard something prowling around close by. I never could tell what it was, but I didn't think it was a Murdoch. Those things aren't usually smart enough to be wary of a pack of men. They just seem to attack and take their chances.

When morning came the morons packed their truck and

headed off to wherever they came from. Once I was sure they were gone, we eased back over to the tower. I felt like an idiot, again. The generator they had been there to steal the generator from the base of the cell tower. They busted the small building open, and wires were strung out everywhere.

"At least they weren't after us," I told June. She nodded and looked around in wonder at the state of the place. It surely was amazing how much destruction rednecks high on cheap liquor could do in one night. I was suddenly glad the whole gang wasn't there, assuming it was the same group. That could've been a hell of a mess.

Those idiots had left a small campfire burning after breakfast and I saw no reason we couldn't take advantage. I popped the top on a can of beans and tucked them into the coals. Once they heated up a might, I fished out my handy dandy foldin' utensils and gave June the spoon. I chuckled a little. June the spoon. Teehee. Yeah, I know, I never claimed to be Shakespeare. The stupidity of that one actually made me laugh. I took the fork, still smiling, and we tucked into a gourmet meal of baked beans for breakfast. June sat looking at me the whole time like I was a few marbles short of a full bag.

When we finished, I policed up our equipment and hid the pack in the shadows of the brush. June and I decided to have a look around. Well, I decided, and since she still wasn't talkin', she had to go along. At least June seemed up to walking. That, my friend, was real progress if you ask me.

There really wasn't too much left after the Wonder gang finished their rampage. I pulled together any wire I could easily salvage and a few other odds and ends. I even found a screwdriver left by some long-gone repairman or perhaps just a drunk idiot. Either way, it was mine now. I showed June that it could make a pretty effective weapon and she latched onto it. OK, not mine now. June's now. Ah well, easy come, easy go.

I was about to suggest we take a nice siesta in the shade by my pack when I heard the sweet song of our lady. She was purring up the road toward the tower and I thought I'd just about jump for joy.

Not completely overcome with stupidity and with June tugging on my hand, we disappeared into the brush.

"It's OK June, it's my family. We'll just stay hidden to be sure but I'd know that truck anywhere." I said. June looked at me a little funny. I realized I just called her June.

"Oh, the June thing. Well, I had to think of you as somebody. That name popped into my head and it's been stuck there. If you want something better, you're just gonna have to give me yours."

For the first time, I thought I saw a hint of a smile on June's face. I still didn't get a name.

The truck came up the road at a slow, steady pace. It was easy to tell that the driver and passengers were carefully examining the sides of the road and what lay ahead. The devastation of the night before had to be making them even more nervous. They crept through the gate and into the clearing near the base of the tower. I could see movement inside but still couldn't tell who was driving.

I took steady aim at the driver's door waiting for it to open. I was a little startled when I didn't see my mom step down

23

from the driver's seat. To my relief though, it was Jules, my little sister. How in the hell did Mom get desperate enough that she would let Jules drive? That made me even more wary and I began scanning the back of the truck. When I did, it was only when the tugging on my shirt became more persistent that I turned around. Instead of an annoyed little girl, I found a gun pointed at me and June about to wet herself in her frantic tugs for attention. The gun lowered almost immediately when I turned and I saw the brilliant smile of my best friend, Belle.

I groaned inwardly, knowing how much shit she was going to give me over her getting the drop on me. Her smile vanished though as her gaze landed on June.

"June," I said "this is my best friend Belle, short for Annabelle. Belle, this is--well to be honest I'm not exactly sure who she is."

"He" June whispered.

"What?!" I nearly shouted. As Belle began to laugh at my expression, June looked up at me with another defiant glare.

"I'm a he!" June said loudly.

"Well, ahh, I--I'm sorry?" By that time, Belle was in full-on fits of laughter. I sat stunned into a pole-axed statue of stupid and June was looking madder by the minute.

Belle finally managed, "He's really not always this stupid. Well, sorta", as another fit of laughter engulfed her.

Finally getting my brain to function again, I managed to close my mouth and stammer out another apology. Belle laughed herself out and June simmered down into a sullen silence

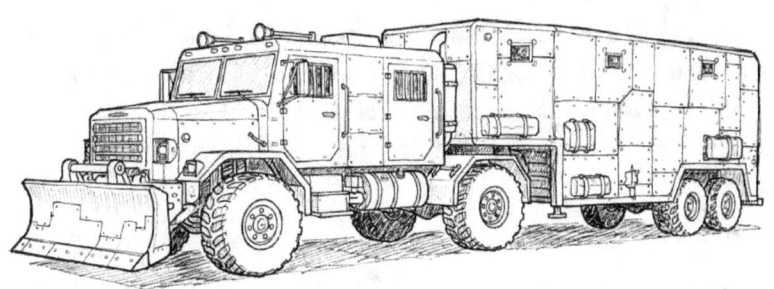

Chapter 3 – Meet the Family

It turned out that Mom was watching this whole scene play out through her scope. After scouting the area, she was fairly sure who was there. Mom was never one to take any chances though, especially since The Fall. She had sent a terrified but determined Jules up the road in the truck while our little clump of bushes was under her scope. Already knowing where we were, it was easy to send Belle down to come in behind me, 90 degrees from her line of fire. It was nicely planned and well executed and I still felt like an ass letting Belle get the drop on me. Here I was trying to be this girl's, I mean boy's, protector. While I'm watching the road, he has to practically rip my shirt off to make me notice the rifle pointed at my head. A real hero in the making huh, I thought disgustedly.

With the kind of attention this area was getting, Mom decided we should move on to a better campsite. I loaded my ruck and loot into the truck and helped my long-haired boy, June, into the back. I swear the long hair is what threw me. That's my story and I'm stickin' to it!

Our Sweet Lady, as Dad had named her, is a customized quad-cab M939 (it looks like a "deuce and a half" but hauls twice the weight). She has a sweet modified Cummings turbo diesel motor, and redundant exhaust to make her "whisper" quiet.

As I mentioned, Dad had always liked to say she was our apocalypse truck. Never have I wished he had been more wrong but sure am glad he wasn't. I had helped him quietly update the beast under Mom's nose, using cash for parts and pretending to work on the tractor. It turned out she knew all along. She actually liked the idea of having a capable all-terrain beast that was EMP-shielded and could burn just about any fuel oil out there. Mom found it immensely amusing to watch us sneaking around thinking we were pulling one over on her.

After The Fall in 2077, we began retrofitting the rig for true apocalypse travel. For more room, and to bring the horses, we customized our gooseneck horse trailer to haul behind. No, it probably wouldn't be DOT approved, and looks like the Beverly Hillbillies went to the rodeo, but it works. We armored everything the best we could. The customization required a lot of material. It didn't take long before we started cannibalizing farm equipment. Did you know that a belly pan of a dozer makes excellent armor? It truly is amazing how much steel is lying around a farm when you no longer care what you cut up.

The rear cargo area was just a bed when Dad died. We made a lot of changes in '77. We built a 500-gallon fresh water tank and nestled it between the frame rails. After the bed was reinstalled we added a custom, lightly armored cargo area. The front already had a 20,000 lb winch and we added an 8-foot dozer blade to help clear anything that got in our way. You could also raise the blade to act as armor for the grill when needed. We even went as far as adding armor over the top half of the tires with a curtain of logging chains hanging nearly to the ground.

The trailer was its own little bit of hell to adapt. For some reason, they were never made to haul the weight of plate armor. It had to be pulled off its original frame and combined with a 35-foot box trailer for a tractor-trailer. The original body was essentially sitting in a steel box with armored doors and shutters. The bonus to all that work came as improved clearance for off-road travel. With the new height, we needed a big ramp. We used heavy steel plate to make a combination ramp and "tombstone" armor plate on the rear. No sense bringing horses only to have some jackass shoot 'em through an aluminum door.

We had excellent cargo space, a 10 kw 3-phase diesel generator, storage batteries, a full-size refrigerator, sofa, flat screen TV, microwave, cooktop, separate commode, shower, fold-down bunks and space for four horses plus tack. It's a real mobile palace, if by palace you mean a utilitarian tiny house. All that and we were still packing stuff on anywhere we could find a spot. With the solar panels on the roofs, finding extra space for anything could be a real challenge.

Now I know you're thinking, a flat-screen TV after this giant EMP and WTF James, how the hell does that work? I really didn't understand it either until I found the copper mesh under the lining of the trunk where Mom had stored it all. The whole damn thing was a big Faraday cage tied into a grounding rod. Turns out Dad may have been an apocalypse freak but Mom was the true closet prepper. That's probably why she ended up in logistics. She told me I didn't know the half of it. I asked and she said it would have to wait because I needed to finish welding the new hitch on the trailer. That seems like a lifetime ago.

The whole thing had become more of Mrs. Frankenstein

than Our Sweet Lady. It only made sense to re-christen her the Franken Lady. Ugly as hell but she could sure get the job done.

Mom slammed the passenger door bringing me out of my daydream. I looked around to check if everyone was good to go and smiled at June. He seemed quite pleased to be seated between two pretty girls who kept checking him over and asking how he was doing.

"That boy's had a hard time. Despite that, I think he's going to be just fine." Mom observed with a Cheshire cat grin. I nodded and started backing the Franken Lady down into the road.

"Where we shootin' for tonight?" I ask as we began picking up speed. "We only left Americus four days ago and I already feel like we've been traveling a month. I'm beat."

"I know, honey. We won't travel long tonight. Just enough to clear out from all these idiots. We're near Geneva now. I'd say they're all coming out of Macon trying to scavenge the outlying communities. If you'll just drive for an hour, I'll start looking for a good hole to tuck into for the night."

We finally found a Dollar General that clearly had nothing left inside. The glass from the shattered doors lay strewn across the interior with the frames hanging limply from the hinges. The entire interior looked bare as the headlights cut across the space. There wasn't even any trash piled up. It was as if someone just loaded up the entire store and drove away. Which was probably exactly what happened, come to think of it.

I pulled into the grass behind the store, completely hiding us from view. As soon as I stopped, Mom jumped out to scout around while we waited in the truck. It was just faster that way and we were ready to roll if something went south. A tap on the window made me jump. "Holy crap JC! You nearly made me jump outta my skin. What are you so skittish for?" Belle admonished.

"Sorry, Belle. I dosed off. It's been a long couple of days." I mumbled sleepily. Clearing new campsites was nerve-racking work but I was almost too tired to care. The stress of the last 48 hours had left me totally exhausted.

I saw Mom waiting and opened the door. She climbed up and started giving orders. "Jules and Belle, stake the horses out while we still have a little light. June, come with me and we'll start supper. James, set up trip alarms at either end of the store and along that path into the woods. Let's get this done!" She barked.

"Oorah!" We all said in unison. I wasn't sure when that started. It just seemed to come naturally after a few days on the road.

Once we had the perimeter established and the horses staked out, we all piled into the trailer to see what was for supper. Mom immediately kicked me back out to keep watch. "James, you know better! Set the example and get out there on watch."

Jules didn't manage to hide her smirk very well and was rewarded when Mom caught her. "And you, my dear daughter, can have 3rd watch since his misery is so amusing to you."

"Mom! I hate 3rd watch. It's too quiet, it's like everything has died. So, so spooky." Jules whined.

Mom completed the assignments with "Belle, you can have the first watch after supper. I don't think James is going to last very long tonight."

"Yes, ma'am"

As usual, 6 a.m. came way too soon. Since everyone else stood watch, I made breakfast. I was in a good mood and made the command decision to break out some bacon and eggs. We had around 15 chickens in a coop I'd built into the old hitch during the trailer retrofit. We kept them locked in but it was a pain finding a balance between fresh air and protection for them. We did a trial run before we left and lost half a dozen before we found a decent balance. It sure was nice having fresh eggs, though.

The coffee was a scarce resource, and we were extremely concerned about how we could resupply. Frankly, I was up for invading Atlanta if we ran out. I thought it would only take a couple days without it to convince Mom that wholesale slaughter was a real option on that one. If we could lay in a stock of cocoa powder too, I knew I could get everyone on board.

Once I had breakfast ready, I fixed plates for me and Jules. I found her perched on the Franken Lady's roof. I handed the plates up before I climbed up to join her. "Rough morning?" I asked.

"Quiet as the dead, at least 'til around 5. Then everything started waking up. I'm not sure which is worse. The quiet or the scattered noises after that much quiet. It's why I hate 3rd watch so much."

"Yeah, it sucks. I used to love it when I was hunting and I didn't have Murdochs and Raiders to watch for. It used to be my favorite part of the day. Now it just sucks. The Fall ruined most things."

"I hate it. I've got nobody. You have Belle while I'm stuck with nobody!"

"I wouldn't say I've got Belle, but I get what you mean. Still, you've got me and Mom."

"Whatever. I mean nobody my age! And no prospects of a boy, much less a decent one. Heck, the only two I know now are my older brother and now a kid half my age. I was supposed to be a Freshman this year JC. I was supposed to have all of high school to date boys. I was supposed to go on a date with David. This sucks!"

"Ummm…." Great, James, real intelligent response, empathetic too. Damn, you're good.

"And the worst part is that they killed Dad!" Jules burst into tears. At least this time my instincts took over and I didn't have to rely on my brain. I pulled Jules into a hug and she balled even harder.

"I know, Jules. I miss him too."

Dad hadn't been lucky enough to die outright. He turned into a Murdoch. It seemed to take him a little longer than some. Mom claimed that was because he had so much to fight for and I guess she's right. Unfortunately, that was one battle he just couldn't win. In the end, it was Mom who shot him. I don't understand how she did it. She is a badass, but still. Afterward, she buried him under the big white oak by the house. She didn't say a word for a week. When she finally did, it was like he had died in a car crash or something and she just moved on. I'm not really sure how I feel about all that.

We stayed like that for a long time. My great morning breakfast was cold, in a lot of ways. We ate it together and that seemed to help. I told Jules to go in and take a break. I'd go check on the horses and keep watch. Jules thanked me, grabbed the plates and disappeared into the trailer. By the time I stuck my head back in, everyone was up and making plans. Mom had decided we needed to stand down and regroup today. The last couple of days were tough and it would be good to take a break. She also needed to debrief me and review our travel plans.

We loaded up and moved over to a nearby lake that Mom found on her map. It looked like an old private pond. There was a good place for the horses to graze and plenty of water. Being off the main road and farther from town meant we had less chance to run into trouble.

During my debriefing, I was blessed with a wonderful lecture about attempting headshots. Apparently, I should know by now that I was only an average shot and there was no excuse for getting fancy when it was a matter of life and death.

I had only redeemed myself, somewhat, by having taken the time to search the bodies and look for supplies. That was certainly minimized by the fact that "any moron would know to look for supplies". Mom was still a bit on edge about the entire ordeal. For once in my life I kept my mouth shut.

It turned out that the rest of the group had managed to slip away unnoticed and circled around towards the cell tower immediately. It was the raider group that scavenged the generator keeping them away for so long. A small contingent of the group had been assigned to block the road, looking to stop anyone who came along. Apparently, they got bored and one of them had the brilliant idea of looting the generator to trade it back in Macon. Mom hid the Lady, gave them time to get on with it, and came on in once she heard the truck leave.

As we wrapped up our debriefing, Mom promised to talk to June and see if she could get his story and his name. She thought that perhaps being my mom and having given him time to see who we were might help.

The break was good for us all. We even took time to go swimming, once we proved to Jules there were no moccasins in the pond. That girl is deathly afraid of moccasins. She will happily stand up to a Murdoch with nothing but a baseball bat, then run screaming from a moccasin if it comes within 50 feet. Go figure.

We had a picnic that afternoon, enjoying the fine weather and everyone told funny stories from before The Fall. For some reason, most of them seemed to center around my misfortune. June even got in on the act with a story about his cat and a peanut butter jar it stuck its head into. The cat ran around bumping into things until he caught it. The more he told us, the more he laughed, and the more he laughed, the more we laughed at him. By the end, I don't think anyone had a clue what he was saying and absolutely nobody cared. It was the most fun I'd had in a long time.

As the sun was setting, we pulled the horses in close and Mom set out the watch schedule. Being back to four on watch made it easier on everyone. It was a quiet, peaceful night with a clear sky and the thinnest sliver of moon peaking back. It all seemed too good to be true.

The next morning was a flurry of activity as we loaded up. No one had time for more than shoveling down a few quick bites before getting on the road. Mom took shotgun again, an actual armament as well as a seat position in this case. She seemed uneasy for some reason, and I think it was spreading as everyone was silent by the time the wheels started rolling.

The original plan was to move up the main highways but stay away from any big cities. Our initial days of travel helped us to decide the back roads were far safer. Even Albany was a nightmare to navigate around.

We made it about 3 hours before we came to an enormous tree across the road. We were as nervous as cats on a hot tin roof, getting turned around but never saw anything. We started trying to work our way around an alternate route and found another blocked road. Only this time, it was more like a dozen trees, all cut. By lunchtime, it was obvious that we were being funneled towards something. Hmmm, wonder what that could be?

We stopped in a long straightaway and started getting ready for war. We double-checked all compartments and closed the armor for the windows. Our Franken truck looked more like a Franken tank. With that done, guns were checked and ammo was laid out close to hand. We rolled down the windows despite the shields. It would keep them intact and allow the passengers to shoot out. With all other paths blocked, we drove on towards Douglasville and Atlanta, ready for a fight.

The attack was not the sudden rush we expected. We came around a turn to find 2 Humvees and a black pickup blocking the road. As soon as we stopped, another Humvee pulled in behind our lady. These guys must have raided an armory, but they were about as military as the average movie star. Plenty of swagger, as though that was a military thing. Mom actually started laughing. She said an old lady and a couple kids could wipe out this whole F'n bunch.

"Hey, you in there, this is Captain Lewis with--"

"Lieutenant."

"What?"

"Lieutenant, you dumbass!"

"Excuse me? I'm Captain Lewis with the--"

"No"

"No, what?"

"You're not a captain and you're sure as hell not with anyone, well, other than these other pendejos. Those bars on your uniform, they're for a lieutenant you dumbass"

"Look, lady."

"Clare."

"Look, Clare."

"Oh, that's not my name, I just wanted to see if your dumbass would say, Lady Clare."

"Lady Clare?" At this point, Jules was laughing uncontrollably and you could tell Captain Dumbass could hear her by the crimson color of his face.

"How many are you up to?" Mom asked quietly.

"9 confirmed including Captain Dumbass. I'd round it to an

even dozen just to be safe."

"Good call, James." High praise indeed from Mom.

"Look, just move your toys out of the road and we'll let you live," Mom called out. Poor Captain Dumbass. He just didn't know when to give up.

"Earmuffs & pick a bandit." She said quietly to us.

"James calls the tall dipshit in the t-shirt at 10." I replied.

"Belle has glasses at 9."

"Jules has rolled sleeves at 3."

"And I have our dear captain." The call only took a few seconds as safety's clicked off.

"Last chance. Move your trucks now!" Mom called out this time with all the authority of a real Marine. I'll give the lieutenant captain credit, if he had as much brains as balls, he might have made general. As it was, he wasn't even going to make the evening meal.

"Now lady, playtime is over. Just bring the kids out, we'll take the truck and I promise you'll live." The group around us chuckled darkly. Mom's reply was a single word.

"Fire."

The "Captain's" head exploded as a 12-gauge slug treated it like a melon on Hickock's range. The other 3 men died a second later with bullets through their chests. They never had a clue what was coming until they were lying face up, staring at the clouds. I dropped my rifle into the scabbard by my seat and popped the clutch.

Our Franken Lady may be slow, but she surely makes up for it with brute force torque. The truck in front slid back into the front of the Humvees as though a child was pushing a matchbox car. Both hummers slammed into the men hiding behind them, causing screaming to chorus through the afternoon sky.

We accelerated up the road, leaving the detritus of decimated trucks scattered along the ditch. I started to look back, only to have Mom yell at me to keep my eyes on the road.

"Looks like there were 2 in the woods. We got 6 or 7 expectant. Count on 5 more and they are Oscar Mike." (on the move)

"Copy."

"I'm popping the hatch," Mom said as she opened the custom roof hatch. She called for Belle's M4 and I knew things were about to get ugly for our pursuers.

"Steady." she called and I eased the Lady into a nice, easy gait. Just after that, I heard the crack of the M4. I caught motion in the driver's side mirror as a Humvee veered into the woods. The M4 came back down through the hatch and Mom settled into her seat again.

"Well, those posers were totally Whiskey Delta".

June looked confused and I heard Belle say, "Don't worry about it. She drops back into military slang when the adrenaline gets pumping and she's having fun. She just means they were weak. She's a Marine and it's a habit. You'll start to pick it up after a while."

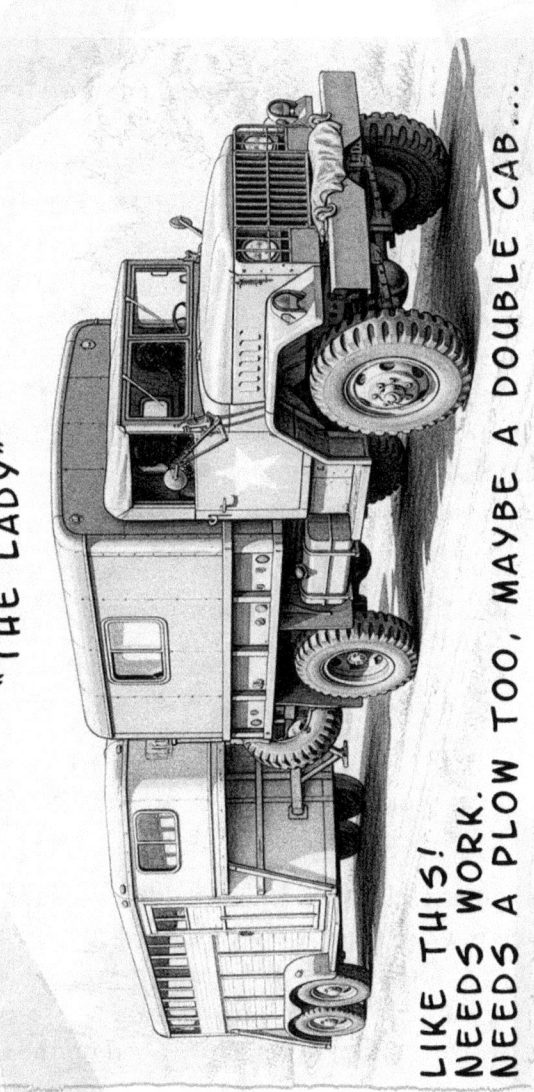

"THE LADY"

LIKE THIS!
NEEDS WORK.
NEEDS A PLOW TOO, MAYBE A DOUBLE CAB....

DAD'S ORIGINAL
CONCEPT - 2075

Chapter 4 – The Burbs

We continued on up the road, nerves and tension building with each mile we traveled closer to Atlanta. A big city was the absolute last place we wanted to go. Every time we hoped to turn west, there was something blocking the road, keeping us on Highway 5. We were talking about turning around to backtrack when it happened. The distraction of our discussion may be why I missed it. It was Mom's shouted warning that made me slam on the brakes. Unfortunately, our rig does many things, but stopping on a dime is not one of them. The homemade spike strip caught both front tires and they immediately started going flat. By the time I had us stopped, we were in big trouble.

"Looks like that dumbass Lewis let someone get around him again", came a voice from the woods.

"Well, they ain't going to have a repeat performance." Came the reply with a chuckle from the opposite side. We were well and truly hooped.

"This is a Charlie Foxtrot," Mom whispered to herself. "Just stay calm and let's see what happens."

"Hey, you in the truck, we're going to do this nice and easy. You're going to get out real slow with hands where we can see them. Leave your guns, knives, fingernail files and any other damn thing you think you might want to use as a weapon in the truck. If you don't, my friend up the road who just stepped out with that LAW rocket, is going to give you a really bad end to a really shitty year. Got it?" As he said it, a figure stepped out of the woods with a long tube in his hand. Mom raised her binoculars and confirmed it.

"Damn, we're fucked. That's a LAW alright."

"And don't try to shoot Sam up there. He's an ass but I kinda like him. Besides, we've got more rockets and if you shoot Sam, we're just gonna blow ya up. Of course, I do like blowin' shit up so I guess it really is a win/win for me!"

There was a long pause while we all turned to Mom, absolutely terrified.

"We'll get through this. For now, we'll have to do what they say. Remember what I've taught you and everything we've prepared. We will get through this and they will regret it. I promise you that." Mom said quietly to us.

"Alright, we're coming out. These are just a bunch of kids, so take it easy." She added in a louder voice to the raiders.

"One at a time!" the voice called back. It began to dawn on me that this guy was calm. There was no bravado like Lieutenant Captain Dumbass. Just a confident calm, as if this was everyday business. I understood why Mom was so willing to comply with this one when she had been so quick to fight the last guy. This man knew what he was doing.

Mom placed her Benelli on the floor and opened the door slowly. She let it open all the way and turned to face the woods. That way they could see she had no weapons. She then turned and very slowly climbed down out of the truck.

"Very good. Now walk halfway to the woods, lie down on the ground, and stretch your arm and legs out like a big ole X. That's right. Perfect. You stay just like that until we come to

41

get you. Passenger side back door next, please."

We followed Mom's example and made an orderly exit. June had the most trouble, both because of his size and the fact that he was shaking so badly that he nearly fell out of the truck. I don't think any of the rest of us were doing a whole lot better, if I'm honest.

Once we were all prone, they started to filter out of the trees. This time, only 5 men and one woman came out. Less than half the number of the last group and they took us down without a shot. It was an eye-opening and terrifying experience.

"Well, well, well. This is quite the haul. Three beautiful ladies and a good, strong back. The boss will be well pleased. I can't wait to see what else they brought us. Not sure I see much use for the kid though."

"Want for me to just shoot 'em. One less to deal with," said the woman.

"Not yet. You and David take 'em one at a time and put 'em in the cages. We'll let the boss decide. He'll like that, although I suspect you're right and he'll just kill that one anyway. Make good bait for the Zoombies."

"Whatever you say, boss."

"And Sue, keep that lady separate. I don't want them getting any ideas, and she looks like a tough one"

"If you say so, but I don't think she looks all that tough. Gave up pretty easy, didn't she?"

"Yes. And that worries me a bit. Check her out good. No weapons, you hear?"

"I know! Damn, you're like a mother hen sometimes."

Sue and a big burly guy they called Bear walked over with rifles pointed at Mom and told her to get up slowly. They stripped us down to our underwear and put us one by one into cages on a trailer. Then dumped our clothes into a trash can on the front. Mom and I were both put into what looked like big dog kennels while Belle, Jules and June were put into one large cage. It looked like a bunch of hog panels they had bolted together with cable clamps; simple but effective.

The leader, I heard them call him Chuck, looked over the Franken Lady then came over to the cages looking like Christmas had come early.

"Well, I can't tell y'all how much I appreciate you bringing me this rig. I should be able to talk the boss into lettin' me use it as my new outpost. Those horses will make some good eatin' too."

"No!" Jules screamed.

"Oh, don't you worry sweet girl. You're going to have plenty to keep your mind off them horses."

"Touch those girls and you will die," Mom told him with a growl in her voice.

"Now, now, settle down, Sweetie. You've got your own problems to worry about. If I don't miss my guess, the boss will just sell you to DFW in Atlanta. You'll fetch a fine price. Load up, everyone. Sam, you stay here and put out some more spikes just in case we get more visitors. I'll make sure you're rewarded for missin' the party."

"Should we send someone to check on Lewis?"

"Fuck him. Either he's fine and will drag ass in or he got what he deserved and he's dead. No need us wastin' fuel on him. Now, let's get these tires changed for those spares and get moving."

It didn't take long for them to get our spare tires on despite the size & weight. That Bear fella was an ox and every bit as strong as he looked. The trucks started up with Chuck driving the Franken Lady. It wasn't hard to tell he didn't have much experience with a straight drive, but he managed somehow. The horses would be terrified, but that was the least of our problems. At least Georgia in September isn't cold so we wouldn't have to worry about frostbite riding in open cages on the trailer.

The drive was shorter than I expected. We must have been in Douglasville or somewhere close to it. We pulled into an old Home Depot. Driving through reinforced gates into what had once been the garden center, it was easy to tell this was no small group of 10 or 15 people. What's more, nearly everyone here seemed to be wearing Georgia National Guard uniforms. It looked like they had a good time helping themselves to the armory in town.

It was no surprise that the Franken Lady caused quite a stir when she pulled through the gates. People poured out of the building to check her out. I counted at least 47, but they kept milling around so it was hard to be sure. They were all walking around the truck and chattering non-stop. Sounded like a bunch of 5th graders at a big assembly.

The entire crowd grew quiet as a monster of a man walked out into the afternoon sun. His gaze fell on the cages and he grinned. As Chuck climbed down out of the lady, he walked over and clasped his arms like they were in some damn movie like Sparta.

"Well done, Chuck. Well done indeed." The big man growled.

"Thank you, sir."

"This calls for a celebration, but first let's see what you brought me in those cages."

We were all hauled out and lined up for the boss's inspection. He came to Mom first.

"A fine woman, but looks like trouble. Set a sale with DFW."

He came to me next and looked at me with surprising curiosity.

"That's a fine truck there, boy. Did you build it?"

"Yes."

"Yes, sir, boy. Show some respect to your betters. Or would you prefer to spend some time letting Bear educate you on how things work here?"

"Yes, sir!" I practically spit the words at him.

"Better, but we'll need to work on that tone." His hand shot out so fast I can't remember seeing it move. I certainly remember it hitting me in the stomach, though. I fell to the ground, gasping for breath. He moved on to Belle beside me.

"Well, now, by your darker skin, I'm assuming you're not part of the family. What's your story, beautiful?"

"She's my wife." I gasped.

"Well, now. Isn't that sweet? You be nice and work real hard hubby, and we might even let you have a turn."

Jules stood defiantly beside Belle, grasping her hand. A terrified June latched around her waist.

"Oh, now you are special. I think I'll keep you for myself. And is this your little brother?"

"Yes... sir." Jules replied in that petulant way that only a teenage girl can manage.

"Well, that's nice. I think he'll make a fine servant. You need to understand something, my dear girl. You two are going to depend on each other. If either of you fail to please me, I will torture the other while the offender watches. Displease me enough and you will both die. Understand?"

Jules blanched and swayed on her feet as though she might faint. All of her earlier defiance seemed to vanish in an instant. The boss strolled back up the line, and as he came to Belle, he reached an arm out around her waist, pulling her to him. My lunge at his throat ended in gales of laughter fading quickly to black.

Chapter 5 – Garden Center

It was nearly evening when I woke up. I was back in my kennel with Mom in the one beside me. I glanced at the cage and saw the others there. Jules was in a pink lace body suit like she had just stepped out of an adult store in Atlanta.

I learned later that Sue had made her put it on for her "big night" with the boss. When Jules complained about it being too small, Sue slapped her hard enough to leave a handprint across her cheek. When he saw Jules, the boss turned around and punched Sue, breaking her nose in spectacular fashion. It seemed that rather than being mad at the boss, Sue was now swearing to kill Jules at the first opportunity.

I could smell cooking meat on several grills at the back of the garden area. My stomach growled despite our desperate situation. While the tempting smell of food seemed to pull everyone's attention in that direction, Mom leaned closer to me and started talking fast.

"James, this is everything we feared. It's going to be up to you to free the girls if we can't find a way out of here tonight. They told me I would get to meet my new owners tomorrow. If you get the chance, use your legs to force open the end of your kennel. You're on the end so you should be able to manage it. I will be looking for every opportunity to cause a distraction. You must get the girls away from here. These men will use them until there is nothing left and then kill them. I'm counting on you, James."

Great, at least there is no pressure. Just perform a miracle,

47

James. You got this. Fuuuuck.

Mom had barely finished when they came for Jules. She was openly crying at this point and tried to hold onto the cage until one of her captors reached over and punched June in the stomach. Jules' cries turned to screams of desperation as she let go in shock while June crumpled to the floor. They escorted Belle out just after Jules. Mom was apocalyptic with impotent rage, her fists clenched so tight every knuckle was white. I began to fall into despair.

"Pull your head out of your ass and start working on a way out. We don't have time for your pity party, James!" Mom hissed with rage.

I had never heard Mom that mad, especially at me. It worked though and I started thinking about how to get out of here.

They took Jules to the offices where the boss had set up his quarters. They handcuffed her to the bed and left her like a mint on his pillow.

Belle, on the other hand, was brought to a stage where they put her in what appeared to be a stripper cage looted from a local bar. They told her to dance when the music started, or they'd bring her husband up and just beat on him for entertainment. She said the women were worse than the men, reaching in grabbing at her and taunting her continuously.

After about an hour, the boss came on stage and made a short speech about how bad deeds and good work bring such wonderful rewards. He called Chuck up to the stage and told everyone that for his dedication and good work, Chuck would be amply rewarded. He would get to keep the new truck as his mobile outpost and could test out the new living quarters with the "tasty morsel in the stage cage". This was followed by whoops and catcalls by the drunken crowd. He wound up his speech with, "Well, it looks like the grub is finally ready. Dig in y'all!" Cheers erupted from the crowd. I could hear every syllable over the amplified speakers and felt like I was going to be sick.

Chapter 6 – Chuck's Prize (Belle)

Chuck immediately went after his prize and dragged me back to the camper. He handcuffed me to a bunk and went back for food. While he was gone, I began working out the thick, stiff wires I had sewn into my bra. I tossed one over to the side of the bunk Chuck had folded down and tucked the other down my leg, held in place by my panties. When Chuck returned, he was simply delighted to see me standing there with no bra.

"Well, I see you're bored with that boy husband and looking for something new with a real man. I guess the food can wait."

He came quickly over and unlocked the handcuffs, pushing me roughly towards the middle of the bunk. I reached up and pulled him into a kiss, surprising him and guaranteeing he thought he had won the lottery.

Chuck responded in kind, then suddenly felt a sharp pain in his temple and tried to jerk away, but I was having none of that. I clutched him to me with inhuman strength born of desperation, my legs wrapped tightly around his back. Meanwhile, my hand gripping the wire worked back and forth, making sure this was the last time Chuck came close to winning any lottery. As soon as he hit the floor, I pulled the knife from his scabbard and slid it into his spine just like Ms. McKinney had shown us. He barely knew what had happened.

I stared at him, feeling nauseous, but took comfort in

knowing what would have happened to me if Chuck had his way. Then I thought of Jules and sprang back into action.

Chuck's reward helped in several ways. I was now alone, free and back in my own quarters. I dressed quickly and pulled out the two hidden pistols. With Chuck's rifle and knife, I was at least ready to go down fighting.

I quickly searched Chuck for anything else useful and found a set of keys and an FRS radio. Unsure how they found any working, I decided that it was something to think about later and just tucked the radio into my vest.

I pulled off Chuck's shirt and finally managed to get him into the bunk. Once there, I used the pillow to make a long lumpy shape beside him and covered it and most of him with a sheet. I stepped back to look at my work from the door. I smiled to myself. In a dark trailer, you could easily mistake it for two sleeping people.

I eased open the door and peeked out into the dark lot. Everyone seemed to be inside enjoying the party, except for a single guard by the cages. I slipped out and worked my way over to the main gates. Using Chuck's keys, I unlocked them, getting ready for our escape. To be sure the gates would open easily, I pulled them slightly ajar, leaving them mostly closed. That way you wouldn't notice from a distance.

With that done, I moved back along the fence towards the cages. I wasn't sure what to do about the guard. Sure, Ms. McKinney had taught me to shoot and everyone here deserved all the violence I could visit upon them, but I needed to do this quietly. I was no soldier, just a farm girl from South Georgia.

Lost in thought about what to do, I walked down the fence line and I stepped on an unseen pipe. I hit the ground on my back with a whump. The air rushed out of my lungs and I struggled for breath as footsteps came running in my direction. The flashlight beam seemed like a spotlight as it lit up the fence behind me. As quietly as possible, I rolled onto my stomach and began to crawl away.

The guard was wary as he came around the cages towards the fence. He had definitely looked like he heard something. He had to hate being alone on guard duty. Even inside the fence, you couldn't believe you were really safe from the Zoombies, as they called them. I mean, those damn things were fast and by now everyone had seen a few that could climb almost as well as they could run. Guess that's why their boss called them Zoombies.

The guard at least seemed happy to have a gun-mounted tac-light based on his grin as he swung it around. His 12-gauge would make short work of anything that made it over the fence. To him, that had to be exactly what it sounded like, something dropping down over the fence. He raised his radio to call for backup when his world went black.

I stood over the guard with that damn pipe in my hand. I had been crawling away when my hand landed on it, nearly pushing it across the ground. That would have been the icing on the cake. First to trip on it, then to knock the damn pipe across the concrete; yeah that would have been brilliant. With all the noise it would have made, I may as well have stood up and shouted "Hey, over here, I'm over here". Luck was on my side this time though, and I managed to slide my hand across the concrete to stop its roll. It left a nasty bit of road rash and it was worth every painful second.

The guard was so intent on the fence that I had no problem sneaking up behind him once he walked past. My only surprise was how loud the impact was when I brought the pipe down on his skull. I shuddered as I remembered that sound.

I hurried quietly over to the cages. I tried to open Ms. McKinney's cage when I saw the lock. Pulling out Chuck's keys I began trying them one at a time. My hands were shaking making it take twice as long.

"Easy, Belle. Take it nice and easy. You've got plenty of time." Ms. McKinney said in a soothing voice. Just then, the radio crackle to life.

"You done yet, Chuck? The rest of us want a turn." I froze.

"It's OK, Belle." Ms. McKinney coached me, "Just hold the radio up to James and he can say he's busy. You can do that. James, try to imitate Chuck the best you can." My hand darted to my vest and I yanked out the radio, nearly dropping it. I recovered quickly and held it up to JC's cage.

"Busy. Fuck Off!" JC said in a passable mumble of Chuck's voice. We heard a howl of laughter from inside the building.

"Come on, buddy. She needs a real man. Surely you've finished up by now."

"Fuck Off!" was JC's only reply. It seemed to be the right one though, because another howl of laughter was the end of the radio traffic.

Of course, I lost my place with the keys and had to start over. Getting through that little drama seemed to have relaxed me a little. My hands had nearly stopped shaking, and it took much less time to sort through the keys the second time around. In what seemed like only a few seconds, I found the right key.

Ms. McKinney practically burst out of the kennel. With the look on her face, I was immensely glad I wasn't one of those men.

Of course, the lock on JC's cage used a different key. No wonder there were so damned many keys. While I found the right key, Ms. McKinney began pulling clothes out of the trash can and putting hers back on. She sorted the rest as she came across them. By the time JC was out of the cage, Ms. McKinney was retrieving her shotgun from the truck. She had apparently grabbed my M4 as well. She handed it to JC along with 2 spare mags.

"I know you love that M1 but we don't have time for fucking stripper clips. Use Belle's M4." She ordered.

I turned to the big cage to get June out before I realized he wasn't there.

"They came for him right after they took you", JC explained when he saw my lost look. "Something about ensuring the boss had his handmaid to serve him for the feast."

"Belle, I want you and James to disable their trucks. Sabotage if you can, the flashier the better. They probably have fuel stored along that back fence. I've seen what you two can do. Get on it, and don't forget to watch your back. One stands guard while the other works. Got it?"

"Yes, ma'am!"

"I'm going after the other two. As soon as you finish with the trucks, get the Lady ready to travel. Wait to start her but I want you in that truck ready to haul ass when I get back."

"Yes, ma'am."

"And James, remember to shoot for the chest. No fancy shit, just good clean shots center mass."

Ms. McKinney pulled down her balaclava and disappeared into the dark.

"Your Mom is scary pissed." I said, my voice quavering.

"I know, so let's not disappoint her, shall we?" JC replied.

"Yeah, no doubt!"

JC and I headed to the back fence and found the fuel. They had a few drums of gas and one of those short tankers nearly full of diesel. JC began filling empty beer bottles with gas and told me to open the valve on the big diesel tank. The fuel was running off the side towards the fence. That was no good I had an idea and pulled the hose off the reel in back, flipped the switch for the electric pump, and started spraying fuel under each truck.

As soon as JC had a bottle for each truck, he started rigging them to blow. He'd pop the hood, wire the fuel in (no, I'm not going to tell you pyros how he did it, but trust me, it works) for an ignition-fired ignition. It's simple but effective, my favorite kind of device. As soon as he finished with each truck, I would spray diesel over the motor and quietly close the hood. It took us nearly 15 minutes to finish. While he worked on the last few, I topped off the tanks on the Lady. I even found four spare jerry cans that I filled and jammed into the cargo hold.

"Done," JC said, now completely drenched in sweat. "It

should be quite the show. I've run a little cannon fuse between several of them and the tanker just to keep things interesting".

"Are you insane? What if some drunk comes out to take a drive."

"Well then, I suggest we leave."

"Oh, dear God! If they don't kill us, you may do it for them."

"Nah, we'll probably be long gone by then. Probably," he laughed. I just stared at him. Dumbass.

We sat for just a minute before he jumped up and headed for the pumps.

"Where are you going?" I half whispered.

"I got an idea." JC called over his shoulder.

"Oh shit."

He filled a 5-gallon bucket with about a third gas and two-thirds diesel. He started pouring a trail from the trucks back to the doors for the building. There he emptied the remainder in front of the doors. He finally seemed to hear my panicked attempts to get him to stop. Naturally he continued on in typical JC fashion. You could tell he clearly thought this was such an awesome idea. He came back to the truck with a shit eatin' grin and I slapped him. I mean, I slapped him hard.

"You dumbass! What happens now if this whole thing goes up before your Mom gets out?"

"Well, shit. I didn't think about that." JC replied.

"No fucking shit you didn't think about that. JC, sometimes

you are such a dumbass! Like a monkey and his favorite football. This Tom fuckery of yours could end up killing your entire family. Are you fucking listening to me? Damn it, JC. Now we just have to pray they make it out in time. I swear, sometimes you've got the mind of a badger in heat. Just go, go, go, with no other thought than what's in front of you!"

"I said I'm sorry," he whined.

"Ummm, actually you didn't. You... What was that?" I asked.

"I heard it too. It sounded like a gate. But that couldn't be. The gates were locked. I heard the guard report that he closed and locked them." JC said.

"Get down!" I whisper shouted. Thankfully, he dropped without knowing why. It was then that we saw the Murdochs slipping in through the gates. The now wide open gates!

Chapter 7 – Angel (Lindsey McKinney)

I left the kids to work on the trucks and started into the building. I'd noticed a couple other raiders wearing lightweight balaclavas. It seemed like a pretty safe disguise. Of course, when I entered the building, no one had one on. I guess they thought it looked tough until it was party time now, who needed that? Well, nothing I could do now but go with it.

I walked in carrying an empty beer bottle like I'd been at it pretty hard. It wasn't too hard to pull off since most of these asshats were totally sloshed at this point. My focus was on finding Jules and June. I saw the one they called Sue standing guard near the office hallway, so I headed in that direction. Before I could get there, a voice behind me said,

"Now come on sweetheart, don't run off when the parties just gettin' going." I groaned and turned to face the next moron to enter my life.

"Just looking for you sugar. Now what do you say we find a nice cozy place to relax together." I said.

I turned him back into the store and down one of the darker aisles. He was drunk enough that he was easy to guide. He seemed to think I was somebody named Mary. Well, Mary it is then.

"Come here, Mary and take off that damn ski mask. Hell, you can take off more than that if'n you want." He chortled.

"Oh sugar, don't you worry your little head. I got just what

58

you need." He reached out to grab my waist. Before he could, I grabbed his wrist. I damn near spun him too hard. He was too drunk to resist even a little and I had to jerk him back to keep him from falling flat on his face. As soon as his back turned to me, I dropped his wrist and grabbed his face. The knife in my other hand slipped between the vertebrate in his neck and he slumped back against me. That done, I dragged him over to a shelf and propped him into a half-seated position on the floor. Damn, that fat bastard was heavy.

As I was about to turn out of the aisle, the boss man himself came strutting towards the office hall. As he approached, he asked Sue, "How are you enjoying the party?"

"You're hilarious. You broke my fucking nose. I can barely breathe."

"And you're going to have two beautiful black eyes in the morning. Hell, I wouldn't be surprised if they don't swell completely shut. Maybe next time you'll remember to respect what's mine. Hmmm?"

"Yes boss."

"See, it's not all that difficult to show a little respect. Now, I'll go spend a little quality time with my prize and you can join the festivities. Run along now, little Sue."

The boss disappeared down the hall and Sue started toward my aisle. As she passed, I slipped my hand over her mouth and dragged her back into the dark. My knife found the same sweet spot in her neck. Now Sue wouldn't have to worry anymore about that broken nose or those black eyes. I'm such a humanitarian some days.

Killing that bitch put me in such a good mood, I dragged her over and laid her out in a lover's embrace with the moron that slowed me down earlier. Those two really deserved each other, so sweet.

Now, back to Gran Jefe. I really did need to sit down and have a talk with that man about how he treats young women, especially my daughter! I slipped quietly down the hall and nearly ran face-first into one of the drunks coming out of the Men's restroom. Training is a wonderful thing and before I even thought what to do, one hand clasped his mouth while the other brought my knife into his throat. I pushed him back into the alcove, hitting the wall and driving the knife deeper. Just to be on the safe side, I twisted the knife around and did my best to lean out of the arterial spray. As soon as he stopped struggling, I dragged him into the Women's restroom. I got him just inside the door and dropped him on the floor. I really didn't have time for that shit.

Looking back out into the hall, I thought it might be better to go ahead and empty the Men's room of any other potential problems. The smell of stale urine nearly knocked me over when I opened the door. This lot was just nasty. I went in quick, finding only one man at the urinal. I threw a sidekick into the small of his back forcing him to gain intimate contact with the porcelain potty. He reached across for a shoulder holster. Who was this guy, Inspector fucking Clouseau? I shoved his elbow up into his face, breaking his nose. I thought this might help him learn the error in his choice of holster, though he certainly wasn't going to have time to use that knowledge. As he gasped in pain, I grabbed his hand and pulled his arm back across his own mouth. My knife came out and found its second home once again, in someone's spine. I checked the stalls just to be sure. Yep, we were all alone. Maybe now I could go pay my respects to the boss.

When I opened the door, the hallway was clear. Excellent. Now I could get to Gran Jefe. I did the best I could to wipe the blood from my boots on Clouseau's pants but when I looked back there was a light trail behind me. It must have been dripping down through the tread. I scuffed them along the floor as I walked down the hall to keep them as clean as possible. The trail couldn't be helped. I just didn't want to slip when I could least afford it. I heard a high-pitched whine from up ahead and picked up my pace.

When I opened the door, I saw my daughter completely naked, sobbing while she tried to dance for that fat bastard. That big son-of-a-bitch was sitting on a wooden chair holding a knife in one hand and June's hair in the other. June was shirtless and had streaks of blood across his tiny chest. As Gran Jefe started to turn towards the door, I launched myself through the air.

He spun out of his chair and threw June at me like a hammer. The boy collided with me and knocked me into the chair the boss just left. Instead of trying to stop, I rolled across the chair and back onto my feet by the wall. July screamed and ran to the fallen boy.

Up on his feet now, the boss looked surprised, but not upset to see me there.

"Excellent. First a little fight, then a little fuck. Of course, I mean your daughter. You'll be dead. She is your daughter, right? Not just some tramp you picked up? I admit, you do favor each other."

61

I moved towards him and he laughed as I approached. Laughed ,that is, until I kicked his knee. I looked up into his eyes with my own wicked smile of satisfaction as it broke, bending completely backward. As he stumbled forward, my elbow lashed out towards his face. He managed to raise an arm, turning it into a glancing blow. His blocking arm then darted out with a quick jab aimed at my kidney. I hopped back and his blow hit my thigh instead. My leg collapsed from his heavy blow, causing me to fall flat on my face. As I hit, I rolled left and narrowly missed the knife blow intended for my back. The boss was practically immobilized by his shattered knee, so I had plenty of time to get back on my feet.

"Come on, bitch! You think you've got me beat? Nobody beats The Boss!"

Dear God, this bastard was referring to himself in the third person now. My answer was the wooden chair. Apparently, the boss expected all women to be weak and compliant. He seemed stunned when both the chair and his blocking arm shattered. This time, he screamed. I grabbed a chair leg and walked slowly forward. The boss began a tirade of useless screaming curses. Honestly, I was disappointed in his lack of creativity. I'd heard newly enlisted recruits who could do better. The length of swearing between breaths was impressive, but that was certainly the only impressive thing about him.

"Did you really think you could rape my daughter? Did you think I would do nothing? I've spent time in a hell you can only imagine. Let's see what we can do to acquaint you, shall we?"

For the first time, there was real fear in the boss's eyes. To have someone beat him so thoroughly and then casually discuss his end seemed to unnerve him enough to break through his arrogant persona. The chair leg came up, seemingly from nowhere, and shattered his other arm. He screamed in rage and pain as he attempted to lunge at me. He was so focused, he never even saw the snap kick that shattered his other knee. As he began another tirade, I decided to shut his stinking hole for him and brought the chair leg up into his jaw. The blow slammed his mouth shut, shattering teeth and splintering bone. His sobs were all that he had left.

"That's it, sweetheart. Now you're beginning to understand. The world isn't quite what you thought it was, is it? Your days as boss are over; in fact, all your days are over."

His screams began in earnest when my foot began to grind what was left of his knee into the hard tile floor. It took a minute before I realized his weren't the only screams I was hearing. I turned to see July cradling June against her chest, screaming at me to stop. I stopped immediately and ran to my baby. I pulled them both to me, whispering in her ear.

"I'm sorry, baby. You're going to be OK. It's almost over. I need you to carry June, OK?"

July nodded, unable to speak through her sobs.

"Come on. Let's get back to the Lady. James and Belle are waiting."

I opened the door and checked to be sure it was clear.

"July, wait right here for me. I need to finish this real quick."

July walked into the hall without a reply. I pulled the fire axe from the box by the Emergency Exit and walked quietly back into the room with "the boss". A long 5 minutes later, I returned to the hall and we started out into the warehouse. It was then that we heard the screaming from the main building.

It dawned on me then that nobody had responded to the boss's screams. I was so enraged that I had welcomed anyone who wanted to join the party. Still, I was glad to take it all out on him. After I walked back into the hall, I realized it was impossible. There was no way they hadn't heard him.

When we reached the end of the hall, we could see the Murdochs were everywhere. I'd never seen that many together in one place. There must have been a hundred or more ripping, biting, and tearing. The raiders tried to fight back. Even if they had been sober and prepared, it would have been a tough fight. As they were, it was hopeless.

We hugged the wall, trying to let the Murdochs pass us by for the noisier prey beyond. As we turned the corner into the garden center lot, we came face to face with 3 Murdochs. The first Murdoch exploded backward as the 12-gauge slug caught him in the chest at point-blank range. I swung my aim to the second one before the first even hit the ground. That one caught buckshot through its side, spinning it away like a crazed, bloody, spinning top from a demented haunted house. The third one seemed to just appear at my side, grabbing the gun before I could turn. She lunged for my neck with teeth bared to rip out my throat. Her head exploded before she made it 6-inches from where she stood. I looked across to see Belle lying on the Lady's roof, M4 aimed nearly at my head.

I reached back, grabbed July, and pushed them both ahead of me.

"Run!" I yelled.

Belle's rifle continued to fill the night air with a deafening roar. Some shots were so close it seemed like I could feel the wind off the rounds as they sizzled past my ear. The rear door on the truck slung open and I practically threw July up the steps and into the truck. It had already started to move as I grabbed the handle and hauled my ass up and through the door. I slammed it tight only to look up and see a butt in my face. I started laughing as the butt shook with each report of the rifle above.

James glanced around to practically stare at the mad woman in the back that was covered in blood and laughing hysterically. He turned back around to focus on driving.

As we backed through the gates into the parking lot, I heard a rifle report followed by the whoosh of fire. As flames spread through the fenced lot, small explosions popped off followed by one that shook the truck. I could see a sudden bright orange fireball through every crack in the armor.

Belle dropped down into the front seat, slamming the roof hatch as she did.

"Hit it, lover boy. I hope I never see this burg again!" Belle yelled as she punched James' right arm.

Chapter 8 – Flight (JC)

We drove hard for an hour before I was willing to slow down, much less stop. It was murder on the fuel but I didn't care. There was no way I was going to let Raider, Murdoch or DFW gang members find us sitting idle on the roadside anywhere near that town. We were somewhere outside of Cartersville when Mom finally convinced me to pull over. When I felt a little safer, we pulled to a stop in a gas station parking lot parallel to the road with the engine running.

Jules and June lay curled up together under a blanket, passed out. Mom quietly woke Jules and got her to put on some sweatpants and a T-shirt. I hadn't even realized she was naked when she came hurling into the truck. Everything had happened so fast and she had lain curled up, wrapped in a blanket ever since.

Belle pulled out the first aid kit and we cleaned up the cuts on June. None of them were very deep and they had all stopped bleeding long ago. We just couldn't afford an infection in this world. We pulled one of Jules' old t-shirts over his head and laid him back down in the seat against the door. The boy had never woken up and Jules never spoke.

Mom and Belle walked back to check on the horses. It gave Mom a chance to wash up and get some clean clothes. She was coated in blood and had to shower before there was any point in putting on anything clean. It took far too much water, far too much time and nobody cared. Mom came back to the rig with watered-down bleach and towels and we proceeded to clean the back seats where she had left a bloody mess. In the old days, I think she would have just tossed the towel. Those times were long gone.

"Thank you, Belle. You saved us. That was some incredible shooting back there." Mom said softly as she climbed back into the truck.

"I'm glad I was able to. That first shot. I was terrified I would hit you or Jules."

"You did great."

With the cleaning finished, Mom swapped seats with Belle and we took a long, hard look at the map. We decided to head east and then north, straight up into the Appalachian Mountains. It seemed to us that the likes of Chuck, Sue and The Boss weren't likely to be attracted by such rugged country with so little to loot.

We were still wired and decided to drive on through the night and find a good place to stop in the light of day. I ran with all the off-road lights on to help me spot any surprises. It wasn't as though I worried about oncoming traffic or the cops. As I drove, Mom seemed to be in the mood to talk.

"It looks like the horses got a feast to enjoy on the ride. Was that your doing?"

"Oh yeah, we forgot to tell you about that. After the Murdochs started coming through the gate, I went back to set up a lantern, we had to sacrifice one by the way. We figured the raiders may be too overcome to start any vehicles and Belle could shoot the lantern to light things up. Anyhow, while I was doing that, I found a box with six LAW rockets in it. I didn't see any more, but I thought they might come in handy, so I tactically acquired them. Had to have a place to put that box. I pulled a bale of hay for the horses to make room. You always said the best place to carry a meal was in your belly, right? I kept one out. It should be rolling around under June & Jules somewhere, a rocket, not a bale of hay."

"Oh shit. I forgot about that." Belle said and quickly dove under the seat to find it.

"Dear Lord, you two are going to be the death of me one day."

"That's guaranteed if JC keeps coming up with brilliant ideas." Belle's muffled voice came up from the floor.

"I don't even want to know what that's about." Mom replied.

We lapsed into a comfortable silence after that.

We traveled like that for some time before something made me look over at Mom. She had this evil-looking grin on her face. Uh oh, that couldn't be good, I thought.

"So James, you and Belle are married now? Is that right?" she asked.

"And so it begins," I said. "I thought maybe it would help."

"No Freudian slip there?"

"With Belle? Hell no!" I might have said that part a little too quickly and perhaps a little loud as it woke Jules up again.

"What is lover boy in denial about now?" she mumbled.

"Nothing. Not a damn thing. And what's with all the lover boy crap all of the sudden?" I quickly replied.

"So what is wrong with me, lover boy?" Belle seemed to place particular emphasis on those last three words.

"Not, what, nothing, stupid" My brain was beginning to seize as I sputtered out a nonsensical reply.

"Oh well, when you put it that way, it's easy to see that you should have been on the debate team in school. Of course, it was a really small school." Mom teased. Her grin just kept getting bigger as I floundered.

"I just mean that Belle and I, best friends, not--nothing more."

"So, there's nothing wrong with Belle?" Jules chimed in, starting to get in on the verbal beating.

"Didn't I just say that?"

"Ya know JC, you're really good at not saying what you think you said. I'm beginning to wonder what else you've supposedly said and where I fall into this whole 'Belle's not good enough but there's nothing wrong with her' thing. Oh, and I'm stupid?"

"I--look, this is not. I mean….Damn it!"

"Oh, good comeback, James." And all three of them burst into giggles. I'm still not sure what happened and if it was a good thing or a bad thing.

We drove for a few more hours with a whispered conversation from the two girls in the back punctuated periodically by fits of giggles. The first rays of morning sun were starting to show when someone mentioned food. We had crossed into North Carolina and were driving through the town of Murphy. I think the McDonald's sign is probably what prompted the food idea. We decided to drive a little farther to get away from town. For some reason, towns weren't big on our priority list at that time.

The area seemed to be a long valley of old agricultural fields. It looked like a nice enough place. We found a field we could pull off into and stopped to stretch and eat breakfast. It was a nice, quiet breakfast with plenty of open fields where we could see everything within a quarter mile of the Lady.

It was such a fine morning we decided to make it an extended break. The horses seemed overjoyed to get out of the trailer. Jules and Belle saddled up and took them all for a gallop out through the fields. I'm not sure who was enjoying it more, the girls or the horses.

Mom and I fixed breakfast while they were gone. Remarkably, we hadn't lost a single chicken during the excitement of the last few days. It looked like eggs were on the menu. I had been afraid it would be fresh chicken instead. By the time the girls returned, we were all famished and ate like Murdochs held in isolation. Mom even managed to wake June up for a bite.

"He's in shock." She said, looking over at June. He was eating slowly as though he had no idea what he was actually doing. "We'll need to keep an eye on him. He's young and should recover. I'll see if July will talk to him. It would probably do them both some good. They went through a lot together back in that little hellhole. I'm not sure that I helped," she added cryptically.

"How long do you want to stay?" I asked.

"Let's give it another hour before we pack up. We all need a good break."

2078: THE FALL

We were road weary, but spending the morning out in the fresh mountain air had made it almost tolerable when we had to climb back into the Lady. Belle made a comment about my dip in the river improving the atmosphere as she climbed back in. Maybe it was more than just the mountains that helped improve the air. I certainly felt better regardless. Even the horses seemed happier about going back into the trailer. The exercise and my proficient skills mucking out the stalls seemed to make all the difference. Of course, the little bit of grain I put in their buckets probably didn't hurt either.

If there had been a question before, there was absolutely no doubt we were in the mountains now. Luckily for us, we had the Franken Lady. She damn near idled up the mountains and since I was in such a fine mood, I let her ride the jake all the way down the other side. I admit, I did get more than one dirty look from the back seat for all the noise I was making. It was worth it though, just to listen to her roar. Besides, where the hell did they expect me to find new brakes out here for this beast? That was one thing that we hadn't factored into our decision to drive through the mountains. It would be a huge tradeoff but it was either the noise or the brakes.

When we entered the Nantahala Gorge I began to wonder if this route was doomed to failure. The first few trees across the road weren't bad and I was able to just push them out of the way. Our blade had a sturdy mount and I wasn't too worried about damage to the truck as long as I kept it slow and steady. As we traveled deeper into the ravine though, we came across a big locust tree hung in the guardrail. The roots were still attached and the truck just couldn't get it to budge. When I tried a little more speed it slung us backward toward the river and nearly into a jackknife with our trailer. We had to stop and walk the horses back to the small field we passed at what looked like an old rest area. We had a saw and an axe with us but locust is like iron. It would take at least an hour to cut through with the axe and was too hard on a new chain for the saw, at least in our circumstances. I decided to walk past the tree a ways to see if it was even worth the effort. Two turns past the tree I came to a landslide. Well, that explains all the trees on the road. I walked back and told everyone the bad news.

Looking at the maps we found that we could go back up the mountain and around the gorge through a town called Robbinsville. It was the shortest way around, but it looked like it would take several hours. We were all more than a little worn out and frustrated with how little progress we'd made since breakfast. I suggested we just get the truck turned around and camp where we were. It was nice there along the river. There didn't seem to be anyone around, and we had plenty of water and grass. Everyone agreed, and I went to get the truck.

By the time I backed the Lady up to the fields, the horses were staked out and everyone was down by the river. I found a nice level spot to park and headed down to see what they were into. Apparently, June had found an old fishing rod left on one of the picnic tables. It had a faded old fly on it that June dressed up by pulling threads from a discarded yellow vest he found in the bathrooms. Turned out our June was quite the fisherman. By the time I got down to the river, he already had two trout on the bank and was working on his third. He was grinning from ear to ear. Still wasn't talking, but that smile was worth a thousand words. Our June was still with us.

"Alright then, looks like trout for supper. I'll get a fire started in the pit over there and go dig out the lemon pepper. Belle, can you see if you can track down the iron skillet? I think it's in the Lady's cargo area. It should be on the top shelf, driver's side, near the front."

"Of course, it's near the front. Yeah, I'll get it."

After June pulled in his fifth trout in 20 minutes, Jules couldn't stand it anymore and just had to try her hand. Fifteen minutes later, we had five trout. No, not five more trout, just the five trout June caught. He was now giggling at Jules' frustration. Mom sat cleaning the fish just down from them on the bank, smiling as she watched the pair.

Finally, June took pity and reached for the pole. He showed Jules how he held the rod and how smoothly he cast. He pointed to where the fish would be and then where to cast. He demonstrated the technique, letting the fly float down over a deep-looking hole. The trout struck hard enough to jump out of the water. Jules half screamed, half growled in frustration as another grin split June's face and he slowly coaxed the fish to the bank.

They kept it up until Jules finally caught a fish. By then, June had caught twelve, but I do believe Jules was more proud of her one than he was of his twelve. And believe me, that was saying something. If I had been a taxidermist, she'd have made me mount the damn minnow on the Lady's hood.

The fishing had brightened everyone's mood and we had a fine dinner. Mom always said that good food was the key to keeping good morale. I was beginning to see that for myself. It seemed like everyone was always in a better mood after eatin' a good hot meal. I guess that's why she insisted on bringing the chickens. I only wished we could've brought some cows.

I woke up early the next morning. Dang, it was cold up there in the hills. It reminded me of the fall huntin' trips I went on with Dad. It made me a little sad thinking about it, but gave me an idea too. I grabbed my rifle and walked back up the river. It was more open up that way. It looked like there were some old houses that must have burned down a few years back. The yards were grown up and shaggy. I thought it looked to be a likely spot for large game to be pokin' around.

I sat along the edge of the woods downwind from the nearest opening. After about an hour, a whitetail deer parted the brush. Her head was down grazing and I slowly brought the rifle up. I had to stop and wait while she looked around for a bit. Then she turned away from me. The last thing I wanted to do was just wound her. When she turned away, I squeezed the trigger. She dropped where she was, sprang back up, and staggered toward the river. I waited, holding my breath and hoping she wouldn't make it into that fast-moving current. I saw her go down again and this time, she didn't get back up.

I jumped up and nearly sprinted to the river. The deer lay only three feet from the water's edge. I pulled my knife and got to work. I had her field dressed and was dragging her back to camp before I figured the others would even be awake.

"You jackass!" was Belle's good morning greeting, from behind me, rifle in hand.

"What!? I got us a nice doe. Just think Belle, steeaak."

"Yes, JC. You disappeared from camp. Didn't leave a note, and then proceeded to wake everyone up with a rifle shot.

Nice job! " She practically shouted at me. "Damn it JC, we had no idea what happened. After everything that happened this week and you just take off to go hunting without telling anyone? Jules is in tears and June is hiding under his bunk. You really are a thoughtless bastard sometimes!"

"I think that's enough, Belle." I heard the implacable voice of my mother say. She had walked out of the weeds appearing like a ghost only a few yards from me. She scared the shit out of me, if I'm honest. Belle glared at me, whirled around, and walked stiffly back towards camp.

"I do believe you owe her and everyone else in camp an apology, James. More than that, you've got to stop acting like a child. You're twenty years old and I need you to be the man you are. We can't afford for you to keep acting like a teenager. You're acting on your impulses without any consideration of the consequences for the others in our family. We can't make it through this without each other. We need you James and I need to be able to rely on you. Do better." She turned and walked away.

I don't think I've ever had a beating like that and neither one of them even touched me. I walked slowly back to camp thinking about what my mother had said to me. I'd always taken pride in being impulsive and spontaneous. It always seemed so cool, like a free spirit that lived for today, ya know? She was right though, I wasn't being spontaneous but childish. Damn, I went from feeling like a hero to feeling like shit in less time than it takes two rabbits to make four.

I cleaned the deer and bagged the meat in zipper bags. We have a full-size refrigerator that was full when we left, but four, now five, people eat a lot of food. There was plenty of room even with the leftovers from June's fish.

I tried to give everyone time to settle down a little. That was partly because I wanted to give them some personal space. Mostly it was because I didn't want another ass-chewin' like the two I'd already had. Belle just kept glaring at me and calling me an asshole if she needed something so there was no point going there.

I went to June first. He had come out of the space under the bed and was sitting on our little couch. I kneeled on the floor beside him.

"I'm sorry, June. I got caught up thinking about hunting with my dad and I guess I got carried away. I hope I didn't scare you too bad. Forgive me?" He nodded. "Can we go fishing one quick time before we hit the road?" He nodded again and I took his hand. I picked up the rod as we walked out and sat on the bank watching him fish. He caught another six trout. I just sat beside him cleaning each one he handed me. The smile slowly returned to his face. By the time Mom called us back to the truck, at least one of us looked happy again.

We hit the road late that morning and headed back the way we came. It wasn't the start to the day I had expected after such a fine evening the night before. I hadn't realized how much my little screw-ups were hurting everyone else. I know, Belle tried to tell me, but it never sank in. Not until hearing what I'd done to Jules and June, followed by that quiet ass-chewing by Mom. Belle would hardly speak to me and Jules just looked, well, pitiful. She just sat looking out the window, hugging her knees. Yep, I felt like shit alright.

We made it up the mountain and down to Robbinsville without any trouble. Unfortunately, that damned highway took us right through town with no way I could find to go around. Our luck in towns wasn't exactly good. Our shutters were up and Mom had swapped her shotgun for a LAW rocket. The swap made a pretty good exchange as far as force multipliers go. As we pulled into the intersection to make our turn, Belle grabbed my arm.

"Movement" was all she got out before we heard the ringing of shots off of the armor.

I hammered down on the gas and let the coal roll. They had a couple of old trucks strung across the road just through the intersection. They had them hidden from sight by a tractor-trailer in the parking lot next to the road. I headed straight for the rear axle of the truck on the left and saw Belle reach over to the blade hydraulics to angle it. We barely even felt the mild jolt when the mass of the Lady slung that truck to the side like a pissed-off toddler.

We saw a small group jump into a truck in the parking lot and I heard the hatch on the roof open. Out of the corner of my eye, I thought I caught the Dragunov with its big scope being pulled through the hatch. Mom didn't pull it out very often, but lord, help anything down range when she did. As we pulled into a long straight stretch, we heard three evenly spaced heavy reports. Yep, that was the Dragunov.

"That should discourage any more mischief," Mom commented as she climbed back down.

"Return the favor they offered us?"

"No, just ruined their afternoon. And put a permanent end to that old Ford they were driving. Although, it did do a pretty little pirouette when it hit the ditch before it landed on its roof. Ah well, play stupid games. Win stupid prizes." She monotoned with a hint of a grin.

"Excellent, because something's not quite right with our little Lady. We can keep going for now, but we'll need to stop for maintenance soon."

"Damn. The hits just keep on comin'!" All trace of Mom's grin had vanished.

Chapter 9 – The City

As we headed toward Bryson City, the road opened up into a four-lane highway. It made us a little nervous, thinking of possible implications.

"I thought you said this was a small town ahead?" I asked Mom

"It is small. This area used to be a popular tourist destination. They probably needed the big road to handle all the summer traffic." Mom's explanation sounded reasonable, but her tone was not convincing.

As we drove by a gas station, we saw two people just standing outside talking. One of them turned and waved as we went past. At the next cut through, I made a u-turn.

"What are you doing?" Belle asked nervously.

"Recon."

"What? Are you crazy, JC? Haven't we had enough trouble for one day!"

"Look, we need to know the lay of the land because, like it or not, we're gonna have to stop. The Lady isn't running right and I've got to figure out what's wrong before we do some real damage. For that, we need a safe place to stop. They seemed friendly and there didn't appear to be anyone around. So I'm going back to talk to them."

"Really JC, we can find ..."

"No Belle, I think James is right. The thought occurred to me too, and it wasn't a good place for an ambush. I think they were just what they seemed." Mom unexpectedly came to my defense.

"Can we at least put the shutters back up?" Jules pleaded

"No. I think that would be a mistake. What would you think if our truck passed by and then came back looking like it was ready for battle? We'll be ready, but let's stay friendly for now." Mom decided.

"Besides," I said, "we're already back to the station."

When I pulled in, the people had disappeared. A reasonable precaution I thought. It still made me start to question my own reasoning. I stepped down from the truck with just my pistol in its holster and no rifle.

"Hello?" I called. "Hey, we're friendly. I just wanted to talk."

I saw a figure step around the corner of the building. I didn't miss the rifle barrel poking out of the window.

"Like I said, we're friendly. Just want to get the lay of the land. You seemed friendly when we passed and we've found mighty little of that lately."

The woman who stepped out of the shadows of the building was surprisingly young. Her dark hair pulled back into a braided ponytail that fell down the back of a worn flannel shirt. Tight blue jeans tapered neatly into riding boots. Compared to her, I looked like I just stepped off a military base. No wonder they were wary.

"That's close enough. There's a man in there with a gun and strangers make him awful nervous. What do you want?"

"Like I said, just to get…"

"Yeah, the lay of the land" She interrupted. "Whatever the hell that is supposed to mean. Like I said, What do you want?" she spaced those last words out real slow for me this time.

"Sorry, I just get a little nervous with a rifle pointed at me. My truck is running rough and I need a safe place I can work on it. I got parts, I just need time and a relatively safe place for my family here."

"Your family?" You look a little young for that."

Seeing that nobody had started shooting, Mom stepped down from the truck. She didn't approach. Mom called out from where she was, "Yes, his family. I'm his Mom, Lindsey, and the rest of our family is in the truck. We can take care of ourselves, but it sure would be nice to have a safe place for James to work. Do you mind if I walk over there?"

"No, I guess that'd be alright. Come on over." There was a hissed protest from the building but she waved it off.

"Thank you," Mom said as she approached. "We just came through a town to the west and our reception wasn't nearly so friendly."

"I bet not. The Raiders moved in there about a month ago. They killed most of the locals in town. The rest either joined 'em or ran. A few made it here. I'm pretty impressed that you made it through. That's a tough lot, according to those that survived."

"We didn't slow down to talk. With the shutters up, our Lady is pretty much a tank." I said proudly.

"I can see that. Mind if I ask what the hell kind of trailer you're pulling. It almost looks like a horse trailer but I've never seen anything quite like that."

"You've got it right. It's a horse trailer. I had to build it out to support the weight of the armor."

"Make sense I guess. You used, what, a semi-trailer?"

"Exactly!"

I walked toward the trailer with this strange young woman, continuing our animated conversation. It quickly became obvious I'd found a kindred spirit.

Mom could see us both pointing at different things and discussing them excitedly. The man who appeared beside her nearly caught an elbow to his chest when Mom jumped in surprise.

"Dear God. You startled me!" she breathed out.

"Sorry, wife was always gettin' on me about doing that. Said I walked too damn quiet. They sure seem to have hit it off, don't they? I'm Ronnie, Jess's uncle. Guess I'm everything now. It's been hard, this last year."

"I'm Lindsey and, yes, it has. Is there a place we could work on our truck?"

"You could do it here but I'd recommend you go on into town. They're friendly, if maybe a little skittish. Of course, who isn't these days? We can ride ahead and let 'em know you're OK to let you through the barricade. That's really what we're doing out here. We're scouts and if someone stops, we check 'em out. Hold on a minute." Ronnie let out a piercing whistle. It was a nice long one followed by two shorts.

"Sniper?" Lindsey asked.

"Yeah, she's a way up on the hill. No way to see her from here. She's got a Dragunov that she can pluck the eyes from a squirrel with it, or so she says. Her grandma was a soldier in the old desert wars and brought it home with her. Looks impressive and she surely can shoot well. I'm just not sure about that squirrel business."

"I know the gun. It's a good one." Mom replied.

"Anyway, let me drag Jess away and we can take you into town. Our sniper can keep an eye on things for a while."

For some reason, we were expecting horses. We were all a little startled when the big Harley started up behind the gas station. Ronnie pulled over and motioned Jess onto the back. We all piled into the truck and followed them up the road towards town.

"So James, who's your friend?" Belle asked as I pulled out. "James? Earth to James!"

"Oh, ah what?" for some reason that elicited a fit of giggles from Belle and Jules.

"I asked who your new friend was. You two seemed to hit it off."

"Oh, ah, yeah, I mean, sure, yeah. Her name is Jess. Yeah, she's interested in the modifications I made to the Lady. I mean, who wouldn't be, right?"

"Yes, I did notice the guy driving the bike fawning all over your explanations. Oh, wait, he stayed back there talking to your Mom. I remember now."

"What? Umm."

"Come on James, not even you're that oblivious."

"You really think so, Belle?"

"That you're that oblivious? Well, maybe, but I was trying to give you the benefit of the doubt."

"No, that Jess is interested in me?"

"You were paying attention?"

"Well, sorta."

"Yep, there's the James we know and love."

"Love?"

"Oh, shut up."

"Love you too, Belle."

"Ass."

We only drove about a mile before we passed under the first overpass. Or is that through the first underpass? Anyhow, we went past the first exit off the highway. The entire bridge looked more like a fortification than a highway exit. These people weren't taking any chances. The entire thing from the wood line to the bridge was a log palisade. They must have used an old track hoe to dig a trench and stand logs on end until they had massive walls barricading the ramps. Even the bridge itself seemed to have walls tall enough for a man to walk across unseen.

This was the first time we had seen a group so intent on keeping their community safe. I guess that's why the Raiders chose the next town over. Or maybe it was just the first one they came to from Atlanta?

The next exit was an overpass that appeared to have a single ramp open. The others were barricaded in a similar style as the first. We had to drive over the bridge and then make a sharp turn back down the ramp. It was clearly done to slow down any approach. The entire time we were within view of a hotel. I'd be willing to bet my M1 that there was someone up there with a rifle, and probably a flare gun, watching our approach.

At the bottom of the ramp, we came to an enormous set of gates. It reminded me of pictures of the old log forts built back when Europeans first came to North America. The gates were open, allowing us to pass through. I also noticed them close behind us. Apparently, they saw us coming with our escort. I turned to tell Mom about the gate closing and saw her checking the Benelli. She caught my glance and just shrugged. You never can be too careful, loud and clear, Major.

They brought us down a side street and led us into a large gravel parking area. Surprisingly, there was an old steam locomotive sitting in an open shed behind the parking lot. It looked as though someone had pulled it apart, working on it. I thought this just might be the strangest little town I'd ever visited.

Jules and June seemed perfectly content to stay in the Lady while the rest of us explored. Mom checked Jules' Remington 30/30 and handed it back to her.

"Lock up when we leave, but please don't shoot anyone you don't have to. OK, July?"

"Yes, Mom." Jules seemed calm, but there was no doubt that she wouldn't leave the truck until we were absolutely sure these people were OK.

Ronnie and Jess were waiting by the Harley when we finally made it over from the truck.

"What's with the train?" I asked.

"Oh, that? It was a big thing for the tourists back before the Fall. They would come from all over to ride a train. The town and railroad got this big idea to bring even more people here. They bought that old steam engine and had somebody rebuild it. They converted it to run on oil. Now the engineer and a mechanic in town are trying to see if they can convert it to a wood burner. Could be handy for commerce if our little corner of the world ever gets its shit together again." Jess replied.

"Makes sense. Oil's gonna get scarce and I doubt the rest of the world is going to bother helping us after what our government did. Although, have they thought of just using biofuel? I mean, if you have excess grain. I also saw a lot of kudzu coming into town. "

"Yeah, we got plenty of kudzu. We're using it to feed cattle right now, though."

"You got cows? Damn, what I'd give for a steak!"

"Easy there, cowboy, no need to request your last meal now. We were gonna wait until tonight before we asked." Jess said, with her hand resting on the holstered revolver on her hip.

I just stopped, mouth open. I couldn't decide if I should go for a gun or run for the truck. I saw Jess look over at Belle and both girls burst into laughter.

"Oh god," Jess gasped, "you should've seen your face!"

"Ya know JC, I think I like this girl," Belle said as they both continued to laugh, walking away arm in arm.

I just stood slack-jawed, the color of a slice of fresh, ripe watermelon, and watched them walk towards what must be the main street. Looking over at Mom didn't help. She was obviously trying hard not to laugh and Ronnie just stood there grinning and shaking his head.

As the two girls rounded the bend ahead of us, I heard Belle shout, "They've got a market."

Sure enough, there by the road, in a little strip mall parking lot, were several tables set up with food and other goods for sale. It was a bizarre scene, with a few horses tied up over by the road and everyone carrying guns. It looked like the old West meets small-town America.

The crowd had turned to follow our progress into the... market? A few looks of apprehension until they recognized Jess and Ronnie. Then everyone seemed to relax.

Mom and Ronnie walked over to a nice-looking lady sitting in a rocking chair with a desert eagle in her lap. This was just weird, and yet, somehow comforting at the same time. Yep, totally bizarre.

"See anything that interests you, young man?" said a voice behind me. I spun around to see a lady with white hair next to a table full of various jars and home goods. It had been a year since I'd seen anyone with white hair, so I just stared.

"Please excuse him, ma'am. He isn't always this rude. I think today has him at a total loss." Belle said as she walked over, digging her elbow into my ribs.

"Yes, ma'am. Sorry ma'am. I mean, no ma'am, I'm just looking right now."

"Eloquent, isn't he?" Belle asked.

The lady just smiled, "Well, you just let me know if you do, son."

"Yes, ma'am."

In the end, Mom haggled a bit and finally settled on some canned bear meat, green beans, and corn. She even convinced the lady to throw in a fine-looking fishing pole with several flies for June. For our part, we traded the salvaged wire from the cell tower and 100 rounds of 5.56. It wasn't a big trade for anyone. Just knowing that some bit of civilization survived seemed comforting.

Ronnie introduced us to several people in the market and said we'd be staying over in the train parking while we worked on our truck. He must have had some pull around town because no one questioned him. They just nodded and welcomed us.

We gathered up our purchases and the man that traded for the wire followed us back over to the truck. When we got back, we found June and Jules both asleep in the back seat. Apparently, the two could see us occasionally in the market, and when it became obvious that we weren't in danger, they had slowly dropped off to sleep.

Before they left, Ronnie pointed over to a house near the post office and said that we should come over and join them for supper in about an hour. It seemed odd to have such a normal conversation after the last few days.

The house turned out to be an old bank. Seems there's no use for banks when all the electronic currency is gone and the paper money doesn't have anything backing it. Besides, everyone had cleared out any valuables long ago. When Ronnie and Jess moved into town, they just took over the old bank as their new home. It was a sturdy brick structure and looked like it would be warm with the big wood stove Ronnie had installed. I did wonder about the glass doors, but Ronnie pointed out that the double doors would keep it warmer than most single-wood doors.

"We may have to rethink it if we ever get running water again. For now, this has everything we need."

"You think you'll get power back on?" I asked

"Probably not. There are a few in town working on a plan to use gravity-fed lines to pressurize the town water. That's the advantage of living in the mountains, James. You don't need a water tower if the water's gotta come down the mountain anyways."

"I'd never thought about that. Will it work?"

"Maybe, if we can funnel enough lines together, shut off everything we're not using, and if there aren't too many leaks, then maybe."

"You seemed a little hesitant on the power. Is there a chance you might?"

"Oh, well, that same group seems to think they can rig up a water wheel on the river to run some of those ole house generators. If they can get enough to work, who knows, I guess it's possible."

"Dang Mom, maybe we should just stay here. Y'all taking in any new blood?"

"That would be up to the council."

"That sounds awful nice, but I think James is getting ahead of himself." Mom added. "Regardless of where we settle, we need to visit my dad's farm up north."

"Where's the farm?" Jess asked.

"West Virginia."

"Ooh, that's pretty country. They even still get snow, don't they? I've never seen snow."

"They do occasionally. Not like when Pops was a kid, but every now and then."

This had all been a big mystery to us. It was fascinating to hear Mom talk about it. Ya see, here's the thing; my Mom is from Georgia, her dad wasn't called Pops, and he most definitely did not have a farm in West, by God, Virginia. We have absolutely no idea where we're headed; Mom refuses to tell us. Apparently, we can't let slip our destination if we don't know it. Op Sec she says. It's always nice to know your Mom trusts you.

June and Jules, those two had become quite the pair and hung back together in the shadows. They had at least decided it was safe enough to leave the truck. Mom had promised them each a present if they would come to supper with us and visit with Jess and Ronnie. Besides, you know, food. Food is a good motivator for just about anyone and Mom had promised that no food was coming out of our stores tonight. That is, no food that wasn't already going over to Jess and Ronnie's house.

We ate there just like normal times meeting up with new friends. We talked about everything but particularly the travel conditions. Mom and I soaked in any information we could get about road conditions and rumors of raiders. Mom had brought out our 3-gallon jug of sweet tea. Seems we weren't the only ones who appreciate that southern nectar. They both commented on how generous it was to share such a scarce thing. Mom's only reply was that we would enjoy it while it lasted and what better way to enjoy it than with new friends.

We set our normal watch that night. Since we were in town I doubt any of us were very alert. There was a sense of safety and it was just hard to stay wary of danger. Our lack of attention came to nothing though, and the morning greeted us with a cool breeze and an overcast sky.

With breakfast came the demand for the promised gifts. The fishing rod seemed to practically vibrate in June's hands. It was love at first sight. You could tell he was just itching to go down to the river and try it out. His enthusiasm seemed to spill into Jules as I think it occurred to her that the old rod may need a new home. As soon as Mom gave her approval, June grabbed his old rod and shoved it into Jules' hands.

"Let's go!" he yelled with excitement.

"Coming!" she replied.

"Back in time for lunch, you two," Mom called after them as they sprinted for the river.

"Looks like it's time for me to get to work. Belle, do you mind giving me a hand?"

Belle slow clapped with a sardonic grin, then said, "Don't I always?"

It was looking like a long day…

In the end, it turned out to only be a loose wire. Either the vibration from the big diesel or all the relocation of inappropriately parked vehicles must have knocked it loose. Either way, it was soon fixed and I was looking forward to seeing what June would bring us for lunch.

When they returned June had a stringer full of fish and a huge grin. Every time he looked over at Jules, he just giggled.

"Should we even ask why he's laughing, you have no fish, and your clothes are wet?"

"NO J-Z, you should not!" she huffed. Yep, she calls me J-Z when she's mad because she knows I hate it. Her baiting didn't do much good this time though, because it only made everyone laugh. I thought I saw a slip of a grin as she stomped off towards the trailer to change into dry clothes.

With Jules in the trailer, June was more than happy to tell the story.

"I told her the rocks were slick and not to reach out so far. It doesn't help anyhow, but she wouldn't listen. When I started to warn her about that stick, she just shushed me. Well, she tried to. It was more like a shurgle."

"Shurgle?" Belle asked laughing

"Yeah, you know, shush gurgle. She followed that with a lot of screaming about cold water, which brought Jess and Ronnie running over. They offered to bring Jules some soap. Said if they'd known she wanted a bath they'd have even brought a towel. By then, a couple other people were coming over. Jules had almost made it out when she slipped again, falling back into the river. Ronnie came down the bank to help her out but he was laughing so hard he nearly dropped her back in a third time. When she finally made it back up the bank, she started running around trying to hug Jess and Ronnie, yelling that they looked hot and needed a hug to cool off. I think the whole town had come to watch." At this point in his story, June was in tears he was laughing so hard.

"Ha, Ha, Ha, very funny," Jules said in a mock stern voice from behind us, but she ruined it with a big grin she just couldn't seem to hide. Mom shook her head and said, "I suppose I have to hang up the clothes you just left lying on the floor."

"How did you know that?"

"July, I've been your mother for 15 years and some things have never changed. Even with The Fall."

Needless to say, the story made it around quickly to anyone who hadn't been there. Good entertainment was not something to pass up these days. What surprised me more, though, was when two men came by the trailer to talk to June. They were amazed at how many fish he caught in that part of the river and wanted to know if he'd like to come out on the lake with them.

Chapter 10 – Big Catch

When all was said and done, June, Jules, Mack, Jess and I loaded into a small modern sailboat at the local marina. Mack, one of the locals impressed with June's fishing, said that it had been something of a joke before The Fall. A rich retiree's toy he'd brought from Florida. The problem with sailboats on Lake Fontana is all the wind shadows, he explained. Too much of the lake is surrounded by ridges that often block the wind. Since The Fall, they had discovered a remarkably high-tech solar-powered electric motor hidden in the boat. Mack said they could use the sails on the open water when wanting to travel longer distances. Most of the time they just used the electric motor. The compromise for the slower speed was not having to fight the sails, tack back and forth, or "any of that other nonsense," as Mack put it. I think he secretly enjoyed sailing. He wasn't about to admit it within earshot of the townspeople.

The electric motor wasn't the only thing hidden. It turned out that Jess had a hidden talent for fishing. By Mack's telling, she might even give our June a run for his money.

We set out early in the morning the day after I found the loose wire on the Lady. Mom and Belle wanted to come along, but there simply wasn't room for everyone. They volunteered to stay behind and work on supplies and planning. I garnered a spot on the boat as a sort of guard/guardian for June and Jules (please, for the love of god, don't tell Jules I put it that way).

Since there wasn't a lot of room on the boat and I didn't want to risk my M1. Instead, I just brought along my pistol and a buck knife (a country boy can survive, right?).

Mack and Jess discussed where to go fish while the three of us just enjoyed the scenery. It was quite possibly the most beautiful lake I'd ever seen. There was just something about that glass-smooth water flowing through the coves with the mountains reaching up around you. We motored down the lake for nearly an hour before pulling into a large cove.

"We haven't been over here in a while, so there should be some good fishin'," Jess said. "June, why don't you leave your pole in the cabin for now and try one of Mack's heavier poles. We've got some big bass and even some walleye, if you're lucky. Although, I think we'll have better luck with them on towards dark."

June rushed to find a safe place for his Precious. Only then would he pick out his pole for the day. Mack had more poles than it seemed possible to ever use. While June headed below, Mack started picking out poles for each person. It didn't take too long to realize that each pole was either different or had different bait pre-rigged on it. I was really starting to see why Mack was the master fisherman for the town. It was obvious Mack abso-f'n-lutely l-o-v-e-d fishing. When he tried to hand me a pole, I declined.

"I ain't much of a fisherman and besides, it'd be good to have someone keepin' an eye out."

"JC, are you scared you're gonna be embarrassed when we all skunk you?" Jess teased.

"No, that is pretty much a given. I'm just scared of what my

Mom would do if she found out I let us relax in this cove with no guard."

"He's not wrong about that," Jules added. "Mom can be scary when she…" she trailed off and seemed to slip into a dark memory.

"Jules?" I nudged her with my elbow.

"Yeah, I'm OK. Just remembering… something. Anyways, you better keep an eye out."

Despite that dark beginning, it didn't take Jules long to become lost in fishing. The serenity of the lake just seemed to pull your worries away as the boat slowly swayed in the water. Mack used a trolling motor he had rigged to the front and we traveled up and down the banks catching several smallmouth bass.

It was Jess, instead of June, who landed the first largemouth, and let me tell you, it was a beautiful thing to watch. (The bass, not Jess. Well, maybe Jess too.) Before we knew it, we were all cheering her on. Mack grabbed a net and stood ready while the rest of us whooped and hollered as she reeled it in towards the boat. When Mack finally swung the net into the boat, he had the biggest bass I'd ever seen. We all broke into loud cheers and congratulations. Jess had a huge smile on her face that seemed to radiate around the boat.

As Mack leaned down to put the bass in the livewell a red mist seemed to erupt around him. He held momentarily suspended, then seemed to spin towards the deck in slow motion as we all stopped and stared. It was as if time stood still until the report of the rifle reached us. That sound seemed to break the trance, and everyone hit the deck. I immediately began crawling toward Mack and yelling for everyone to stay down; no use being quiet now.

Jess had already managed to grab the first aid kit out of the cabin by the time I reached Mack. She half threw, half slid the kit at my head. I managed to stop it before I became the second victim and started my assessment of Mack's wound. It looked like his turning to put the fish in the livewell probably saved his life. The bullet had burned the back of his neck and cut through the meat across the top of his right shoulder. He had been knocked unconscious and was starting to moan as I felt around for broken bones.

"Jess! Can you drive this thing from inside the cabin?" I whisper shouted.

"No. Look at the size of this damn thing. It's a sailboat, not a yacht!" She yelled back as tears ran down her cheek.

"He's OK." I said quickly, "Just a flesh wound that looks worse than it is, but we're all in trouble if we don't get out of here!"

"Jules, pull that anchor to you and make sure the rope is tied to a cleat. Once you're sure it's secure, throw it overboard. We've gotta get out of here now and we can't take the boat. Can everybody swim?" Everyone nodded except for June, and Mack of course, who was still only half conscious. June had curled into a ball and was rocking slightly.

"June," I called.

"June! Look at me. Look at my eyes. I need you to look at my eyes." He turned slowly and met my eyes with a look of absolute terror.

"June, you're OK. We're going to get out of here. I got you away safely last time and I'm going to do it again, but I need your help. Can you help me?"

He nodded slowly, still staring into my eyes.

"Good. I need you to crawl down into the cabin and find life jackets. Get a small one for you and put it on. Then find a big one I can put on Mr. Mack. Can you do that?"

He nodded again, faster this time.

"Jules, can you help him, please. While you're in there grab a bag and any food, water, or other supplies as well as extra life jackets for us."

Her look was almost as terrified as June's. I could see in the set of her jaw a mirror image of Mom's steely determination peaking around the corner. She mumbled something that sounded like "yes," and the two of them disappeared through the tiny hatch.

I pulled a couple gauze pads from the first aid kit and used them to mop up the blood on Mack's neck and shoulder.

"Jess, give me a hand?" I could do it pretty easily, but Mom always told me to put people to work in a crisis. "James, if they are busy, they don't have time to panic." She told me.

"OK, I'm going to pull the skin together and I need you to put these butterfly bandages on when I tell you to. Put them about a half inch apart and we'll see if he needs more when we get done."

"OK, James." I don't think she even realized she called me James instead of JC, like she had been.

"OK, Let me wipe it dry one more time. Now get this one."
We continued like that until we had his shoulder in decent
shape. Wipe and tape. Wipe and tape. When we finished I
pulled duct tape out of a side compartment and used long
strips to tape over the bandages. I hoped that would keep the
water out.

"As long as he doesn't try to use his arm that should hold."

As I said it, Jules returned with an extra-large life vest.

"Perfect! Thanks, Jules. How's June doing?"

"I think he's right behind me. He wouldn't leave his fishing
pole."

"That's ok, we may need it before this is over anyhow."

I pulled the vest over Mack's right arm and up into his armpit.
Then we rolled him onto his side and laid the vest beneath
him. That allowed us to roll him back onto the vest and he
had it halfway on. Getting his left arm through was a little
awkward but we managed. With Mack's vest on, we started
buckling him in. He had been slowly waking up while we got
his vest on and managed to look over at me with a pained
expression.

"What the ever-lovin' fuck hit me?" He asked.

"I'd guess a 270 so keep your ass down. The good news is
with the way you dropped; I'd bet our Franken Lady they
think you're dead."

"Oh, well, yeah. I guess. They still around?"

"Oh hell yeah! No way they left. Probably headin' our way
looking for a boat or supplies or worse."

"Great. What's the plan?"

"We can't sail away with that rifle out there. The only choice I see is to make for the shore. We've dropped the anchor so the boat won't float away"

"Jess, turn off the battery disconnect and pull the main fuse. You know how long it took us to find that damn thing. Maybe they won't bother to steal her if they can't get her under power." Mack said almost pleadingly. Jess disappeared through the hatch.

"Hurry, Jess!" I called after her. "We don't have much time. We've been sitting still too long already."

Jess returned a few minutes later looking satisfied, a worried-looking June in tow.

"Don't worry, Mack. They'll play hell trying to get this girl to move under power."

"Good."

"OK, we're ready then. Everyone, crawl to the far side behind the cabin. Try to use it as cover and slip over the side into the water. Be quiet as you can. Mack? Can you make it over or do you need help?"

"I've got it."

"Good, just don't try to use your bandaged arm. Once you're all over, I'll hand down the first aid kit, June's fishing pole, and the dry bags Jules brought up. Everybody ready?"

I saw nods all around.

"Let's go then."

As we crawled toward the far side, I saw Jess duck back down into the cabin. Just as I started thinking I'd have to go down after her, she popped back out. In her hands, Jess carried the most beautiful thing I'd seen all day, a .300 blackout with a 30-round mag and iron sights.

"Sorry. I forgot I left this on here last week. I've kept meaning to get it off. Every time I started to, something else came up. Now I'm glad I never did. I've got 2 extra full mags but that's it for ammo."

"It's gorgeous." I beamed. "Doesn't' really change our plans with such a short range. Still, it may be the difference in us all getting home."

I helped the others down into the water making sure everyone had something to carry. Jules and Mack each used a life jacket to rest their bags on to make sure we kept the dry stuff dry. June meanwhile, had a death grip on his rod and tackle. I'm not sure a raider could have pried it from his cold dead fingers without a fight from the grave.

I was about to drop in when I looked over the deck. An idea, a good one this time, came to me and I crawled back over to where Mack had fallen. I dragged my life jacket through his blood and then slid it across the deck towards the rail, making sure to drag it over the rail itself. The effect was a blood trail that looked like someone had dragged a body over and dumped it into the water. Satisfied with my work, I slid in after the others.

We climbed onto shore over some shaded rocks without hearing another shot. I looked back at our lonely little boat drifting out there with a blood-covered deck and it just made me mad.

"I don't know about you guys, but this really pisses me off. I'm getting really tired of being shot at for no reason. Jess, you up for a little revenge?"

"Oh hell yeah!"

"Mack & Jess, you know the area. Where should we head?"

Mack spoke up this time, "We're on Chambers Creek now. They'll probably expect us to head around the shoreline more or less straight towards town. I'd recommend we head up the cove, a ways deeper into the park. Then we can climb over this ridge and drop down the other side. We should be able to pick up a trail that will make walking much easier. It'll take us back toward town, dropping us down onto the Road to Nowhere."

"The what? Road to Nowhere? Ya know, never mind, you can tell me later. I like that idea with one exception. Jess and I will stay behind to greet our guests. Mom always told me to show guests the proper hospitality. It just wouldn't be right to let these assholes feel like they're being ignored."

"I don't like it," Mack said. "We need to stay together."

"I agree, but once the adrenaline wears off you're going to slow down. No offense June, but you and Jules are gonna have a hard time climbing these mountains. Me too, for that matter. We're just not used to the elevation or the steep hills in these mountains. We don't know who is coming after us so we have to assume they won't have that problem. We need to slow 'em down and make 'em think twice about coming after us. We do our best to ambush them. No more than two volleys before we fall back to catch-up with you guys."

"OK, I don't like it, although, you make some good points.

Even if I'm fine, you're right, y'all are gonna have a hard time coming from the coast to the mountains."

"It's settled then."

"What about us?" Jules chimed in, "Don't we get a say in this?"

"You want to take on this bunch with your fishin' rod?"

"No, you ass. I want you two to stay with us. Mom wouldn't like us splitting up!"

"No, Mom wants you safe and would understand the plan and the tactics. We have to show them that we're not prey and there's a cost to coming after us. If not, they'll come on twice as hard. Especially if the guy with the scope saw you and Jess, which I'm sure he did. What raider scum isn't going to push hard to capture two beautiful women?"

Jules was silent, thinking back to her recent time at the hands of the boss, I'm sure. She just nodded and turned away.

"I'm sorry, Jules, I can't let them take you again and I'll do whatever it takes to prevent that."

"That's what I'm afraid of." She mumbled as she started walking up the cove.

Mack gave a kind of half-shrug and turned toward Jules. "Come on, June. Let's make tracks. Good Luck you two and please be careful!"

Jess and I stood in the shadows for several minutes watching them go. I don't think either one of us was looking forward to the unknown fight coming to us. Finally, we tugged our gaze away and started making plans.

There was a steep hill to the west of us where Jess thought she could get a clean line of sight. While she made her way up the hill, I circled around to the east. The plan was to let them get to the sailboat and climb onboard. We would let them check it out and see that nobody was around. It should help them relax and drop their guard. Once they did, Jess would open fire on whoever had the rifle. When they turned toward her, I would shoot from the opposite side at whoever was closest to me. We chose where I would hide before Jess left so she would know exactly where I was, and hopefully not shoot me.

It was a great plan. Our only problem was that the enemy also made plans.

We waited for over two hours. Something was wrong, very wrong. They should have been here. Maybe it was just a shot from some drunk raider having fun? Jess had said there was a campground or some such over on the opposite shore. That was why we didn't fish that side. No, that didn't make any sense. That was a hell of a good shot at Mack and only chance had saved his life. Something was wrong.

The shot from Jess scared the hell out of me. The scream behind me was even worse. I had become focused on the water; I hadn't noticed the raider sneaking up behind me. I spun around so fast that I lost my footing and slammed my shoulder into the tree I was crouching behind. It nearly caused me to drop my pistol.

A second deep crack from the .300 made me jump as I looked up the hill behind me. Jess was a great shot and I am damned lucky. The man just up the slope was clutching his stomach with both hands as blood seeped between his fingers. His time was done, his body just didn't know it yet. His screams had settled into quiet moans by the time I climbed up to him. I was as skittish as a bacon-wrapped cat running from a wolf but I couldn't pass up the opportunity for intel. I crawled over to him, keeping one eye on his hands.

"How many?" I demanded.

"Screw you. Danny's gonna pick you off one at a time." He sputtered.

"Yeah? I don't think so, asshole. We got you, we'll get that guy too."

He laughed between his gasps. "That bitch'll make short work of you. And then she'll sell your women back down in Atlanta. You ain't ever been up against someone like her, boy!"

"Guess she couldn't do it without help though, huh?" I said with as much contempt as I could muster.

"She took down that big dude by herself and only brought the three of us over here to finish off the rest of you. It won't take long." He sneered.

"Thanks, dumbass. That's what I needed to know."

He looked confused until I jabbed the muzzle of the pistol into his stomach and he passed out from the pain. I quickly searched him. I took away a Remington shotgun and a 1sling full of shells, a Berretta 9mm with two extra mags, a decent folding knife, some para-cord and a Mickey Mouse watch. That last one confused me but I thought June might like it. As soon as I finished I ran along the slope towards the hill where Jess waited.

I told Jess what I'd learned after we made sure no one was following me.

"I don't like this, JC. They must have landed on the other side of that point and then come through the woods. I'd bet they split up and the other three are heading toward the trail to cut us off from town. We've gotta get back to the others and fast."

"I think you're right but what if one of us goes back to the boat and sails around to the point. We could take their boat and circle back here to pick everyone up."

"Nice idea, but I don't think we've got enough people for that. Jules is right, we need to stick together. If they do catch up to us we'll need everybody."

"Yeah, I guess you're right. I just hate to leave our boat for a running battle through the hills."

"Well, let's get moving and maybe we can avoid that running battle part."

We headed north up the mountain parallel to the cove. Keeping to the middle of the slope made it harder to walk, however, thick brush grew above and below us. The clear area through the middle made much faster travel despite the awkward footing. It also meant we were less likely to lead someone to our group's trail. Even starting over two hours behind, we thought we could catch up in no more than another two hours. Of course that assumed June and Jules were struggling with the terrain and elevation as much as I was.

When we crossed the west fork of Chambers Creek we turned toward the main branch and started looking for their trail. It was Jess who found it. She had crossed over and we were working back and forth up the slope as we hiked, each taking a side of the creek.

"Got it." She said just loud enough for me to hear.

"What?"

Jess just pointed at the ground and I started walking in that direction as I climbed. We passed a deep cove on our right and Jess's face suddenly lit up.

"I know where he's headed. There's another backcountry campsite on the other side of this ridge. I'd bet anything he's planning to go through Cherry Gap and pick up the trail at that campsite."

"Makes sense, I guess. I take it you've been this way before?"

"Not really I've camped there before and we wandered around a good bit. There's some pretty good fishin' in the park if you're willing to put in the effort. A lot of us who grew up around here have fished these streams."

We climbed onward, not talking. It was all I could do to keep moving and not be sick. Between the rough terrain, the high elevation, and me worrying over our people; I was starting to wonder if my breakfast was going to make the hike all the way to the gap with me.

When we finally had the gap in sight I thought I heard rustling in the leaves up ahead.

"You hear that?" I whispered to Jess.

"Yeah, they've probably heard us coming. You stay on this path and keep heading the way you are. I'll circle up onto the ridge and get a look from off to the side, just in case, ya know?"

"Sounds good to me. Just don't miss if it ain't them."

"Damn straight. I gotta protect the man who thinks I'm beautiful!"

I swear I must have turned twelve shades of red but what can you do? Just roll with it and drive on.

"Thanks, beautiful!" I replied with a grin.

Jess skipped, I mean actually, honest-to-god skipped, off into the brush. What in the hell was I getting into? I almost rather just take on these other 3 bandits bare-handed and take my chances than get tied into a relationship during the apocalypse. Oh well, I guess it could be worse, she really was beautiful.

I started climbing again and wished I hadn't stopped. My legs burned and it felt like every muscle was protesting the abuse. Even my arms burned from carrying the shotgun.

When I was about ten feet from the top of the gap, I heard a rustle behind me. At the same time, a figure stepped out of the shrubs in front of me. Before I had time to react, I heard Jules' voice.

"Oh, thank god it's you! We weren't sure when we saw two people with long guns. I take it you've been looting again?"

"Yep, he didn't need it anymore."

"Hey, where's Jess?" Mack called.

"Behind you." She answered.

Now, I've seen a cat do that jump-twist spin flip thing, but this was the first time I'd seen a man do it. If it hadn't been for raiders hunting us I might have burst into laughter. As it was, I had to settle for the huge grin on Jess's face.

Chapter 11 – Thompson

"Damn it, girl. You just about made me piss myself. Don't DO that." Mack complained.

"Sorry, Mack. It was just too easy and you know I can't resist that kind of temptation."

"We didn't expect you this soon. You must have made pretty good time. I'm bettin' that's not a good thing."

"No Mack, it's not. They pulled one over on us. They came ashore as soon as they hit the point and came through the woods. One split off and came down on JC. He might've had us both if we'd stayed together. Luckily we didn't quite play into their plan, either. The good news is that JC has a new shotgun and we only have three raiders remaining. The bad news is that the group includes the sniper and they were heading this way to cut you off. We've got no idea where they are now."

"Damn. Who'd of thought they'd pass up the boat to come after us."

"This lady sniper sounds like a real piece of work. I'm betting she wants it all and figures the boat ain't going nowhere."

We argued a little about what to do. In the end, we decided to head deeper into the park, over to a place called Hazel Creek. We needed time and distance and the only way to get them was to go in an unexpected direction. Farther from help seemed like a terrible idea so that's the direction we chose.

We reached Cold Spring Gap at noon and stopped to rest. Our group was in bad shape considering how little we'd traveled. Most of us were not accustomed to the terrain and none of us had prepared for a long hike. We did have our packed lunch and a couple MREs that Mack had stored in the boat emergency locker. Our lunch was mostly perishable foods. We ate all that and shared the water in our two canteens. Like I've said before, food's easier to carry in your stomach.

Our plan was to make it down to one of the campsites on Hazel Creek. Mack thought he remembered a place called the bunkhouse where we would have shelter. He said as best as he could remember, it was near the end of Cold Spring Creek at Hazel Creek. Since we were walking down Cold Spring Creek, we figured we should get there sometime during the late afternoon. Plenty of time to have a small fire for supper and have it put out before nightfall.

When we came around the last bend in the cove approaching Hazel Creek we smelled wood smoke and all stopped as one. I handed the shotgun to Mack and pulled out my pistol. The Beretta I gave to Jules. We spoke in quiet tones.

"As much as I would like help, I don't want to bring trouble to someone else, or risk having to fight on two fronts. I say we circle south back towards the lake. To be honest, I'm too tired to head north uphill and there's got to be another campsite downstream." I suggested.

"There is. A bunch of them sites. If this one's occupied, though, I'm afraid the others may be too." Said Mack

"I say let's chance it. We can go slow and keep a careful eye out for people and traps."

"I really don't see any other good options. We'll head over this ridge and down the other side to Hazel Creek. Maybe ole June there can catch us a couple trout for supper and we can cook 'em before night settles in."

We started diagonally up the ridge. Since the stream was heading down the walk was more level than turning up. Good thing too because we were beat.

We made it down to the creek without seeing a soul. Sure enough, June caught several small trout and we made a small fire of the driest wood we could find. Mack wove a few green saplings into a kind of grate and he cooked the fish on that while I refilled our canteens. The iodine pills I added to the water tasted like crap but at least we wouldn't get sick. As soon as we finished cooking, we doused the fire and moved off up the opposite hillside to eat. We were all quiet, contemplating our long day and what lay ahead, too tired to talk much.

"Let's move on up the ridge and find a place with good open woods where we'll have a view and can rest a little. We can set a watch and maybe all catch a few hours of sleep. I know I could use some."

As I said this, I watched June's eyes close while he leaned against Jess's shoulder. Everyone just nodded in agreement and we headed up into the open woods above. I took up my old job of carrying June. I sure was glad we didn't have far to go, he was getting heavy fast.

I set the watch for two people at a time since we were all

exhausted. We couldn't afford for the watch to fall asleep and I figured two could watch each other as much as the hills around our camp. It all stayed pretty quiet until the early morning hours. June shook me awake and with a frightened tremor in his voice he said, "Jules thinks she heard something."

"Ok, I'm awake. Just keep calm. It's probably an animal. Go ahead and quietly wake the others though, just in case."

As he did, I made my way over to Jules.

"What did you hear?" I knew Jules wouldn't have woken me for an animal. We'd spent enough nights on the farm working and camping that she knew the difference.

"Someone's on the ridge across the creek. Sounds like they're moving toward that bunkhouse place Mack mentioned. Maybe those Raiders circling it? I'd say there's more than one."

I listened for a few minutes with her and it didn't take long to know she was right. I turned as Mack and Jess approached us.

"Looks like our raiders have caught up to us. We think they're circling up to attack that bunkhouse you mentioned. We can try to go help out but I don't like the idea of doing that in the dark. Especially since we don't know who's in that bunkhouse or what they'll do. Just as likely to shoot us as the raiders."

"I agree," Mack said. "Let's fade back to the west, parallel to the lake. I'm betting the smoke from that camp attracted them. They should be focused on the attack. Maybe they won't notice us."

We moved out west through a low gap and down into another

drainage with a dense laurel thicket. Jess found us a dry spot away from the creek and we did our best to catch a few more hours of sleep before morning. I doubt anyone managed it, I know I didn't.

Sunrise greeted us with a distant rifle shot. It seemed to echo all around but we all figured it must have come from the bunch we heard in the night. Several other shots answered the rifle, from different guns by the sound of it. I could only hope they killed that lady sniper.

Now wide awake, we decided to eat breakfast and make our plans for the day. We had a few granola bars we split up for breakfast while we passed the canteens.

"I'm tired of being prey," Jess said with murmurs of agreement from Jules.

I looked at Mack who seemed to be avoiding the suggestion.

"OK," I said, "June, are you up to go hunt the hunters?"

June looked at me in surprise. Then his look seemed to harden. That's a really weird look on a small kid, weird and really damned unnerving.

"Hell yes!" he replied.

"Fine, you guys know the stakes. I'm not going to bother with any speeches. We'll split into two teams. Move up this ridge above the bunkhouse and see if we can get an idea of who's left. June, Jules and Jess; y'all can be our sniper team. Jess has the rifle and Jules can watch her back. June, you help Jules watch or use those keen eyes to help Jess scout, whatever she tells you. Mack and I will be the team for close work with the shotgun and my 1911. Neither have much range so we're stuck with it. Remember, for now, we're just scouting. We'll go ahead and y'all follow once we get a couple hundred yards out. I want us to split up. Then we can watch each other's back."

We were lucky. The ridge we followed must catch the wind pretty well because the leaves were thin and we made very little noise. The morning dew helped with that too. We were able to get directly above the bunkhouse when we heard voices. The first was more of a moan than anything.

"Hold still, damn it," a woman's stern voice said.

"I told him not to get that close but you know Slim, thought he was a real woodsman. Guess he did OK until he stepped in that trap."

"Well, he's fucked now. I can't get the bullet in his side and that foot looks like somebody beat it with a spiked club."

"Hey! What the fuck are you doing?" a man yelled.

The boom of a rifle echoed through the mountains.

"Damn it, Danny, he could've made it."

"I've told you, Joel, you gotta know when to cut your losses. Slim was going to slow us down and I want to find those girls. Those two alone are worth ten times what the crap in this camp is worth. Besides, none of this junk can walk and I ain't gonna carry it."

"Fine, but what about that old timer that shot Slim?"

"I killed his boy there and he ran off, you really worried about some old man? You're getting soft, Joel!"

"I just remember the old timers back home were nobody to

mess with and that one looked mad as hell when you shot that boy."

"And he ran! Do I need to spell it out for you? HE RAN! Now focus on the job or I'll make it a solo mission, which means solo money." yelled Danny.

"Fine. Let's see what they have to eat. I'm starving." Joel mumbled as he wandered toward the cabin.

We could hear the two start rummaging around inside. Pretty soon we heard Joel say, "Well I'll be damned. They got bacon. I'm stokin' up that fire and we're gonna eat good."

"Fine, I guess I can wait for bacon, but as soon as we're done, we're huntin' those girls," the one called Danny replied.

The smoke drifted our way and my stomach began to growl. Mack glanced over at me. It must have been pretty loud but he didn't look to be doing any better. I'd swear I saw drool before he licked his lips.

We slowly started easing down the hill, quiet as a mouse. After another 20 minutes, we were close enough to see them through the trees. Joel was a medium-sized guy with blond hair and had a huge slab of bacon lying across a grate in front of him. Danny was pacing in from of him. She was tall with short dark hair and a mean look about her. She was the type that looks like she's never smiled once in her life. Jules would say she's afflicted with perma-pole. I'd have to agree based on what little I could see.

Joel bent down and poked at the meat with his knife.

"Looks nearly ready," he said.

"Good. I'm getting tired of waiting."

He leaned down and stabbed a slice with his knife, the fat popping as it dripped into the flames. Holding it up, he blew on the meat to cool it off. Licking his lips, he brought it up for a taste and, I swear, both Mack and I leaned in with him.

We both jumped when his head exploded. The boom of what sounded like a cannon echoed down that little cove. Danny didn't miss a beat. Her rifle came out of nowhere and she was looking down the sights up the hill when another shot spun her around and she hit the ground. The third shot was another cannon blast from up the cove that parted the air where she had just been standing.

Mack and I froze, looking for the first shooter. When we looked back, Danny was gone.

A grizzled old man stepped from the shadows upstream of the bunkhouse. He was carrying a Winchester .300 Magnum and did not look happy. My dearest hope was to escape without that old man trying to kill me. To that end, I began pleading for my life.

"Excuse me, sir? Can we come out into the open without you shooting us?"

"You with this scum?" He growled.

"No sir. We've been running from 'em and circled around to try to ambush 'em."

"Well, ya sure screwed the pooch on that, didn't ya, boy?"

"Yes, sir. I think we did and I'm awful sorry about that, sir. That woman there needs to die in the worst way."

"That she does son, that she does. Well, you ain't Jesus and I'm growing tired of talking to a bush. Get your ass out here where I can see ya."

"Yes sir."

I stepped out with Mack, our guns pointed down, and I stuck out my hand.

"Name's James McKinney, sir. That crowd tried to bushwhack us down on the lake. She clipped my friend Mack here. Been running us all over this mountain ever since."

"Who ya got up on that ridge James?"

"That's my sister and our friends. Sorry, Jess spoiled your shot. I can't understand how she didn't kill that rat. I ain't seen her miss yet."

"Vest."

"I'm sorry?"

"She had a vest with a trauma plate. You can see ceramic shards in the dirt there. Must have been a glancing blow for her to have moved off that quickly. Probably from her turn when she lifted the rifle. Not Jess's fault, I don't reckon. She's a good shot, but shit happens. Just wish it hadn't made me miss. I owe that woman."

We could hear the others coming down the hill.

"Jess!" the old man called, "you best come around the way your James here did. I've got a couple surprises over thataway that you don't want to get into."

"Thanks!" she called back.

Before no time they were hopping across the small stream and into the clearing beside us.

"Damn, no blood? I know I hit her." Jess asked.

"Yeah, you hit her, girl. She had a vest with a plate. Probably knocked the wind out of her and bruised her up good. Unfortunately, that's about all you did." The old man replied.

"Damn."

"Yep, pretty well sums it up."

"What now, sir?" Jess asked.

"First, my name's Thompson not sir. I'd hoped we was far enough back we could make a go without folks around. It's turned into a regular Grand Central station and now my grandson is dead. I'm sure enough gonna hafta kill that bitch or die tryin'."

"We'd like to help, Mr. Thompson," I said.

"Just Thompson boy, and I'm not sure I want you kids getting in my way again."

"Yes sir, it's just that I don't think we can get home while she's still out there. You heard her. She wants to kill us and take Jess and Jules to sell. I can't allow that to happen and I think we've got a better chance working together."

"Maybe. Ya'll set a spell and rest. Get ya some water while I scout out where she's gone. I'll do that better without a bunch of you scattering the tracks all to hell 'n gone."

"Yes sir. Much obliged."

After a half hour of waiting, Mack turned to me.

"Ya know JC, I do believe that old bastard has took off after our rabbit and left us on the porch."

"Yeah, I reckon you're right, Mack. Let's go find 'em and make damn sure that woman's dead."

Now, I don't claim to be no tracker, but I've hunted enough deer to know a thing or two. Half of tracking is in the head. Knowing what a wounded animal is likely to do gets you there and the tracks just keep you on the path. The first instinct is a quick getaway. That means the easiest path and hers was downhill. We started downhill following fresh marks in the dirt. A scuff here from a boot that slipped, a heel print there where the trail was soft, and so on. Suddenly all the tracks just stopped.

"Stop. She's cut off the trail." I said.

Mack took the left and Jess the right looking for sign. I went on down the trail to make sure she hadn't cut back in farther down. Before long Mack called out, he'd found where she came out of the creek on the other side and started uphill. He said there were two sets of tracks in the sand. It looked like old man Thompson was on her trail.

We carried on that way for most of the day. We'd follow for a while then lose 'em. Sometimes we'd pick 'em right back up. Twice it took nearly half an hour. It was late afternoon when we heard that big rifle boom again. Jules started to run ahead when I yelled at her to stop. She spun around and glared at me.

"He got her. It's OK now. We can go see!"

"No, Jules. All we know is that that shot was fired from his rifle. I hope he got her. Maybe he did, in which case she's not going anywhere. Maybe he missed. Maybe he's not the one who pulled the trigger. We're going to find out, but we go together and we go easy. Understand?"

Jules sighed, "I guess."

"Love you, Jules."

"Oh, shut up."

We did pick up the pace since we had a definite direction and it didn't sound too far away. As we got closer, we dropped back in to a slower walk. With a few nods and hand signals, we split out into our groups again. When we found old man Thompson he was leaning against a rock. His rifle was lying on the ground about ten feet away and he was bleeding out, gut shot low down.

"Never thought she'd get the drop on me. I've been hunting these hills all my life and could just about slap a deer on the ass before they noticed I was in the world. I must have got sloppy in my old age. She hit me from behind and when I came to; there that bitch was standing over me with my own gun. Shot me with my own damn gun. Least I'll get to be with Toby again now." With that final pronouncement, Old Thompson closed his eyes and stopped breathing.

I turned toward Jules when I heard her sniffle then saw her face contort into a scream as something slammed into my head and everything went black.

The first thing I heard when I came to was sobbing. My first thought was poor Jules had lost her rabbit again. WTF? Not sure where that came from. Repressed childhood memory, anyone? My second thought (or was that the fourth?) I gotta admit things were real fuzzy there. My next coherent thought was damn my head hurts. Yep, that one about summed it up. I blacked out again.

Now, I have to admit, it was easy to get focused on one enemy in our post-apocalyptic world and totally forget there are others out there. I'm guessing that's what happened to dear ole Danny. There she was, gloating over her victory. I'm blacked out, bleeding in the dirt from a head wound. Mack is concussed and tied to a tree and June, Jules and Jess are bound hand and foot and tied together like a little chain gang. Yes sir, she was on cloud 9. It had been a long, tough road but just like every time before, she'd got the job done. And this was going to be a fine payday, indeed. Two women and a kid would be a damned fine payday. She could probably even sell all the extra hardware for a pretty penny. She'd make the girls pack it out for her. Best of all, she wouldn't even have to split it with those 3 morons.

The first Murdoch hit her like a freight train. It knocked her off her feet and 15 feet down the hill. Her rifle went flying into the bushes out of sight and well out of reach. Danny was quick though, she'd dealt with these fuckers before and she'd do it again. Nothing was going to stop her payday. She smoothly drew her pistol and shot the Murdoch twice in the chest. Another shot to the head as she got up. That was most definitely that. She was Danny, by God, and smooth as fucking silk. No damned zombie stood a chance.

Apparently, that was very fucking well not that. The mother to that young Murdoch was very much planning to make the bitch pay for killing her young. As Danny turned to find her rifle, the mother tore the pistol from Danny's grasp. I don't mean the Murdoch pried the gun out of her hand. I mean she tore the pistol away along with Danny's thumb and forefinger. Danny screamed as a geyser of blood sprayed from her hand. As Jules told me later, that was the point at which she glanced over at me and saw a smile, though I was still nearly unconscious.

Danny was definitely no longer smiling and she was very much done fucking around. She grabbed at her ankle as the female Murdoch flung her bodily down the hill. Danny hit a large white oak 25 feet down the hill and we heard a sickening crack as her lower vertebrae shattered. She slapped again at her unmoving ankle until she was able to knock her pants out of the way and grip her .45 hideout gun. The big .45 boomed as the first hollow point tore out of the 3-inch barrel and plowed into the charging Murdoch. She fired again and again and again until each successive pull of the trigger only brought another click. The foul-smelling Murdoch lay dying in her lap. It's warm blood soaking through her pants. She couldn't stand the stench and the feel. The feel? She couldn't feel the blood. She could see it soaking her lower half and knew she should feel the warm slick blood coating her but she couldn't. She couldn't feel anything below her waist. Oh God. She couldn't feel below her waist.

Danny slumped down as the realization of her imminent death flooded through her mind. She had been so close, so unbelievably close, to the biggest payday in months. She could have started up her own crew. A real crew of professionals, not the backwoods dickheads like Slim and Joel. And now it was all gone. All gone because of the assholes who dared to run from her, as though they could escape. Dared to hunt her! Well, she'd killed one on the boat and the other guy would be dead soon. Them and these damned zombie fuckers. What a bunch of bullshit. She'd been cheated. Cheated! She screamed in rage. She screamed again and picked up the pistol, put it to her temple and pulled the trigger. The click was loud in the silent woods. She screamed an incoherent diatribe against everything that wasn't her. She screamed in impotent rage at the world.

Chapter 12 – Such Sweet Sorrow

With Danny no longer a threat, Jules told Jess to scoot closer and unhook her bra. No, nothing like that, she told her how to get the razor blade she had hidden in the wide strap near the clasp. Jules had become even more paranoid after our brush with the raiders in Georgia. This was just one new addition to her wardrobe. Once she had her hands free, Jules was able to get to the knives Danny had piled on the ground. The rest of our party was free in no time.

Before anyone else had time to rub the circulation back into their wrists, Jules grabbed the shotgun and bandolier. The look on her face said quite clearly that anyone suggesting otherwise would probably not see another sunset. No one did. Jess went down to check on Danny. She found her panting under a mauled mound of naked female Murdoch, pretty disgusting by all accounts. She took the .45 and made sure Danny couldn't move (I didn't ask how and I'm not really sure I want to know). Then, she just left.

Jules, however, was not in such an apathetic mood and promptly walked down and shot Danny in the chest. Twice, 'in case it didn't take the first time'. Jules was definitely not the forgiving type when you attacked her and her family. I think she may be related to our Mom.

They checked to make sure I was still alive and then four of them made a travois and drug me down to the lake. We were only about a quarter mile from a cove and they managed it by nightfall. It was too far to drag me all the way back to the boat. Mack and Jess went to get it while Jules stood guard over me and June.

We made it back to town after midnight 2 days after we left to go fishing. I didn't wake up again until the next day, whereupon I promptly wished I hadn't. I felt, well, I felt like I'd been shot in the fucking head, which of course I had. Like Mack though, the turn had saved my life. The bullet hit me harder and deeper than Mack's but it was still a glancing blow. The town doctor declared I'd be fine with time and rest. At least he said there didn't appear to be internal swelling. Until I recovered, he said, I'd probably be kinda whiny and I'll admit that he was right.

Belle kept a close eye on me over the next few days. I'd never spent so much time staring into those big brown eyes, to which she promptly told me not to get any big ideas. Besides, she had a date with Mack. I found I wasn't real crazy about that idea. I couldn't complain though as Jess came to visit on several occasions while I was on bed rest. We enjoyed talking and I found myself dreading the time when we would leave this sleepy little town.

A few days after our return, break time was over. Ronnie helped me pull the spare tires off the rims and patch the holes from our fight in Georgia. After they held air overnight, we winched them back up into place. We made a few other minor repairs like fixing a leak in the camper's sink drain. It was nice to have help and I picked up some good tips from him.

Mom seemed the same as always although she did seem to keep a closer eye on us after our little adventure. That's what Jules started calling it and I guess it worked as well as anything. "Our little adventure" sounds like a fun family holiday trip, a cross between National Lampoon's Vacation and Zombieland, with a little Die Hard thrown in for good measure.

Five days after our little adventure, we began preparing to hit the road. We topped off our water tanks and restocked our food stores. The smoked trout and venison from a deer I killed hunting that morning with Ronnie were more than we'd eaten. I tried to split it with him, but he insisted that we keep everything for our trip. The Franken Lady was in fine shape, it was her occupants that were a little reluctant to leave.

The night of our final supper in town, Mom offered to bring Mack, Ronnie and Jess with us to the farm. All three said thank you, but no. In return, they offered us a place in town. We had proven that we could be an asset to the community. We too said no, although not without some hesitation. It was very tempting to stay. Mom left directions to the farm with Ronnie, imploring him to keep them a secret. We didn't want a map for raiders, but our invitation to them would remain open if they ever changed their mind. Now they would know how to find us.

"Hey, that's more than I know!" I protested when Jess told me.

"Gotta be careful who you trust with sensitive information," Jess said with a sad smile.

We all said our goodbyes that night with plans to get on the road at dawn. Jess and I spent the early evening walking around town. We didn't talk much, just walked enjoying each other's company.

"I wish you would come with us, but I understand staying here. You have a home here and we don't know what we're driving into. We'll miss you all, though. I'll miss you."

"Enough sappy talk," Jess said as she leaned closer. "Things will settle down and one day it won't seem that far to visit. Maybe by then you'll have established a home for us."

"Us sounds nice."

"Yes, it does." We leaned into the kiss that seemed to only deepen as it lingered. My hands began sliding up Jess's waist tugging her shirt as they went. Jess pulled me closer, both of us breathing hard and moving deeper into the shadows.

"JC?" Jules called "Oh, there you are."

"Damn." I breathed

"Oh, sorry. JC, I'm sorry but Mom sent me to find you. She needs you to go over the route with her for tomorrow. She said you better do it now. That way you can get some sleep before we hit the road. I am sorry." She blushed and quickly walked back toward our rig.

I leaned into Jess, our foreheads pressed together breathing deeply. Our lips brushed as she spoke.

"You should go."

"No."

"James. I know. Trust me, I don't want you to go but you should and so should I."

"I know."

"You're not moving"

"No, neither are you."

"No."

I leaned into another long kiss and when we finally pulled apart, I looked into Jess's piercing blue eyes. "I better go. I will miss you. You and Ronnie take care of each other and come find us if you change your minds."

"We will. Be careful, James."

I turned and walked back toward the Lady, only looking back once to see Jess watching me walk away.

The first light of dawn was just peaking over the mountains as our Lady pulled through the gates and back onto the highway. We headed into the rising sun toward our new life.

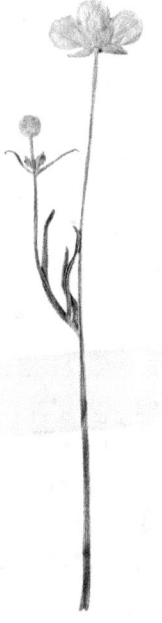

Chapter 13 – Franken Hell-Beast

Our original plan was to head through the Cherokee Indian reservation to the Blue Ridge Parkway. Then, take the parkway up into Virginia. Unfortunately, the Cherokee were well organized against outsiders. According to Mack, they had blocked all the roads within the first few days of the Fall. We could still take the Parkway. We'd just have to pick it up north of the reservation between Sylva and Waynesville. That left several communities and one decent-sized town we'd have to go through before we could get off the four-lane highway. With that in mind, we left early and hoped to be on the Parkway before raiders and bandits bothered rolling out of bed.

The plan almost worked. We had made it up to Sylva without seeing a single soul. As we came around the bypass, we saw the blockade up ahead. Normally we would slow down or stop, assess our immediate surroundings, and then scope out the distant barricade. Apparently, the melancholy mood had affected Mom, too. This particular morning she just said, "Enough of this bullshit. Drop a gear and pour on the fuel."

Out of the corner of my eye, I saw the short tube in her right hand as she reached up to pop the hatch. Not sure if it was my imagination, but I thought I heard the snap of end covers and slide click of the tube as she extended the LAW preparing it to fire. I hit the switch to dump extra fuel into the mix and our Lady began to blow a cloud of black smoke. Belle reached over and hit play on the mp3 player. The forward-facing PA began to blast Tactical Nuke by The

Acacia Strain (yep, more electronics from Mom's Faraday stash). Mom slapped the roof and Jules reached over my shoulder and began yanking on the air horns.

I can only imagine that we must have looked and sounded like a pissed-off aberration from Hell. We were barreling down the highway towards that blockade boiling black smoke and the dulcet tones of death metal. This particular group was a little slow on the uptake because someone moved a truck across the gap they had for a gate. They never even got the chance to get out of the truck. The rocket shot away from our Franken Hell Beast and detonated against the driver's door. It blew the truck backwards and rolled it onto its side sliding across the asphalt. One particularly stupid raider stepped out into the space and raised his gun just as we closed the gap. The blade caught him square in the chest, the impact tearing his head from his body. The few remaining raiders just stood staring in disbelief.

I flipped the fuel mixture back to normal and shut off the PA as we cruised on up the highway. Mom slid back down with a grin on her face. Belle just sat in the passenger's seat staring in morbid fascination as the stupid raider's body slowly slid down off the plow.

"I sure do wish we had more rockets. That is definitely the best way to deal with bandit roadblocks. No fuss, no muss." Mom said more cheerful than she'd sounded all morning.

"Easy for you to say, I'm the one that'll have to clean the plow," I replied.

"Beats being captured." Jules chimed in.

"Preach," Belle said giving her a high five.

I'm not sure what it says about us, not to mention our new world, but blowing up a truck and killing a couple bandit raiders seemed to have put everyone in a better mood. Even June looked like he had just stepped off his first rollercoaster. There's just something about explosives in the morning.

We pulled through the Balsam Gap and found the gate to the Parkway closed. Now, as much as I might have been considerate of such a gate before The Fall, I just wasn't even in the mood the get out. I dropped into first gear and eased up to the gate. The pipes tried to resist as they bent and started to wrap around the edges of the blade. Then we heard a loud ping and the Lady lurched forward, both gates shooting off to the sides. We eased on up the ramp and onto the Parkway.

As we climbed up the mountain, we began to leave the fog below. We passed several overlooks and could see the mountains below, like islands in a cloudy white sea. The brilliant morning sun sparkled on the wet dew-covered leaves. In the midst of this violent new world, it was one of the most beautiful scenes I can ever remember. It looked like a mysterious land straight out of the pages of a Tolkien novel.

We continued on to a parking area called the Devil's Courthouse. I liked the name and pulled in to take a break and stretch. It had been an eventful morning and I figured we could all use the stop.

"Paps?" Belle called.

"Coming." Jules replied.

I explained the acronym to June and he just giggled like it was the funniest thing he'd heard all week. He seemed to like it though and it stuck with him immediately.

"Paps too," June said to me.

"Yeah, OK. Let's go. We'll go over there to the other side of the parking lot."

Mom walked back to check on the animals and talk to the horses.

"JC?"

"Yeah, June?"

"Are we brothers now?"

"Yeah June, I think we are."

"OK. Well, if we're brothers…"

"Yeah?"

"Well, if we're brothers can you call me Ben?"

"Sure, Ben. I'd like that. Was that your name before?"

"Yes. I like June OK. I like my old name better. I just wasn't sure before, you know."

"Sure, I can understand that. Mom always says knowledge is power and that is why she keeps a lot of things private. We can't let the enemy have power over us. So, sure, I understand, June. I mean Ben."

Ben just grinned and said, "Thanks!" before running behind a bush.

We took a few minutes to walk up to the rocks that made up the courthouse and admired the view. I introduced the family to Ben and everyone showered him with excited appreciation for trusting us with his real name. Perma-grin set in and I wondered if Ben would stop even when he went to sleep that night. Jules walked over towards the edge and nearly fell when a Peregrine Falcon shot away from the rocks just below her feet. Once we had her back from the edge, we sat and watched the bird watching us. After a few minutes, we decided we should leave her in peace and all walked back down to the Lady.

The Parkway seemed to have mourning in mind as we left Devil's Courthouse and drove on past Graveyard Fields. Who named these places? Progress was slow along the winding road. Still, the magnificent views were worth the extra time. Not to mention we hadn't seen a soul in hours. That was likely to change as we were coming down toward Asheville.

We stopped at an old burned-down building marked by a worn sign as the Pisgah Inn. Knowing we were closing in on the city of Asheville, we wanted to raise all the shutters and make sure we were ready for another battle. Besides, it was a good place to enjoy the view while we ate lunch. There were even a couple old rocking chairs left on a part of the deck that hadn't burned. It was a glorious moment of peace.

Chapter 14 – Funky Town

We made it down and across Interstate 26 without any problems. Tensions were high as we headed toward more populated areas and while crossing a bridge over a four-lane city street we saw several old trucks on the road ahead. They were even up on the grass banks.

We stopped the truck and Mom popped the hatch. I noticed our old friend Thompson's .300 Win Mag go up through the hole with her.

"I didn't realize we even had that gun." I commented when I saw it.

"Yeah, Jess said she couldn't leave it for some bandit or raider to grab. She didn't want to keep it herself though," Belle replied. "Y'all actually came out of the park with a bunch of new guns. Most of them we left with Mack and Jess. Your Mom grabbed that one up and wouldn't let go. It was a lot like Ben and his fishing pole. My Precious!" Belle laughed.

It appeared we had interrupted a holdup and everyone was just staring at the Franken Lady trying to figure out their next move. A beast like the armored Lady and a mobile sniper were definitely not a part of these bandits' plan. To make things worse, a few moving shadows in the edge of the woods had to be Murdochs. That idea seemed confirmed by several of the bandits facing out and a naked body was lying in the edge of the shade near the trees.

As I may have mentioned before, Murdochs are not mindless

zombies. Mom said it was important not to call them zombies because we could fall into the trap of thinking of them as the old stereotypes, slow and mindless. Even so, I hadn't seen them act like this before, waiting around the edges as if waiting for some signal to attack. It unnerved me.

"Hey Mom, could they be waiting for backup?" I asked.

"The bandits?"

"No, the Murdochs."

"Well, shit. Hadn't thought of them doing that. That could be a problem. Damn sure looks like someone is and these guys look too scared to think they've got backup coming. We better move now before anyone else joins the party. Hand me that PA mic."

"Somebody better start explaining what the fuck is going on and you better do it quick!"

"Just trying to mind our own business when the men stopped us, ma'am!" yelled the tall man with the group of three lined up in front of the big Ford.

"Fuck off, bitch!" added one of the men we assumed to be bandits.

Mom turned to us, "Easy enough, target anything that isn't one of those 3 by the Ford. Let's start with the bandits. As soon as they break, start hitting the Murdochs. No need to bother with stealth just go ahead and run 'em out" (she meant we could slide our barrels out through the firing ports).

"Ready?"

By tradition, we left the apparent leader for Mom.

"10 o'clock hippie with a scarf." I called.

"2 o'clock dark coat toboggan." called Belle.

"2 o'clock red shirt, should've worn his brown pants" called Ben. Wait, WTF? Called Ben? When the hell did he become a shooter? Oh well, fuck it.

"10 o'clock rainbow skirt by JC's hippie."

"Bag your bandit on my mark. Fire!"

Five rifles fired as one and five bandits hit the ground. Ben's shot was a little high and hit the target in the shoulder but he got 'em. No way was that dude going to be picking up a rifle to shoot back. Two of the three by the Ford dropped to the ground. The third bolted for the woods. It was a damn teenager who panicked at the sudden gunfire. Everyone else had already started firing at targets in the woods. I just called "Runner," and jumped from the truck slamming the door behind me. The firing from the truck behind me never let up.

I hit the woods right where I saw him bolt and stopped to let my eyes adjust. As I stood there, Belle slapped me on the shoulder.

"Go in 3," she said.

After a quick 3 count to let her eyes adjust too, we started moving into the woods looking for the boy.

"Dark clothes, about Jules' size," I said.

"Damn, gonna be hard to find in this," she said as she fired to our right catching a Murdoch through the side.

"Hey, kid! We aren't here to hurt you. If you don't get your ass out of these woods, we're all gonna die!" I yelled.

137

We continued forward following his tracks in the soft ground. It looked like he'd been sprinting, so the tracks were easy to see. We moved at a quick pace and kept scanning for Murdochs. I could hear the Lady release her air brakes and start to move back on the road. There was some shouting but I couldn't tell what they were saying.

We were practically running and only noticed the drop-off at the last second. I started to slide and Belle reached out, grabbing my flailing arm. She yanked back and we both fell to the ground. The Murdoch running behind us had a puzzled look as his dive took him over us and out into space. We heard him hit the railroad tracks below and I was real glad it hadn't been us. Unfortunately, it wasn't a long drop and I could already hear the Murdoch scrambling to find a way back up.

After a quick look around, we found the kid's tracks again and I groaned as I saw that they turned away from the road. We started to break into a jog when I heard a strange voice call my name.

"JC?"

I turned to see who called and it was the tall man from the Ford. "That's me."

"I'm Ramirez. We're chasing my son, Con. Damned fool kid is still pretty skittish. I only found him a couple days ago after we got separated. Those bandits y'all killed captured him. We tracked them down and were trying to escape with Con when they got ahead of us back there on the road. That's when y'all showed up."

"Good to have help. Hopefully, he'll listen to you if we ever catch him." I panted as we ran down the edge of the drop following Con's tracks.

"The lady in the deuce threw me this radio. Said she'd be on Seven."

"Copy." I was beginning to think I hadn't quite recovered from the little adventure.

"May I?" Belle said as she grabbed the radio from Ramirez's hand.

"Sure?"

"Major, we have Ramirez and we're heading North along the railroad tracks."

"Good copy, Belle. Keep me looped in."

"Yes ma'am."

We picked up the pace as we broke into the open and saw a figure up ahead.

"Con!" Ramirez yelled. "Damn it, Con, stop!"

"I think he's too far to hear you, or too far gone," I said.

"Copy that."

Con was heading straight for what looked like an apartment complex. In my experience, that was bad. Sometimes they held raiders. Most often they seemed to be full of Murdochs. Some of them seemed to head back to their old homes like a dog returning to its bed. In a lot of ways, they weren't too different, except they would defend their bed or nest to the death. Usually, it was your death, which just meant food for them. Win/win, if you're a Murdoch. It's almost like

Grubhub for Murdochs. Con disappeared through the bushes and into the apartment complex.

When we emerged from the far side of the bushes, I froze. The place was crawling with Murdochs. A few were wandering around looking bored, one couple was busy making baby Murdochs against an apartment wall and at least two were fighting. The majority of them seemed attracted to the fight and were moving in that direction. I just hoped it wasn't a fight over a teenage boy.

"How attached are you to this boy of yours?" I asked Ramirez.

"Well, he's my son."

"That would be pretty damned attached, I'd guess."

"Yep, pretty damned attached."

"OK, good to know. Why don't you lead Ramirez? I have no idea where the kid would go from here."

"Makes sense, let's head right toward the back of the complex. That's away from the fighting and I think he'd move in that direction." Ramirez said. I liked the way he thought.

We circled around three buildings looking for any sign of Con with no luck. When we got to the fourth we heard a muffled scream and saw someone dragged into the central stairway. Ramirez sprinted to the stairs and raised his M4 as he ran. The concrete corridor leading through the center of the building amplified the crack of the rifle. We ran after Ramirez and found him on the first flight of stairs holding a teenage boy with dark hair. The kid looked terrified and Ramirez was examining his ankle.

"I'm sorry, Dad. I didn't mean to, but when they started shooting I just knew they were shooting at us. I know you said to drop down, but I just knew they were going to shoot us in the back. I knew it! I had to run. You see, don't you? I had to run. I-"

"Con!" Ramirez interrupted him, "We can deal with that later. Right now we're all in danger. We've got to get out of here."

"All?"

Con hadn't even noticed Belle and I standing right beside him. Man, that kid was out of it.

"Ramirez, they're coming. We're out of time." I interrupted.

"Up the stairs." He yelled.

We ran up to the third floor where we saw an open door. We followed Ramirez in, acting as a rear guard while he carried Con who suddenly seemed to have fallen limp in his father's arms, all energy expended. Belle quietly closed the door and locked it while Ramirez set Con down on a sofa in the living room and I checked for occupants. We finally got a break and there was no one in the apartment.

Con started to babble again and I saw Belle walk over and slide a finger over his lips. He seemed startled that she was there. He jumped back and started scooting towards the end of the sofa.

"It's OK, Con. I'm Belle. This is JC and we came with your dad to find you. We're here to keep you safe. Do you understand?"

Con nodded slowly at Belle's soothing voice. She seemed to transfix him and he just stared at her. Well, better than incoherent babble, I guess.

"How's the ankle?" I asked Ramirez.

"Just a sprain, I think. I couldn't feel any broken bones and I've felt my share. I'll look in the bathroom for an ace bandage or gauze."

"I'll check the pantry to see what I can find. I doubt there's any food but it's still worth looking. Maybe Murdochs can't or won't open cans."

Belle pulled out the radio and turned it back on to transmit.

"Major?"

"Go ahead."

"We're trapped in the first apartment complex north of your position. We've got about fifty Murdochs outside our door."

"Copy, escape plan?"

"Working on it. Just made it inside. We'll need to assess and evaluate our options."

"Copy that. We'll hold at our last."

"Good, copy. Signing off for now."

"Copy, I'll remain on the air."

Ramirez came back with KT tape he found in a gym bag and began wrapping Con's ankle.

"How are you doing, son?"

Con just stared, first at Ramirez and then at each of us in turn, always stopping on Belle, not that I blamed him.

"We're going to be OK, Con. These nice folks are going to help us get out of here. Then we're going to go find a nice safe place to live. Somewhere away from the raiders and bandits and zombies."

"You mean Murdochs." I corrected without thinking.

"Mur what?" Ramirez asked.

"Sorry, we call them Murdochs. Mom, the Major, says calling them zombies could cause us to fall back into the stereotypes of slow, mindless creatures and that could cost us our lives. We needed a new name so we named them after our billygoat. He was a right bastard of a goat. Mean and faster than he looked, not too bright but still smart enough to catch you if you weren't paying attention. Although, my sister Jules will tell you the name came from the A-team character because they're crazy murder monkeys. Since the goat is named after the character, it's really the same thing."

"Well… OK, umm Murdochs, I guess."

"Sorry for the rambling, I guess I'm just burning off adrenaline."

"No worries. I get it. I've been an adrenaline junky all my life. That's why I joined the Rangers."

"Well, that just won't work." said Belle.

"You got something against Rangers?" Ramirez said a little defensively.

"Nope, the major is a Marine."

"Well just damn," said Ramirez laughing, "I travel all this way into the hills and get stuck with a damn jarhead."

The apartment was a mixed bag. We found some canned food, Band-Aids, antiseptic, gauze, duct tape, and some super glue. I found a kid's room that had clothes that looked about right for Ben. I stuffed those into a backpack. Unfortunately, there were no guns, no hunting or camping supplies, and no working electronics. There was more Grateful Dead crap than any ten people should own. That was only exceeded by the amount of Phish paraphernalia. And yes, I do mean paraphernalia, like the Phish bong on the coffee table. We definitely weren't in South Georgia anymore!

After an hour Ramirez had Con's ankle well wrapped and ready to run. Con himself had finally calmed down enough to realize he was staring at Belle. Now he just stared at her legs. Of course, that's probably because she was wearing a tactical vest zipped up and loaded down. The vest was covering the other things boys like to stare at.

Our plan to get out was simple, we would cause a distraction and then go out the back and into the woods. After that, run like hell. Simple, unless of course, you were on the 3rd floor of an apartment building. Not to mention having limited supplies and at least 50 Murdochs milling around the building looking for the next tasty treat. That tended to make things much more interesting.

To deal with the first problem Belle and I found some scissors and cut sheets into strips. We braided the strips and tied each section together. We got about five sections per bed and each section added around five feet with all the knots. Two beds and most of an hour later and that problem was solved.

The distraction was a bit more difficult. Since the Murdochs were cannibals, we tried shooting one on the other side of the complex. It did distract some of the Murdochs. It also seemed to draw others towards the noise. Ramirez tried an improvised suppressor. Unfortunately, we didn't have any decent materials to build one. Paper towel rolls or 2-liter bottles were not going to cut it, no matter what you see in Hollywood. We had hoped for some sort of flammable liquid. Unfortunately, the only thing they were burning in this apartment had seven leaves and a big fat bud.

In the end, we decided to sacrifice a few of Belle's shotgun shells and that lovely pink bong. We packed the bong tight with gunpowder and cut strips of sheets for wadding. We made our own fuse using a mortise and pestle from the kitchen to grind down the gunpowder. Add in some spray oil and finely braided thin sheet strips then voila, a fuse. It wasn't great but it would work well enough.

The only trick was getting our improvised munition away from our location. In the end, none of our great ideas proved to be practical. The loot in the apartment just plain sucked for our needs. Ramirez took the bong and the three lighters we found and loaded them into a book bag. While he prepared to climb down from the rear of the balcony on the end, the rest of us opened windows along the front of the apartment. When he said go, we began to throw light bulbs and a few cans of SPAM we had opened. The popping light bulbs and smell of potted meat seemed like a Murdoch magnet. Ramirez disappeared and Con moaned a little as he watched him go.

"Don't worry Con, we'll all meet up at the trucks if not before." Belle consoled him.

"Let's go get ready. Belle, you're first. Con, watch how Belle goes down. Let the balconies and rails take your weight as much as possible. I'll come down last."

We had all rigged slings using more strips of cloth and I had the backpack. Ben better appreciate this added weight I was lugging around for him. We waited nearly 10 minutes and I was beginning to get worried when the bong went off. It was on the far side of the complex and you'd have thought someone just rang the dinner bell. The Murdochs were off like a shot.

Belle made short work of the climb down and took up a position to watch the Murdochs. Con surprised us both by descending like an experienced rock climber making it in less time than Belle. To my shame, I was the slow one who struggled and nearly fell when I slipped on the rail of the second-floor balcony. I made it down without the rope breaking though, so I was happy enough.

We all ran directly into the trees and began a slow jog to the Southwest. Con surprised me again by not complaining or trying to turn back for Ramirez. I was beginning to think the Con we first met was not his normal persona. Our route took us over a small hill and as we started down the other side Ramirez ran up beside us jogging easily.

We had run a quarter mile when we heard the Murdochs coming and this time it sounded like all of them. Belle reached into her vest and pulled out the radio.

"Major, we're a hundred yards out and we're bringing the whole damn town with us."

"Inbound with company. Good copy."

Never let it be said that our family stood idle while we were on our rescue mission. As we broke from the trees, I saw a flare streak towards us. The edge of the woods we just passed through erupted in flames. I could have jumped for joy. Instead, I just ran harder as the trucks started to roll. An M4 began to fire from the Franken Lady's roof hatch and Ben was holding the rear door open.

"Everyone in here!" Mom yelled. The Ford in front had already accelerated well out in front of the Lady and was moving up the road at high speed. It was quickly out of the range of the Murdochs. As Belle leapt up through the door, Ben dove out of her way across into the front passenger seat. Con was right behind Belle, with me struggling to climb in after with my pack. I felt a big shove from behind and practically flew into the seat Con was already in.

"Pack it in tight and get that door closed," Mom yelled at us. When I finally heard the door slam Con was in Belle's lap and I was somehow facing backwards with my pack in the seat. Ramirez was in the seat by the door laughing.

"Drive hard, baby girl," Mom said to Jules as she dropped down into the passenger seat with Ben.

"You and I are going to have a long talk when this is done, James." She said to me.

"Yes ma'am," I replied dipping my head. I knew I was in for another ass chewin'. What else could I say?

"If that bunch back there gives up, we'll meet Amy up here about a mile ahead. We can get you boys back in your truck and then pull around to lead the way with our plow. I'm not putting up with any more little adventures today." Mom said with the authority of years of command. The truck remained quiet aside from us shifting into more comfortable positions.

Between the wall of flame and the speed of our departure, the Murdochs hadn't been in sight for several minutes when we caught up to the big Ford. The driver pulled the truck just slightly to the side with only two tires off the blacktop. The engine was running and the woman driving did not get out to greet us. I could tell that Mom approved.

"Alright, you two," she said to Ramirez and Con. "Here's the deal. I talked to Amy and she said you're looking for a place to settle. She also mentioned that you're a medic and a Ranger. I'll forgive the Ranger part since you brought that idiot back in one piece." For some reason, she pointed at me when she said that last part. "We're heading to a farm up north in West Virginia and I'll not turn down a medic if you'd like to join us. I'm not looking to start a commune but a farm can always use a few extra hands. For now, the offer is provisional. You seem like the sort we need. I don't see any reason it can't become permanent."

"That sounds nice ma'am and thank you for letting the idiot and Belle help rescue my son."

I scowled at the second reference to my lack of mental fortitude. I did see the corner of a smile on my mother's face. Score one for Ramirez.

"We'd like to accept your offer on the same provisional basis. We don't have a destination in mind. That said, we're open to the idea. Still, we'll have to get to know each other better as well as a tour around the farm before we commit to anything long-term. I'm sure you can understand."

"Solid plan, soldier. Let's get a move on."

Ramirez and Con piled out of the truck and we all settled into more comfortable seating. The transfer was quick with everyone just jumping into empty seats and we were off again, Jules and Amy driving the rigs. Jules settled into a nice comfortable speed and we moved on up the Parkway uncontested for a good 5-10 minutes.

Asheville wasn't quite done with us yet. The Murdochs almost seemed to be waiting on us as we approached the exit for Tunnel Road. Tunnel Road? I was beginning to think the owners of the apartment must have named the streets. What's next, Overpass Alley or Left Turn Lane? What was it about this place and the names?

There must have been 150 Murdochs just milling around doing what Murdochs do; all over the road, in the grass, in the edges of the trees, everywhere. I thought this was a good time for an experiment and as Jules dropped into a lower gear and Mom angled the plow, I switched the PA back to the mp3 player. The low throbbing growl of Tactical Nuke began to pulse ahead of the Lady. I hit the switch to change the fuel to a rich mix again and watched the black smoke boil out from under our belly.

The Murdochs seemed puzzled at first seeing this bellowing behemoth appear in their midst. A few turned to charge us. Most of them backed away, wary of the growling beast barreling down on them. Just for that special touch, I grabbed the air horn and let her rip as we slammed into the first Murdoch. The body, well the remains of it, were flung clear of our truck as we plowed forward into the rushing arms of our next victim.

Honestly, it was pretty disgusting. I was not looking forward to cleanup and I could practically guarantee that based on the idiot references, that was going to be all me. On the plus side, of the 150 or so Murdochs out there, we only hit around 20. Somewhere around 10% seemed like an improvement to me.

"How did you know that would work?" Jules asked as I turned off the PA and flipped the mix back to normal.

"I didn't really, but it made sense that it might. The Murdochs seem to be more primitive in the way they approach life. I figured an angry growling beast would strike that predator/prey instinct. With the Franken Lady's size, she is most definitely the predator in that scenario."

"Not bad, James, how about next time, let's discuss it before you try something new."

"Yes, Mom. Sorry, it just seemed like it should work and I didn't think we would have any problems with that crowd while we were at speed."

"No, we probably wouldn't," she said stressing the word we. And then it hit me, the truck behind us with Ramirez, Con and Amy. My face flushed and I felt the triumph leave as quickly as it had come.

"Good. I see that you understand what else was at stake. James, you must think before you act. You have a good instinct for strategy. Now you need to expand your thinking to include the big picture. Get that down and I'll start teaching you the real key to winning any conflict."

"Logistics!" Jules, Belle and I all yelled in unison.

"Exactly," Mom said with a grin. "I'm glad you three have

listened to at least one thing I've said."

"Oorah!" even Ben joined in for that one.

It amazed me how many Murdochs seemed to be in such a small city. Mom pointed out that Tifton probably wouldn't be too much different. A big town in a rural area is bound to draw a lot of people. Naturally, towns became more crowded as people started moving out of the rural areas and back to the perceived safety of the cities. Besides, small cities like that were too poor to afford the walls the big cities like Atlanta built. That only made it natural for the Murdochs to spread around quicker.

For the next hour and a half, we cruised without seeing more than a black bear and her cubs wandering down the side of the road toward town. Now that would be a battle, black bear vs. Murdoch, hmmm interesting. I think I'd have to put my money on that Momma bear. Anyhow, it was getting on toward dark and we, meaning Mom, decided we'd better go ahead and stop when we saw the exit for the Craggy Gardens Picnic Area.

It turned out to be a good place to overnight. The isolated picnic area gave no sign of man or Murdoch and it had grass for the horses. Once we had a watch established and the horses tied out, I found the well and moved the Lady over closer. With Amy's help, I was able to wire our welder/generator to the pump and get fresh water flowing. Our fuel wasn't unlimited but it allowed us all to have long showers and top off the water tanks when we finished.

The well also meant I had the wonderful opportunity to clean the plow and the front of the Lady. I did it without asking or being told. I knew it would be my job. May as well get it over with while I had good water pressure, I thought. While I was busy with shitty jobs, I thought I better empty the septic tank on the trailer. I know most people these days just dump their tanks in any ole field or depression. They reason that the sun would sterilize the effluent. My mamma raised me better. I used the cleanout for the public toilets to dump our tank into theirs.

The fun stuff over, I got busy cleaning out the horse's end of the trailer. Did I say the fun stuff was over? Well, maybe not. At least I wasn't getting serenaded with an ass chewin' while I worked. Considering nobody offered to help, I thought it pretty good as confirmation that I was moving right along through my punishment for the day. I finished up just as the last rays of light fled over the horizon. Then I finally got my chance for a shower.

We felt isolated enough that night to have a fire. I jack-knifed the Lady and trailer and Ramirez adjusted their truck. That way we had three sides to help block the light from our fire. We tied the horses out along the fourth side. It left room for a small fire that we could all enjoy while we ate supper.

The cool night air felt wonderful and rather than setting up Ramirez's tent or trying to crowd into the trailer, most of us decided to sleep under a tarp. We strung it up over our impromptu courtyard. We talked a lot, laughed a little, and just spent time getting to know each other. Mom surprised Ramirez when she told him she was in logistics. He said he didn't think she acted like a POG during the standoff with the bandits. Her only reply was that she hadn't always been in logistics. That naturally spiked his curiosity. She deflected the questions with surprising good grace.

I mentioned that Amy helped me with the well. That's because she turned out to be an electrician. As we sat around the fire talking after supper, she told us when Ramirez fled DC to find his family he had hitched a ride with her. She had been heading to New Bern to check on her Mom. Amy had grown up in a small house on the Neuse River spending more time on a boat and in the water than on dry land, at least when she wasn't in school.

Her dad had left when she was eight and her Mom had instilled in her a fierce independence. They didn't have money for college but her Mom worked hard as the office manager for a local electrician. When Amy expressed an interest in his work, he began to teach her. By the time she was a senior in high school, she spent all her spare time as his apprentice. Three years after that she took her exams and became a licensed electrician. She continued to work for him until she moved north with a boy she met on the job. When she got pregnant he left her and she too became a single Mom. She mentioned that last part with such a downcast look that no one asked what happened.

Ramirez's story was more straightforward. He joined the Army right out of high school and married his sweetheart once he returned from basic. He worked hard and made it into the 75th Ranger Regiment. Being one of the elite comes with a price though. While he was working his family was growing up without him. As a ranger, he spent more time deployed and eventually, his wife said she'd had enough. When he re-enlisted, she asked for a divorce. He said he understood and never held it against her. "She was a good woman, a great wife, and a wonderful mother. She just couldn't tolerate the deployments. She always looked haggard, thin, and grey by the time I returned home. She said she couldn't eat or sleep, always worrying about who the next knock on the door would bring and what news they would bear. How could I blame her or ask her to stay? I missed her terribly but it was the best thing for her. That made it the best thing for our Constantine." Ramirez explained.

Con stayed quiet. Eventually, I heard soft whispers from his side of the fire and saw Jules sitting beside him. He was a year younger but without any friends to pressure either of them, it didn't seem to matter. Seeing Jules smile her rare shy smile was enough to bring a smile to my own face.

"You really are a good big brother, you know," Belle said. I looked over to see her watching me from the next seat over.

"It's just good to see her smile after everything we've all been through, after what she's been through." My mood turned a little sour, "I'd like to find that bastard in Georgia and spend some good quality time killing him again, assuming he's actually dead."

"Oh, I don't think you need to worry about that. Jules and I talked a little and your Mom may have gone a little nuts with that one. Jules said the major was almost more terrifying than that boss raider. She also said there was absolutely no doubt that he was dead. Honestly, it shook her up. Not just the business with the raider but watching your Mom take him down. It sounded pretty damn gruesome."

"Jules is her daughter. I would hope so!" I said my voice rising.

"Easy, JC. I agree with you. I'm just letting you know that it's been taken care of and that's a topic you should probably steer clear of with both Jules and your Mom."

"Yeah, I'm sorry Belle. I know you're trying to help. It just pisses me off."

"Like I said, you're a good big brother. Jules is lucky to have you, we all are." I glanced over and Belle had a strange look, like she'd said something she didn't really intend to say.

"What's the plan for tomorrow?" she said quickly changing the subject.

"Why's that Belle, looking for more action already?" I teased.

"Hey, you're the one that bolted from the truck trying to act the hero! I was just there to save your ass, on the major's orders, I might add."

"I would expect no less. I must disagree about acting the hero. I can't help being who I am."

"Oh god. Really JC? You, my friend, are absolutely incorrigible."

"Speaking of incorrigible, look what I found in that apartment," I said pulling a small baggy of cannabis from my pocket.

"Well now, that is interesting. Ya know, I always did love what a generous and sharing person you are."

I turned and looked at Belle with a slack-jawed expression. I may have played it a little too hard because she was almost laughing when she asked, "What?"

"I just realized something, Belle. I mean we really screwed up."

"What?" she asked a little more seriously this time with a tinge of concern.

"We should have put some of this in the Spam we threw out to the Murdochs."

"Ya think? I mean, I know it would have slowed them down. It just seems like a waste."

"NO, well yeah but that's not what I mean."

"Well, why then?" she demanded sounding exasperated.

"Because then we truly would have had potted meat!"

"OH MY GOD!" she yelled laughing, "That was horrible, JC! I can't believe you went all that way just for that. That's it, I can take no more. I'm going to bed."

Chapter 15 – Parkway

The morning came bright and beautiful. No, actually, that's a lie. It sucked. The rain had moved in just during the early morning hours and drenched us all. It was cold rain with a howling wind that nearly tore the tarp away before we could get it down and stowed. The horses looked miserable, and Jules' horse tried to bite me twice while I was putting them back in the trailer. By the time we got everything packed up, nobody had a stitch of dry clothing on and there were no smiles to be found. It was shaping up to be a dandy of a day.

It was then that I remembered the backpack of clothes for Ben. We finally saw a smile that morning when he realized what this meant. Ben would finally have something other than the clothes I found him in and the few clothes we had bartered for in Bryson City. There were even a few T-shirts he actually liked. I unloaded the clothes and the meager supplies we had looted into the trailer.

We all changed and grabbed our rain gear. Ben had to settle for a poncho that we had to fold and tie around his waist to keep it from dragging on the ground. I thought he was going to blow away when he stepped out to run for the truck. The first gust nearly picked him up like a bizarre cross between Mary Poppins' umbrella and a hot air balloon. Jules grabbed his hand just to be sure and they ran for the back door together. By the time we made it the 30 feet from the trailer to the truck cab, I wasn't sure changing clothes actually did us any good. I could even feel the Lady sway slightly during the bigger gusts. Oh joy.

I was back in the driver's seat with Mom and her Benelli riding shotgun. Mom had assigned one of the radios to Amy & Ramirez and we kept the other so that we could have comms on the road. Our drive today shouldn't take us close to any big towns. It would be a meandering drive up the Blue Ridge Parkway. It really was too bad the weather was so horrible. Otherwise, we should have had some spectacular views.

Our goal was an early lunch at Price Lake where the maps showed a good size field. It didn't look to be close to any towns, and Mom thought we could take a break to exercise the horses. After that, a run for the border and Virginia by nightfall, we hoped.

The Price Lake stop was better than we expected. We made decent time despite the storm and got there around 10:00. The rain had let up and was more of a drizzle with occasional showers. We decided to go ahead with some horseback riding. It felt great to get back in the saddle, and it turned out that Ramirez was a decent rider too. Belle helped Amy with her first time getting on a horse, and Mom carried Ben with her for his first.

Besides the fields, there were several trails in the area. Everyone had time to enjoy at least an hour of riding. Ramirez said it was great to ride again, but he was already feeling it. He handed Ginger off to me as soon as they returned. Amy, not knowing any better, took Dakota back through the fields with Jules on her beloved Jasper. Nobody was allowed on Jasper other than Jules. That was not our rule; it was completely a Jasper thing. She pretty well hated everyone except Jules. Fox wasn't much better, which is probably why Mom named him Charlie Foxtrot. He was a mess. Damn if he wasn't fast though.

Con finally warmed up to the idea, and I put him up on Gin. She took it easy on him and seemed to have a good time. When Jules finally brought him and Amy back, it was nearly 12:30 and we needed to get back on the road. While they had been out riding, Ramirez and I went hunting. Ramirez managed to kill a nice buck and together we had it dressed out and quartered by the time they returned. We grabbed a quick lunch after loading the horses back into the trailer and were back on the road by 13:30.

The rain had stopped and the day was shaping up to be a good one. Naturally recent experience had taught me to be wary of such wonderful potential. I kept looking around each turn with apprehension until Mom had had enough.

"James, if you don't relax I'm going to lock you in the rear of the trailer with Fox."

"Sorry Mom, I just keep waiting for the other shoe to drop. It's been too nice of a day and things really haven't gone that well for us on this trip."

"Son, if you don't learn to enjoy the good times you're never going to be able to stand the hard times. Don't go looking for trouble when there is none. Stay alert, sure, but enjoy these moments of peace because, as you point out, they won't last."

"I know. It's just been a hard trip."

"It has, that's all the more reason to enjoy today. Besides, the rain seems to be moving back in, does that help?"

"Yes, ma'am, and no, or maybe; hopefully it'll satisfy that superstitious hind brain of mine."

Mom smiled and went back to reading the map.

"We're making good time. There's a decent-looking spot up on the Virginia border that we can overnight if it hasn't changed too much since they printed this map. I'll let Amy know."

Sure enough, we rolled across the Virginia – North Carolina line at 17:36 and found a good creek near exit 89. It was a nice area with rolling hills and plenty of fields for the horses to enjoy. Everything seemed quiet, so we just parked on the ramp up to the highway. The horses seemed undecided about coming out into the rain. After some time it seemed a desire for fresh water and a good stretch overcame their reluctance. They came on out with only a token nip or two. Jasper didn't even put much effort into trying to bite me.

Ramirez came over while I was putting Dakota out on a picket.

"As much as I love putting up a tent in the rain, I'm going to take a quick jog up that dirt road over there and see what's around. Maybe we can find an abandoned house or some other shelter for tonight."

"Sounds good. Take the radio and Belle with you. She's a great shot and you've seen her work back in Asheville, at least enough to know she'll have your back."

"Way ahead of you. She's already waiting by the truck. We'll be back in 10 mics."

"Copy that." I smiled.

There was definitely part of me that did not like that arrangement. I mean, I know Belle and I were just friends and he was way too old for her. Stupid, right? They were just going to look for shelter, and there's Amy after all. She was closer to Ramirez's age and a pretty lady at that.

They returned a few minutes later saying they found a house just up the hill behind the trees. Mom wasn't crazy about the trees so close to the house limiting how far the watch could see. On the other hand, it would get us away from the crossroads, and Ramirez was right. It beat them having to set up a tent. We left Jules and Con to guard the horses while we moved the vehicles up to the house.

Those two seemed to be good for each other, so we kept finding excuses to leave them together. That's not to say they were about to start dating or anything. Just that they were talking and sharing experiences. Mom left Ben with them this time to join in with his own experience. Being able to talk with someone else with similar experience at the hands of raiders seemed to be helping. You could see their moods change every time they spent much time together. It was like watching them set down another 10lb weight they'd been carrying. Not everything at once, but enough to make a difference.

The night was uneventful and the extra 3 people for night watch were definitely allowing everyone to get more sleep. It also made policing the area and packing up quicker in the morning. Overall, having the extra hands added to our group was great. Even just conversations about new topics were a nice change of pace. I'm not sure how many times you can rehash the same old stories about the same old things. We had been getting close to finding out.

After a long debate, we all decided to take the Parkway up to

a place marked Fancy Gap on the map where we could get
onto I-77. The Parkway had been nice and mostly quiet travel.
Unfortunately, it was heading in the wrong direction now.
We hoped the interstate might allow us to pick up the pace.
Higher risk for raiders for sure, but we needed to make some
progress before our fuel started to become a problem.

Chapter 16 – Mountaineer

I-77 was both a blessing and a curse. We were certainly able to travel faster. You still couldn't drive too fast, though, because of the random cars that had died in the EMP blasts. It doesn't seem like a problem until you realize that a stopped car seems to come at you pretty quickly when you're moving at highway speeds. Top that off with the fact that our Franken Lady is a lot of things, but nimble ain't one of 'em. Oh, and let's not forget the trailers behind both trucks, one of which had horses and chickens along for the ride.

Despite all that, we made good time and were approaching the West Virginia border by lunchtime. The Dublin-Newbern area looked like it might be a problem. Thankfully, the raiders there seemed to think twice when they saw the armored rig leading the way. The fact that there was someone pointing a rocket launcher at them might have had something to do with that. I'll give them credit for smart decision-making and having cleared out most of the Murdochs in town. It allowed us to sail straight through unmolested.

We passed into West Virginia at Peterstown around 12:30. The place had a sad, desolate look to it, as though it had suffered greatly since The Fall. We saw a few Murdochs out wandering aimlessly, but little else. The local hardware store was relatively untouched. With only half a day's travel remaining to the farm, we decided it would be worth stocking up.

I disconnected our trailer and brought the Lady around to the back. Using supplies from the hardware store, I was able to fabricate a hitch on the back of the camper trailer to allow us to pull a second trailer. We did the same for Amy's rig.

We left both trailers and the Franken Lady at the hardware store while Amy, Ramirez, and I took her truck to look for new trailers. We found one for Amy at a U-haul dealer. As expected, most of theirs were small, and we wanted a little more room for the Lady since she could easily haul the added weight. We went back to the hardware store and dropped the U-haul trailer with the others. With that done, we were back on the trailer hunt.

In the end, we had to backtrack to Pearisburg where we found a big box trailer at an excavating contractor. It looked pretty new and was around 20 feet long. I also raided their shop, finding supplies most looters would pass by as useless. Things like welding rods, nuts & bolts, belts, acetylene & oxygen gas, and various other supplies went into the trailer.

Around the side of the shop, we found some older heavy equipment that might be worth further investigation in the coming weeks. It was simple stuff without all the fancy electronics and looked like it had been well-maintained. There was even a John Deere 450J. It was a great little dozer whose early stick shifters would drive most prospectors away. All that equipment was definitely worth keeping in mind for closer inspection later.

By the time we returned to the hardware store in Peterstown, it was getting late. We dropped the new trailer in a flat lot that must have been a cleared building site and then went back to get the others. Once we had all the trailers hooked up, we drove back to the lot and formed a circle like a wagon train, the Lady on the outside, nose to tail with Amy's new trailer.

We spent a restless but uneventful night there. We used our impromptu courtyard as a paddock for the horses. Ramirez, Amy, Con, and Ben slept in an old abandoned log cabin on the edge of the lot. They said it was dirty, but it had a roof and walls. Once again, it beat hauling out the big tent. Ben did complain about a mouse running around on his sleeping bag. We weren't sure whether that was just a dream or actually happened. We heard Murdochs and other animals milling about in the night from time to time. Apparently, we just weren't worth the trouble.

In the morning we got to work. We took the Lady over to the hardware store with Amy, Jules, Mom, and me to load supplies there. We kept Amy with us so she could direct what electrical supplies we should take. Belle and Ben went with Con and Ramirez in Amy's truck to hunt for canned and dried food. Once we finished at the hardware store, we visited other abandoned businesses in town. Places like the auto parts store, the lube store, a heavy truck shop, and we even marked our maps with a few likely farms to visit in the future.

It took the entire day to comb the town and load supplies. If there were any unchanged people in town, we never saw them. It was a sad realization that the entire town seemed to be either changed or dead. Hopefully, someone had survived and just left to join others somewhere else.

We spent the night back in the same lot with an identical experience. The only real difference was when Jules, who had promised to stay with Ben in the house this time, woke up screaming with a mouse in her hair. Ramirez wasn't sure what to do. In his words, "I wasn't sure if she was dreaming or possessed by El Sombreron!" He later explained El Sombreron was a demon who liked to braid hair and seemed partial to horses and young women with big eyes and long hair. Jules, with her big blue eyes, definitely qualified.

By the time Jules realized the mouse was gone, she had woken the entire camp, and half the county, if I didn't miss my guess. Mom was standing over her, shotgun in hand, looking for what had attacked her baby. That was pretty impressive considering Mom had been 30 yards away behind a closed door sleeping in a trailer. Jules insisted on cutting her hair right then and wasn't about to stay in the cabin, neither was Ben at that point. After everyone calmed down and Jules showered, we all tried to go back to sleep. Jules volunteered to relieve Belle early on watch. She looked cute with her new pixie cut. I nearly started laughing when she kept reaching up to play with long hair that was no longer there.

The morning was grey with clouds, and a cool mist blew through the air like a cold moving blanket. With the new trailers loaded, we looked around at the lonely town one last time. Our lack of sleep from the night before seemed to amplify the desolate mood.

Amy insisted on getting back in the driver's seat of her truck to test how it would pull the added load. Belle and Jules decided the last few hours of our trip would be girl time and claimed two seats in the pickup. I think this was Belle trying to keep Jules' mind off the night before, more than any real desire for "girl time". After much pleading, they even managed to drag Mom in with them. They reasoned that she should be in the following truck. That way she could help check the new trailer's tracking and let me know if she saw any problems. It was a weak excuse, but Mom went along with it anyhow.

That left the Lady as the testosterone-fueled man rig, called the Lady. Yeah, I know. Irony in action, but my dad did have a thing for naming all his equipment after women. Must have liked women for some reason, because I know he loved his equipment.

We rolled out slowly. The lady was pulling fine. She just had to pull harder than the day before. I actually had to use first gear on flat ground, weird. I was glad that we only had a few hours left in our journey as I was beginning to think we may have overloaded our second trailer just a little. The sagging tires should probably have been a good indicator. Oh well, good thing there were no transportation officers to worry about.

With the added weight and second trailers, we had agreed to keep our speed down. The last thing we wanted was an accident that could destroy equipment or injure someone. That meant our two-hour journey (pre-war travel time) would likely take at least half a day. Oh boy.

The Greenbrier River came into view through the trees around 09:30. It was a good thing we slowed for the turn as we approached the bridge over the river, because I nearly slammed on the brakes at the scene before us. What appeared to be a heavy wooden gate attached to a school bus blocked the far end of the bridge. High walls surrounded the gate with armed guards peering down their rifle barrels at our Lady.

Ramirez stepped down slowly from the passenger seat and walked out onto the bridge.

"That's far enough, stranger!" one of the men yelled.

"Gentlemen, how are you?" Ramirez called back.

"That ain't no concern of yours!"

"My apologies, sir, I didn't mean any offense. Just trying to be polite is all." Ramirez replied.

"Well, you shove your high'n'mighty 'politeness' up your ass you fuckin' wet-back!"

"Now that wasn't nice," came my mother's voice from somewhere off in the bushes to the right of the bridge. In the brief silence that followed, you could clearly make out the slap of her rifle bolt.

"Who the fuck was that? Show yourself!" the same man yelled.

"Look, she is one of the best marksmen I have ever seen, and that is saying something. Now, I've tried to be nice, but she seems to be growing weary of your games. Is there someone intelligent that I can talk to, or does this community rely on your dumb ass for all its negotiations?" Ramirez replied in a tone that had changed from an acquiescent conversational tone to that of the professional Ranger. A Ranger growing weary of taking shit from some useless, bigoted asshole.

We could hear a heated conversation on the other side of the wall followed by the sound of someone running off. We waited a good 15-20 minutes before a tall muscle-bound man in his 30's with dark, slicked-back hair and a weasel-thin face appeared at the top of the wall.

"What do you want?" the newcomer said without preamble.

"My friends and I are traveling north to their farm. We simply want to continue up the highway through town."

"There's a toll to drive through, but if you're friendly and want to do some trading, I may be willing to wave the toll."

"What's the toll?"

"Depends on what you got?"

"Look, friend, we don't mind trading as long as the trades are fair, but I'm not inclined to pay a toll, particularly with no set price."

"Well, those are the terms. If you don't like it, go back up to Caldwell and cross there. Should only be an hour out of the way with those rigs. 'Course the bridge in town is out. You'll have to use the interstate, and without local knowledge of the raiders up that way, well, it could be a long delay."

"Sounds like you have it all worked out. As I said, we're willing to trade. How would this work?"

"Oh, simple enough, this bridge leads onto another bridge. You pull up onto the second bridge and stop before the gate. We'll close this gate behind you, and two of your group can come down to our little market to trade."

"I'd like three of us to come down to town." Ramirez countered.

"No, two is the limit. Typically I'd say one, but I appreciate the lady in the bushes not killing Clem. He's an asshole, yet he does have a few skills that we find useful. In return for that favor I'll allow two."

"OK, I think we can do that."

"And just to make sure we don't have any problems, you'll not be one of the two. Neither you nor your talking bush there." He said with a nod towards the bushes. "Not until we all get our courtin' done and learn whether or not we like each other. Understand?"

"I understand, and Clem?"

"Oh, I sent Clem back down into town. He's not usually allowed up at the gates. We've needed to change the shifts a bit lately and he had to take a turn. You can see that he's not the sociable type and tends to cause more problems than he's worth. Unfortunately, he's a good carpenter, meaning we put up with him."

Chapter 17 – Market Town

The gate began to roll to the side as he spoke these last words, and I fired the Lady back up. I had switched the mixture back to rich to let her smoke and even went as far as pulling the exhaust cutout before the second muffler. It pained me to do it, but I made her seem like any ole ordinary truck with a questionable maintenance record, struggling to pull the load. I added to that impression by starting forward in third gear, unsuccessfully. Then, I used second gear making her appear to really struggle to get the load moving. I know it was a convincing performance because I heard one of the guards comment on what a piece of shit she was as we passed.

We used our two radios to come up with a plan while we pulled onto the bridge. Belle and I would go down to the market to meet the people and trade a little. We made a good team and could play the husband and wife routine again. It seemed to set people at ease, and kept too many men from getting ideas about ways to keep Belle for themselves, mostly.

Mom had slipped back into the pickup unseen. That left the guards unable to be completely sure that Belle wasn't the one in the bushes, a fact that Belle found immensely amusing. The declaration that they wouldn't allow us to carry our rifles was less amusing. She almost refused to go, but they didn't seem to have a problem with pistols, and she was a crack shot with her FN. Belle added an ankle holster with her S&W Shield before walking over to meet me. With her long black hair pulled into a ponytail tucked through a ball cap ,and her tactical vest on, she looked hot. Once she caught me staring at her, I had to revise that to pissed-off and completely done with taking shit for the day. Note to self, Belle was not amused under those circumstances.

We walked down the ramp into their new town. It was actually a nice little setup. The river formed a nice barrier on one side that was open and easy to patrol. Our escort was actually a nice guy named Tim who explained that the biggest part of their town was an old lumber mill and the county park. There was a small danger of flooding if the river got up. The towns' folk all agreed that the easy defenses made it worth the risk. They used the lumber from the mill to build a wall down the edge of the triple train tracks, connecting to the river on both ends. The tracks make footing uneven as you approach the wall and provide a good open area to see anyone coming. The only way left into town now was the road we were walking down.

In addition to the impressive town wall, we were soon walking through the former county park that was now a community farm. Tim pointed out the amphitheater along the river that they used for meetings. He carried on for some time about the great musicians who used to play there on weekends before The Fall. He said they occasionally still had gatherings there with music just to keep up town morale.

As you might expect, the market wasn't large. Something Tim said was mostly due to the small town population with very little time to do things like shopping. They housed the market in the park's concession stand with folding tables stacked along the side. The tables looked like they were easy to set up when the market needed to expand.

Darla was a dear old lady who fawned over Belle and kept commenting on what a cute couple we were. She ran the market, and after a while, I began to suspect all the flattery was part of her sales pitch. She had us dealing for more fresh vegetables and fruit than we could carry in exchange for some of the hand tools we had recently acquired.

A few others from the town came over as they learned of the strangers at the market. Still more just watched from a distance as if they thought we might have some disease, and they didn't want to catch it. Several of those who did come over to talk asked for news of the surrounding towns. I think most were just happy to see a new face and talk to someone who hadn't heard their stories a hundred times before. Overall, our impression of the town was a pleasant place, even if a bit standoffish.

Tim had gone to get a horse-drawn cart to take our purchases up to the trucks and bring their goods back when the man we talked to earlier walked up.

"I believe I failed to introduce myself earlier. My name is Horace, and I'm the town mayor, for lack of a better title."

"I'm James, and this is my wife, Belle," I said, and saw a slight frown as I said wife.

"I'm delighted to meet you." He said to Belle and leaned in to kiss the offered hand. Belle shot me a WTF look. I could tell that rather than flattered, she was more than a little unnerved (and probably on the verge of shooting Mayor Dumbass). There was something distinctly wrong with Horace. He had an almost oily quality about him, and his eyes never seemed to leave Belle as he spoke. He did finally reach over to shake my hand, almost as an afterthought. Even then, his eyes barely left Belle. They had a hungry look to them.

"Now, as Darla seems pleased with the trading, I'll waive the toll."

At the word toll, Darla looked at Horace with an appraising look that I wouldn't call altogether friendly. Apparently, the toll was news to Ms. Darla.

"However," Horace continued without noticing Darla's look, "information is valuable and our town has little enough to get by as it is. With that in mind, we'll need to discuss a trade for any local knowledge. You understand, I'm sure."

"Now, Horace," Darla interrupted, "we'll not be taking advantage of our new friends. We want them to come back and trade with us again. Why, dear Belle here tells me their farm is only a bit farther to the north. We're practically neighbors. And neighbors shouldn't treat each other that way."

Horace had a rapid series of emotions cross his face as she talked. They began with anger at the interruption. His expression quickly moved to interest and something I would almost call greed. Dear ole Horace was one we'd need to watch, I decided. And I was beginning to think we should only watch him through a rifle's scope.

"It's pretty simple, really. There's a group of raiders set up at the old Greenbrier Military School in Lewisburg. It's a big group of maybe 50 or more. They use I-64 at Highway 219 as a choke point to abduct & rob travelers. They've pulled cars and trucks up there all over the interstate to force you down a single ramp at the overpass, ya see? Spotters in a tower built on top of the old Fairfield Inn ring a bell when they see someone coming, that way they have plenty of time to get ready."

"To top it off, they worked real hard to close every alternative route. They have a roving patrol that checks those blockades and, sometimes, man them just to keep all of us locals guessing. Most people from out of town never see it coming. They're down there at the interchange with their hands in the air before they figure out what happened," Darla explained.

"Well, Darla, I certainly appreciate that. It's nothing we haven't seen before, but it is nice to know what to expect. It's too bad they couldn't just let us be. It'll be expensive for them to take us, if they can," I said.

"Oh, they can do it," Horace replied. "Best thing y'all can do is go back to Georgia."

"And keep those nice folks and Lewisburg waitin' on us? Now we just couldn't do that." Belle chimed in, laying that South Georgia draw on nice and thick. Damn if she didn't add in a wink at the end for Horace. He looked utterly dumbfounded.

"Now, I know the fella up there at the bridge looks tough and you've got some armor on that old rig, but you shouldn't underestimate that crowd. We've had a few skirmishes with them here and lost several good men, even with our walls and trained militia." Horace seemed halfway between bragging and condescending. It was a neat trick.

"Oh, we've got a few good rifles, and even JC here is a fair shot."

"We'll they've got a mounted 50 cal. machine gun. Can you beat that?"

"Yep, with just one shot," Belle said more seriously. I was beginning to think she had the same opinion of Horace as I did. Ole Horace was closer to the edge than he realized. One misstep here could be fatal for Horace.

"Thank you, Darla, we really do appreciate the information. We'll be careful if we head up that way. Perhaps we can find another route." I said in an effort to stop the escalating debate.

With the transfer of trade goods complete, we had a long discussion over what to do next. In the end, we decided to take the long way around Lewisburg by going up to Alvon before cutting back to 219. It was going to add an hour or two if all went well. It was still worth it to avoid another fight. I backed Amy's rig down onto the ramp, backing doubles was something I'd grown up doing with silage trailers on the farm. As I was walking back to get the Lady, Tim walked up.

"Brought you a little something for the road," Tim said, "and as an apology for Clem and Uncle Horace. Horace is a proud man and wants everyone to show him deference. We're used to it, but most outsiders take offense, and we'd like ya'll to come back. As for Clem, well Clem's one of my uncle's old friends and frankly he's just an ass."

I laughed at that last part as Tim handed me a golden jar of honey that shone nearly clear when the sun struck it.

"No doubt about it where Clem's concerned. Is this sourwood honey?"

"I see you know your honey. Yes, it is, and some of the finest around."

"That's awfully generous of you, Tim. Regular honey is great, but this stuff is heaven in a jar."

Tim just beamed at that assessment.

"I'd have to agree with that, especially since they're my bees. Looks like y'all are going back?"

"Yeah, thought we'd head up to Alvon and cut over to 219 from there. Just seems safer to avoid trouble if we can."

"I hear ya. Well, good luck, and I hope we'll see you again as soon as y'all get settled in up there."

"Thanks, Tim. We'll be looking forward to it, especially if we can trade for more of this honey!"

I climbed up into the Lady and started the smoky show of backing up an old, decrepit truck that was barely making her way. After all, I wasn't sure I completely trusted anyone in this town. There was no harm in a little innocent deception.

We were running behind schedule, a lot behind schedule. We decided to eat lunch on the road to make up a little. By the time we backtracked and made it up to Alvon, it was nearly 13:30, and the Major was none too pleased. She was really hoping to reach the farm today, and that was beginning to look questionable at best. She had already declared that we would not be rolling up into an unknown situation in the dark. A lot could have happened in the last year's chaos.

We turned onto a small, single-lane road that should take us over to Highway 219. At least it was paved. I could foresee fallen trees or landslides in my near future. Only twenty minutes down the road rewarded me with both. A small slide had taken down several trees and dumped them along with a pile of mud onto the roadway.

Mom took up an overwatch sniper position on top of the Lady while Ramirez faded into the trees behind our rigs. That left me on the chainsaw with the others to help pull the brush out of the way. Even Ben jumped in to help. I let him help only after we talked about waiting until I told him it was OK. Then he could come over to grab the brush.

It took an hour to cut a path through all the storm debris which only left the mud and rocks. Luckily our Franken Lady had a beautiful blade on the front that made short work of the debris. By that time my team was exhausted. Mom gave them all permission to ride in the trailer where they could relax and have a snack while we covered the last hour of our trip.

We settled back into the trucks, and after one solid push, we were back on our way, another hour and a half behind.

Chapter 18 – Fifty for the Road

The trees lining the road made it impossible to see the ambush. We were almost on top of the intersection with Highway 219 before we knew it was coming. Two trucks shot out of the Dollar General parking lot as we slowed for the stop sign. The one in front was a Humvee with a .50 caliber machine gun mounted on top. Before we had even come to a stop, the man on the .50 opened up with a burst high through our windshield. We instinctively ducked, but my Mom had drilled into me that in a situation like this, I should never do the expected. Instead of hitting the brakes, like my instincts were screaming at me to do, I hit the gas. The lady lurched forward and hit the Humvee so hard I saw the gunner slam back against the turret hole and go slack. At the same time, there was a loud ringing twang from the plow. The Humvee shot across the road into the telephone pole on the other side, snapping the pole in half and causing it to drop down across the roof.

The Lady continued, plowing into the Humvee a second time and pushing it down a sloped lawn into a tree where they both came to rest. Mom was out of the Lady before it had even rocked back from the impact. She had blood streaming down her face and her Benelli combat shotgun in both hands. She looked like a crazed Nordic warrior stepping out of Hell and looking for the bastards who sent her there. That woman had vengeance in mind and I was damned glad she wasn't coming after me.

Before I could even finish that thought, I heard the boom

of the shotgun and saw the glass in the door of the Humvee shatter. That would be an unarmored version then. A second boom followed on the heels of the first, and the driver's window blew out along with a spray of blood. Mom walked up to the rear door and slung it open. When a figure stumbled out towards her, she let the shells roll out of the Benelli. He was nearly cut in half by the close-range shots. She barely even flinched as the body dropped across her boots. When the shotgun ceased firing, the remaining windows of the Humvee were crimson with blood. My dear sweet mother looked like she just stepped out of a carnal house.

When I had floored the accelerator in the Lady, Amy slammed on the brakes in her truck. Blocking us front and rear would have been a good move if we had been in two normal trucks. In this case, the Franken Beast in front was more than a match for the Humvee. The double trailers on Amy's truck actually blocked the view of the rear ambushers when the trailers slewed to the side during her skid. Ramirez followed his training and, like Mom, was out of the door, gun in hand as soon as the vehicle slid to a stop. What they expected to be a surprise of overwhelming force had quickly gone sideways into a soup sandwich.

Ramirez hit the ground, fired twice, and was disappearing behind the trees before the oxygen thief in the back of the truck even had time to aim. His next shot came from behind the truck and took his bandit through the back of his head. The passenger was nearly in line with the second bandit. His brains painted the windshield with the next shot.

The driver, finally realizing that he was driving the Barney wagon and was royally hooped, hit the gas. The truck lurched across the ditch on the opposite side of the road and up into the adjacent cemetery. He bounced off a large tombstone as a 5.56 mm hole appeared through the windshield where his head would have been. The truck jerking to the side has saved his life. This seemed to motivate him even further, and the truck screamed through the cemetery on the verge of red-lining the motor. He hit the road again with a crash and more fluids streaming out of the truck than it seemed it could have ever held. Undaunted, the driver finally shifted gears and held the gas to the floor. Smoke was pouring from the truck as he crested the hill and fled out of sight.

The ambush over, Mom ran to the trailer to check on everyone riding inside. As she reached for the handle, the door flew open and the rifle barrel led Belle out into the afternoon light.

"It's over," Mom said quickly as the muzzle swung towards her. It was understandable, as Mom was nearly unrecognizable, covered in gore as she was. Belle nearly dropped the rifle at the sound of her voice.

"Ms. McKinney, are you OK?!" Belle yelled.

"I'm fine, Belle. It's not my blood. Shotguns are messy at close range." An understatement if there ever was one. "How is everyone inside?" Mom asked as she pointed towards the trailer.

"We're banged up, but nothing serious. Con has a cut above his eye that Jules is working on now. She'll have him cleaned up and good to go in a few."

They both walked back to soothe the horses, at least two of which were kicking the trailer. After a few unsuccessful minutes, we just sent Mom to clean up, and we unloaded the trailer. The horses finally began to settle after we tied them to a couple of trees upwind of all the blood and gore. Jules and Belle took turns walking each horse around to calm them further. We had lost nearly half the chickens in the noise and commotion. Guess what we had for supper?

Amy pulled her truck into the Dollar General parking lot, and we began assessing the damage. The Lady was well fouled, and it was going to take time to get her out. Ramirez and Amy dropped the trailers from her truck while Mom set up in an overwatch position. My job was to remove the machine gun from the Humvee.

Ramirez came over to help me clean out the turret. We both nearly jumped out of our skin when the gunner grabbed my arm. The power pole had missed him, still hanging by the old lines. This guy had only broken his back on the turret when the Lady hit them. He'd passed out, and everyone forgot about him. Ramirez looked over to me.

"Why don't you take a walk. My new friend here and I need to have a talk."

"That's OK, I'll stay."

"You sure?"

"Yeah."

Without any further comment, Ramirez pulled his pistol and put it to the gunner's elbow.

"Who sent you?"

"Fuck you."

Ramirez pulled the trigger, and the gunner screamed.

"Who sent you?" He asked again.

"Fuck! You!"

Ramirez put the barrel to his other elbow and raised his eyebrows questioningly. When the raider just glared back, saying nothing, he moved the barrel to his temple and pulled the trigger.

"Lost cause." He said and re-holstered his Beretta.

Note to self, if Ramirez asks a question, answer quickly!

We dragged the body out, down through the cab, and I began working on the 50.

While I worked, Amy and Ramirez unhooked the rear trailer and pulled it back up onto the road with her truck. When they started to unhook the horse trailer, I yelled over to them to leave it. "Ramirez, you're used to military trucks. Jump in and back her up. She's a 6x6 with custom diesel, she'll back out."

He jumped in, and she fired right up. Backing out had me jumping off the Humvee quick, fast, and in a hurry. The damned Humvee was hung on the blade. I jumped up into the Lady's cab and used the hydraulics to finally work it free. Ramirez got the Lady back onto the road, and I went back to work on the gun. I decided it would be quicker to just use the torch and cut the mount free. I could play with how to use the mount when I had time and a safer place. Twenty minutes later, we loaded both the gun and mount into the trailer.

With the salvage complete, it was time to start looking over my poor Lady. I found two broken mounts. One mount on the blade had cracked through the center, and one of the hydraulic rams broke off completely. I pulled out the welding leads and got to work. After finishing those up, I went back to look at the trailers. The heavy-duty horse trailer was fine, but the new box trailer had nearly torn the coupler completely off. Another half hour of welding and we were about ready to roll.

We hooked the trailers back up and started looking at our map again. The farm was beginning to look like a lost cause for the day. We decided to drive up to the Droop Mountain Battlefield State Park and spend the night there. Luckily, the salvage and welding time had been good for the horses, and they loaded up without trouble. With the horses loaded, we hooked up the box trailer and raised the windshield armor to block most of the wind. I used a pair of amber safety glasses to keep it from blowing into my eyes, and we drove on up to the state park.

It was an easy drive straight up the highway. We arrived around 17:00 and circled the rigs around a large log lookout tower. The horses had grown accustomed to their paddock and seemed happy to be free to wander the area, eating down the tall grass. I took the first watch in the tower while everyone else enjoyed some downtime or helped cook supper. The smell of chicken grilling in the skillet drifted up to the tower above where I sat. It reminded me how little I had eaten.

I heard Jules call to everyone that supper was ready just as someone started climbing up to me. When Belle's head popped up through the opening, I smiled. I hadn't realized I was dreading having to talk to someone. Belle was different, she would leave me alone if I didn't want to talk or at least talk about something fun or interesting. Best of all, she had a canteen and a small steel bucket filled with steaming chicken and vegetables. It smelled wonderful!

There we are, on top of a mountain far from any town, corralled up on a state park, and here come three Murdochs. They were just wandering up out of the woods like someone called them for dinner. Called them for dinner, hmmm, gonna have to talk to Jules about yelling at everyone to come to supper. Of course, the smell of the chicken probably didn't help. They did seem to be coming from downwind. Well, time to get to work.

I pushed down the mic button on the radio, "Three Murdochs incoming. Enjoy your supper, firing now."

Belle squeezed the trigger on my M1 as I said 'now'. She caught two Murdochs in a row and dropped them both with one shot. The third leapt to the side and then sprinted for the horses. Belle never so much as twitched. She just smoothly adjusted her aim and squeezed the trigger again. The third Murdoch fell into a tumbling roll and a final thud.

"Nice one, Belle," I heard my Mom call over the radio.

"Hey, that could've been me," I protested.

"Not a chance, sweetie. That was too smooth. Besides, the first shot came while you were still jabbering on the radio."

Oh well, when she's right, she's right.

"God, what a day," Belle said as she leaned the M1 against the rail.

"No kidding. Before you ask who, it could have been Tim."

"No way, Tim was too nice." Belle replied.

"That's just it, right? He was too nice. And there's something else, I told him where we were going when he brought that honey as we started to leave. It was such a natural question that I didn't even think about it until the ambush hit. Since then, I've thought of almost nothing else."

"Maybe he told someone. There would have been no reason not to, right? We were long gone, and Horace comes up and says, 'hey nephew, what were you talking to the strangers about?' He tells him and doesn't think a thing about it. Even if someone had to drive up to the raider camp, they had plenty of time. Their drive was half the distance, and you drive like my grandma."

"Yeah, yeah. I guess that works too, and Horace seems the type. I just hate to underestimate the quiet or overly friendly types, ya know?" I said.

"I get that, but it's gotta be Horace. That guy gives me the creeps!"

We sat up there bashing Horace and eating supper just like old times back home. Even with having to keep watch, it was fun.

"Thanks, Belle. I needed that."

"I know," she said with a smirk and disappeared down the ladder.

A few minutes after Belle climbed down, my Mom climbed up.

"Figured I'd take the next shift," she said. "Should give you time to get cleaned up before everyone turns in for the night."

"Thanks," I replied simply.

"It was nice hearing you and Belle up here together. It reminded me of old times back on the farm."

"Yeah, it was nice."

After a short pause, Mom continued, "I was waiting for Belle to leave. I want to talk to you about today."

I groaned, out loud, apparently. Mom smirked and continued, "Nothing like that, I wanted to tell you I was proud of your work today. Your reactions were spot on. You and Ramirez saved our asses today. Your reaction to the ambush turned their advantage into ours and certainly made it a short engagement. You fought your instincts and thought through your actions. That is exactly what I've been trying to teach you to do. I know you hate hearing it, James, but you have an enormous amount of potential, and you demonstrated a bit of that today. Anyway, I just wanted to say thank you."

I sat quietly, not knowing what to say, just thinking about all she had just said. That kind of praise was rare from Mom. She expected a lot from everyone she worked with, and her children were no exception. Finally, I managed to mutter, "Thanks, Mom."

"You are welcome. Now, go clean up. You stink, and your clothes are just nasty."

I laughed, "Yeah, Belle did mention that."

"Probably why the Murdochs followed us up here."

"Yeah, Belle mentioned that too. Although, I think it was either the smell of the chicken cooking or Jules calling everyone into supper."

"Hmmm, I'll need to talk to her about that. This is not the world we all grew up in."

Perfect, now I wouldn't need to do it, and she might actually listen to Mom. She may not listen for most things, but for anything Murdoch or combat-related, she usually did.

Chapter 19 – Mountain Roads

The morning actually brought the sun along for the ride. It was a nice change and seemed to help push everyone's spirits even higher. We were all excited about making it to our new home today. We ate and packed up quickly, all wanting to be on the road as soon as possible. By 07:00 we were pulling back onto the highway and heading north. Without a windshield, the morning air was actually a little cold once we got moving. I was definitely glad we only had a few hours to go.

We slowed as we started past a town called Marlinton. There was a small hand-painted sign that said Stillwell and pointed across the bridge. The odd part was the "Traders Welcome" added below the name. Despite our curiosity, we were all way too excited to stop and pushed on past. We drove by a lot of old businesses and homes as we continued north on 219. It reminded me a bit of South Georgia and made me a little homesick.

Another half hour up the road, and we came to our turn. It was a road that would take us through the old Tea Creek Wildlife Management Area. Turning onto a single-lane gravel road that hadn't seen maintenance in over a year was not what I'd call exciting. This was especially true with double trailers behind me. Particularly when Mom said, "Oh good, we should only have another hour or so to go." She was practically bouncing with excitement. That was really weird for my Mom. I was afraid, very afraid.

My trepidation seemed well-founded. We would drive 5 minutes and have to stop and cut a tree. Then everyone would climb back in only to stop in another 5 minutes, or less, to do it all again. This occurred so often that I just let Jules drive. Then Belle and I could play trunk monkey and hop out to clear trees quickly. After more than an hour, we finally made it to the top of the ridge with a pronouncement from Mom that we weren't quite halfway yet. Everyone groaned that time.

After a short break, we started down the other side of the ridge. We swapped duties around to give everyone a chance to enjoy the thrilling tasks of clearing the road. (Insert huge amounts of sarcasm here. I mean huge, filling the Grand Canyon kind of huge.) Belle and Jules swapped over to Amy's truck, and Ramirez, Con, and Ben became our trunk monkeys. If anything, this side was worse. We had hardly made it halfway down the ridge when Ramirez called for a break.

Three and a half hours into our one-hour trip, we finally made it to the Gauley River. Down by the river, we seemed to be sheltered from the wind a bit, and we didn't have nearly as many trees across the road. We came to a wooden bridge over the Gauley, and I pulled the Lady to a halt. After a long discussion, examination, and some argument, we decided to give it a try. There was a lot of groaning, and I'll swear to this day that I felt the damn thing shift, but we made it. Once I was across, everyone else crawled back into the truck. Yep, the traitorous bastards left me to go across alone. They all claimed they were trying to "lighten the load" I don't buy that crap for a minute.

We crossed back over the river on a similar bridge, and this time, everyone stayed in the truck to show how they weren't scared last time. No, sir, not scared at all. By this time, I realized that they built these bridges for logging trucks, so they could probably hold a whole lot more weight than what we were hauling. As I thought of that I might have exaggerated the creaks and groans I heard with several shouts of "What the hell was that?" and "Oh Shit! Hold on to something!" Mom was way ahead of me, but seemed to be enjoying the show. She just sat there with a little grin saying nothing. I did get punched in the arm when Belle caught me laughing after she started opening the door, getting ready to jump out.

We drove on up the mountain to a wide spot where Mom told me to pull over and stop.

"Is something wrong? Did I miss the turn?" I asked.

"Yes," she said cryptically.

"Well, that doesn't explain much."

"Something is very wrong, and we passed the turn on purpose. Miles is the caretaker and farmer who looks after the place for me. He always flew a flag on an old locust pole at the turn onto our land. It was an old flag of the Confederacy; they called it the Stars and Bars. It was our signal flag. At the top of the pole, everything was fine. Half-mast was trouble, but nothing too serious. Upside down is, of course, distress."

"But I didn't even see a pole, much less a flag. Did I miss it somehow?"

"Yes, because it was in the river. Someone had torn it down and thrown it in the river, where it looked to have lodged in some other debris, so it's been there a while. That pole was set deep, and locust doesn't break easily. It took a lot of effort to take that flagpole down."

"Now what?"

"Now, Ramirez and I need to have a long talk, and we need to look over some maps. Pull on up to the end of the road. There's a big log landing there where we can set up a camp. It's looking like it might become our forward operating base, but that's going to take more discussion. We're on the property and out of sight. Still, we may be too close. Recon will tell the tale. Let's get up there, and James, slow and quiet as a mouse, ok?"

I was incredulous but said nothing other than the expected "Yes ma'am." Quiet as a mouse, really? I'm pulling nearly 10 tons uphill, but okay, whatever. I did my best.

We pulled up the mountain to the end of the road and into our now customary circle. I could see the puzzled looks on Amy, Con, and Ramirez's faces as they followed suit. When we all stepped down armed, Ramirez seemed to grasp the situation without a word.

"We need to do some recon," Ramirez said. It wasn't a question.

"Yes, I have maps in the trailer. We can talk in there and look over our best options. It could be nothing but Raiders, but I don't like it. Miles, our caretaker, is a retired Marine. He'd not be taken easily, and he has most definitely been taken."

"Signal?"

"Lack of one and no replacements or other warnings in place."

"Damn. We've got our work cut out for us, then. Let's brief up, then I'll start dragging out my gear."

"Jules, you and James pull out something for lunch, and we'll eat while we talk."

While Belle helped us make chicken sandwiches, Mom came in and started up the laptop.

"It's time for you boys and girls to finally see why I went to all the trouble to protect a flat-screen TV and a ruggedized computer. It wasn't so you could all sit on your butts watching movies, I assure you."

Mom entered her login information, and a completely new desktop appeared on the screen. She double-clicked a map icon, and a 3D image of the property appeared, including our current location.

"How the hell is the GPS working?" Jules asked (well, I actually asked, but I'm writing the story, so it was Jules as far as you know).

"Satellites are in space, dear," Mom said slowly in that tone you use when talking to a toddler.

"Oh, yeah, right, so, no EMP for the satellites."

"Nope, they use them too. The PRC was very careful about timing. We may have lost a couple, but nothing the redundancies couldn't make up for."

Con, who had been fairly sedate since we met him, seemed to come alive at the sight of the screen.

"May I?" he asked Mom.

She looked over at Ramirez with a quizzical look. He nodded

with a huge grin on his face.

"Watch this kid work," Ramirez said, "It's pretty damn impressive."

It turned out that the quiet Con was a bit of a computer genius. Part of his morose mood was certainly the trauma of his captivity. However, much of the rest was apparently the complete loss of his all-consuming passion, computers. At Mom's reluctant nod, he took control of the laptop. Within a few minutes, he displayed points showing all the highest peaks, best observation points, terrain obstacles, and ranges from potential firing positions. His dad's influence was apparent in his skills.

"This may not be as surprising as it looks if you knew I've used this software before. I hacked into the base server and played around quite a bit before they caught me. Dad got in trouble for that one, and they threatened to put me in jail, but it worked out OK. Not even Dad knew what I downloaded and hid before they came to the house. I liked this software, so I swiped a copy and I'd been learning how to use it pretty well before the stupid PRC wiped out my system with their EMPs."

It was the most any of us, except perhaps Jules, had heard Con say at one time since we met him. As he talked, the map changed colors, highlighting different approach paths to the buildings. Each approach was color-coded according to the amount of concealment.

"It's neat stuff," Con said, "the software uses lidar data to detect the terrain features as well as determine vegetation heights and densities. That allows it to calculate the most likely sentry posts. It then uses that information to determine approach vectors. All of that is done using predetermined constraints. We can edit those if we want. What I'm using now are generic sentry probabilities. If we knew the nationality, the software would change parameters to match the collected data of preferences for that culture. It's pretty sophisticated. This must be a hell of a laptop to run it. Don't suppose you have a spare I can have?"

"That would be a no," Mom said with a slightly awed smile. She stood in fascination watching the talented, suddenly outgoing 14-year-old manipulate the software. He did it as well as any of the techs she had seen on base. He was even better than a few of the newer ones.

"I told you," Ramirez said with obvious pride, "the boy's got talent! Hell, give him a drone and he's a regular Zoomie." He grabbed Con's shoulder and squeezed gently. Con's smile broadened even more.

"I used to worry that Dad would be disappointed that I wasn't Ranger material like him, but he thinks this is cool too."

I looked over at Jules and noticed her watching Con intensely. She glanced up and saw me watching her, and a crimson blush flushed her cheeks. I raised my eyebrows, and she just grinned and shot me a bird.

The rest of us hung back and watched the show as Mom and Ramirez formed a plan for their recon, using Con as their new computer specialist.

Chapter 20 – Recon

Mom worked her way around the northwest ridge while Ramirez and Amy circled back down to the river on horseback. The plan was for Mom to set up an observation post on the ridge. Once she did that, the sweet young couple would walk their horses down the road across the river from the farm. Ramirez and Amy held up at the bridge to allow Mom time to get ready. At 14:30 they would begin their ride along the river, playing the role of curious locals to draw out the occupants. Then Mom could look for sentries and watch how they reacted.

Mom settled into a fork in the branches of a tall oak up on the northwest ridgeline. With the high-magnification optics of her binoculars, she had a clear view of the farm below. She had already picked out one sentry, and she didn't like what she saw. Although he was in civilian attire, the sentry had a QBZ-95 bullpup rifle. It used a 5.8mm round that was unusual here. More importantly, it was the standard issue rifle of the Chinese People's Liberation Army General Forces. It was possible they were stolen weapons, but that was unlikely. The PRC had not supplied the SSA with weapons, and PLAGF troops were very protective of their equipment. They had to be because their lives depended on being able to account for everything.

When Ramirez and Amy began walking Gin and Dakota down the road, the sentries' reactions sealed it for her. The one she could see appeared to start talking into a radio. A lone figure stepped out onto the porch with a QCW-05

(Type 5) rifle. That was it, no other reaction. Everything was seemingly normal and very professional. They were too professional for raiders or bandits, and that meant military. The Type 5 rifle was a PRC Special Warfare unit issue. This was very bad news. Mom knew she was in for a long wait. She pulled out her own radio and called Ramirez, who was now around the bend in the river.

"Professionals confirmed. High-speed. Will remain on station to monitor," Mom quietly relayed.

Two clicks were Ramirez's only response; he had to be sure to keep the radio hidden in his jacket with no idea who might be watching. They continued the planned route down the river road. They would ride another quarter of a mile before making a long circle through the forest back to camp.

Mom remained at her post high above the ground for nearly fourteen hours. Despite frequent stretching and light exercises to keep her blood flowing and stay warm, she nearly fell out of the tree when she climbed down. It took another 10 minutes of vigorous stretching and more exercises before she was mobile enough to travel. That had truly been a miserable night. She slowly made her way back over the crest of the ridge and down the slope enough to get out of the cold wind that had plagued her all night. She began a fast walk and 3 ½ miles later walked back into camp.

Mom was proud to see Jules' rifle trained on her as she entered camp, but disappointed by the lack of challenge.

"No challenge, Jules?"

"I knew it was you, Mom. I recognized you as soon as I saw you."

"You still need to challenge, even when you think you know who is there. This isn't our old world, July. Challenge and response is there for everyone's safety."

"OK, fine," Jules replied in that way that only a 15-year-old girl could manage.

"Thank you" Mom replied, having to repress her military instinct to chew her daughter's ass.

"Mom?"

"Yes?"

"What took you so long? I was getting worried."

Mom could hear the strain in her daughter's voice and realized the bitchy attitude was probably the stress of her long absence. She had to remember as tough as this was on her, Mom had her training to fall back on. Jules was still just a teenage girl who had watched everything she knew fall apart, along with all her dreams of a normal future.

"I had to stay long enough to confirm what I was seeing and try to get an accurate count of the opposing force. Come on in and you can listen to me brief Ramirez. I'll ask Belle to take watch for a while."

"OK," Jules said meekly. "I'm sorry, Mom, I was just…"

"It's fine, Jules. This new world has us all on edge and more than a little scared. We just don't know what to expect. We'll handle it together. All of us."

"K."

Mom walked into the trailer and asked Belle to take the watch.

"Sure thing, Ms. McKinney." Belle replied.

Ramirez came in as Belle was leaving to take up the watch.

"What did you find? High-speed doesn't sound promising." Ramirez questioned.

"Where are James and Con? I'd rather only do this once and then I need to hit the rack."

"Right here, Mom." I said as I walked through the door with Con.

"Good. OK, so it looks like our squatters are a PLAGF squad led by a Special Warfare operator. I was able to confirm eight soldiers, all with QBZ-95s and an officer with a Type 5. They were extremely professional and were using radios for communication. That group is definitely not local bandits or raiders."

"And the weapons tell us who they are, but why would they be on your farm? Surely that can't be a coincidence," said Ramirez.

"No, probably not." Mom replied, "I bought the property through back channels from the government. It was defunct and on the surplus list. They had been looking for someone with clearance to buy it. Nothing top secret, they just didn't want an unlisted holding talked about. I had to sign NDAs and other paperwork assuring my silence. My guess is the PLAGF used their access while helping the SSA to hack into and plunder all our military computer systems. The new government was desperate for help so it must have been easy. This is probably just a special squad left behind to watch the SSA and provide boots on the ground for any small-scale covert missions. I'm sure an old government farm in the middle of nowhere West Virginia only 6 hours from the capital seemed ideal. There was no sign of Miles or his dog, Xavier. They are either dead or captured."

Ramirez stared at Mom for longer than the explanation seemed to warrant. It was as if deciding whether he wanted to challenge her evaluation. He then stared up at the ceiling as if in thought.

"Is there any way they could station more troops there out of sight that you may not have seen?"

"No," Mom replied, "the buildings are pretty limited and the morning sentry change brought the same soldiers as the day before. I'm certain if they had more men they would spread out sentry duty to keep them more alert. I know what you're getting at, but the barn merely covers an old weapons depot. It was a small cache, not a large facility, and was abandoned years ago. The depot is around 40 x 60 feet with poured concrete walls and large steel doors along one end. The barn covers the entrance completely. It is virtually the same width and only forty feet longer to hide the entrance when the depot was active. Miles used it as a barn. He built horse stalls in the front 40 and we poured concrete walls to seal the old depot behind."

"You sure?" Ramirez asked, clearly not convinced.

"I am sure that the walls are poured concrete, and it was clearly marked as a depot," Mom replied.

"OK, this is all good work, and I've avoided the question because we all have our reasons for playing things close to the vest in this new world. Before we plan any kind of operation I need to know what you did before you moved into logistics."

Mom seemed to ponder the request for a minute, then nodded in agreement.

"I was a Marine Force Recon sniper. I knew I wanted a family, so with some help; I worked my way over into logistics. It allowed me to station close to my husband's family farm in South Georgia."

"Thank you. That certainly makes me feel better about our situation and does explain more than a few questions I've had on our little journey. I still feel like we are out-manned and out-gunned. Any ideas on how we're going to tackle this?"

"Not yet. I need sleep, and then we can start planning. We're not in a hurry. I'd rather take our time and do everything we can to minimize potential casualties on our end."

"Agreed."

"Can you or James brief Belle? I'll get some rack time, and we can begin planning after lunch."

"Sounds good." Ramirez acknowledged.

"I'll tell Belle." I added.

QBZ-95

Chapter 21 – Bait

Lunch was a somber affair as everyone contemplated the soldiers occupying our new home. So it came as a surprise when Belle gasped and then started laughing. Everyone turned to stare, and she only laughed harder. As the laughs began to subside, she turned towards me with an evil grin.

"JC, do you remember those zombie apocalypse books I liked?" Belle asked.

"Yeah, the ones that are kind of eerily similar to our present situation, you mean?"

"Similar, yes, but very different too."

"Yeah, well, those were just books with zombies so, of course they were different."

"Yeah, well, you're getting me off topic. My point is that in those books the bad guys would round up truckloads of zombies to overrun settlements. They would launch bags of urine to attract the zombies to their targets."

"Yeah, that was gross. What's your point?"

"OMG, really? Why can't we do that with Murdochs?"

"Well, I don't think they run around looking for urine for one thing. I mean, urine is urine. If that were the case they'd be scampering around all nimbly bimbly after every rabbit, deer, and coyote in the forest. I mean, if ya think about it…"

"JAMES!" Belle interrupted.

"What?"

"Would you just shut up for a minute? I'm not suggesting we need truckloads of zombies and bags of urine. I am suggesting that we have a big trailer we picked up recently that might hold a couple dozen Murdochs. Those Murdochs could provide a hell of a good distraction."

"Ohh…" I replied intelligently.

"Interesting idea, Belle," Mom said.

Ramirez joined in and the discussion began to progress in earnest. It wasn't long before it seemed I would be unloading the new trailer and rigging it to tow behind the Lady. Our hunting ground would be the ski resorts at Snowshoe. It seemed reasonable that the resorts would still have had a pretty high population during the weeks of The Fall. The resorts had been reasonably well protected, and most people felt safe enough to enjoy a fast-moving sport.

Our experience in Asheville provided our proven and preferred bait. Spam, or whatever potted meat we could find, would fit the bill perfectly with no need for pointless bags of urine. We reasoned that it was soft enough to be versatile, and the strong scent would be a good attractant. Put it in a bag with a hole, and you could squeeze out small amounts to leave a trail. Open a can and throw it through the air, and it would sling meat everywhere on impact. If all else failed, we would kill a deer or bear and use the meat we harvested, but no one thought that would be necessary.

After all the planning, we began the real work. We used handsaws to cut small trees we could place side by side, creating an elevated platform of sorts. We then unloaded the supplies from the box trailer onto our makeshift platform and covered them all with tarps. Not the best, but it seemed good enough for temporary storage.

With the trailer empty, I was able to modify the coupler, raising it so the trailer would ride close to level once attached to the pintle hitch on the Lady. It wasn't pretty, but it was strong, and I was too tired to give a damn tinker's damn about how it looked.

The next morning, we set to work replacing the windshields. We only had one spare set. Luckily, I had noticed a deuce not too far away on our ride in. Hopefully, we could swing by and loot the windows from it someday soon.

I decided that we should make some creative improvements to our Lady before our next foray into evil. We pulled out the swivel mount for the Browning M2 .50 caliber machine gun I'd cut off the Humvee. While Ramirez, Con, and Ben unbolted the mount from the scraps of the Humvee roof, Belle and I worked on removing the roof hatch from the Lady. I had always wanted a mounted gun for the Lady, so I had made the hole the same diameter as those on a Humvee. Wishful thinking I had thought at the time. Now my dream would become a reality. Damn, this was cool!

We bolted on the mount, a turret with armor, and I added stops to keep anyone from swinging the gun back into the rear van. The hatch proved to be a real bitch, and took me the rest of the day to reattach. In the end, I had to weld hinges into the turret and make sure it could swing back completely out of the way. I admit I may have cut up the turret a bit to do it, but at least the hatch made a nice rear shield. Simple gravity latches locked it in place when opened and freed the gunner to concentrate on the job at hand. We only had the nine cans of ammo the raiders had with them, but it was a good start. I mounted the gun and 3 cans of ammo on the turret and we were ready to rock'n'roll.

Well, I thought we were ready to rock. My little project came with a price. Ramirez spent the following day drilling Belle and me for four hours on the .50. We had to open the hatch, load a belt, and rack the gun until we could do it without thinking. We took a well-earned break for lunch, both thankful our training was over. That was when Ramirez let us know we would continue to do the same thing for the next 4 hours. The worst part was that we were so low on ammo we weren't even allowed to fire the gun. Just practice popping up, loading, racking, clearing jams, switching belts, etc., etc. Belle refused to speak to me or Ramirez at all that night. Something about a pinched finger and it being my fault for my stupid ambition to be like my Mom. This alternated with "boys and their damned toys". Ramirez just seemed amused.

Four days after setting up camp we were finally ready to set out for Snowshoe. It was the first time since Bryson City that we'd split up for separate missions. That hadn't turned out too well.

Although Ramirez had been keeping a close watch on Con, with a computer to play with, Con had all but forgotten his dad existed. Besides, the computer wasn't the only thing in camp that had Con's attention. It seemed Jules wasn't the only one that had been enjoying their time together. Amy promised Ramirez she would look after Con. Ben was the only one who seemed perfectly content to stay put with no incentives. He said he didn't want any more little adventures!

Our Franken Lady ate up the miles as we retraced our path back to Highway 219. The journey that previously took half a day, slipped past in an hour. I turned north onto 219 for the half-hour trip up to Snowshoe. About ten minutes later we came across a country store that had seen better days. Since we weren't in a hurry, we decided to stop and see if we could find some extra Murdoch bait.

We pulled to a stop in the road across from the store. Just to be on the extra cautious side, Ramirez locked the doors behind us and popped the roof hatch. With the .50 loaded and Ramirez on watch, Belle and I at least had the comfort of knowing someone would guard the truck and cover our retreat if needed.

We stacked up on either side of the door and turned on our gun-mounted lights. At a nod from Belle, I went in sweeping from left to right. As my eyes adjusted, I took a few more steps inside so Belle could enter. At her signal, we proceeded into the store, sweeping it for occupants. Once we cleared the main room, we moved on to the restroom and storeroom. In the back, we found a locked door. For some reason, I decided to knock. The impulse was so strong I couldn't help myself.

I thought I was expecting a shot but when the boom came from behind me, I nearly fell flat on my face trying to spin around. Half expecting a shot through the door, I had been standing to the side reaching over. My nearly 360-degree pirouette was about as graceful as a drunk cowboy line dancing for an audition to the Bolshoi Ballet. Belle stood behind me, doubled over laughing with a giant ledger lying at her feet.

"What the FUCK, Belle?" I yelled.

Apparently, that must have been the reaction she was going for, because at that point she had to set her rifle down against a shelf. She was actually hyperventilating, completely unable to suck in a breath. It wasn't until I heard another wheeze that I noticed Ramirez in the door, laughing almost as hard as Belle.

"Holy shit!" he wheezed, "That was the funniest damn thing I've seen in years."

Belle was now kneeling on the floor with tears streaming down her cheeks.

"Glad I could amuse you two."

"Do it again", she managed ,and half lifted and dropped the book again. Ramirez laughed even harder.

"Oh god. Please don't. I can't." he said as he turned and walked out the door.

"You gonna make it, Belle?" I said with half a grin.

"I…", wheeze, "…think so…", wheeze, she replied.

Once she finally managed to pull herself together, I reached down and offered her a hand. Belle grabbed my hand and stood up, wiping away tears. She leaned over and kissed my cheek.

"Thanks, JC. I needed that." Then suddenly dropped my hand and pulled away, looking a little embarrassed. I just stood there staring with the sensation of that kiss on my cheek, not quite knowing what to think.

We both forgot about the locked door and walked through the store to see if anything remained after the last visitors.

We found several cans of Armour meat in the corner where someone tossed them, going by the dented cans. There were a couple cans of beans, and a few other odds and ends I thought might be useful, like fishing line for Ben and a couple tubes of Loctite super glue. Even a couple rolls of toilet paper under one upended shelf.

As we headed back toward the truck, Belle turned suddenly towards the house beside the store.

"Funny, Belle," I said, growing a little tired of the joke.

"No, I saw something. I'd swear something moved in that window."

"What do you mean, something? The sun is shining directly into it. I can even see the print on the wallpaper. What was it?"

"That's just it. JC, it was a dark shape. I couldn't see what it was, other than it was tall, like an adult standing in the window. Honestly, it was a little spooky. Like I could almost see it out of the corner of my eye, moving across the window. But when I turned, it was gone."

She wasn't joking. I've been around Belle nearly all my life and she was dead serious. It was starting to freak me out a bit.

"Should we take a look?" I asked.

"Oh, hell no!" she replied without hesitation. "We should leave this place now. I mean, right the fuck now!"

"Good enough for me."

We jumped into the Lady and I hit the ignition. Only she didn't start. I checked our kill switch and flipped it twice, then hit the ignition again. Still nothing. Belle was starting to look pale, and Ramirez just confused. I looked back at the house, and there was a figure standing in the window Belle had pointed to, just staring out at us. It was a pale, thin-faced man in a simple black suit. He slowly turned and walked away from the window. As soon as he did, the Lady started without me turning the switch.

I shoved her into gear and poured on the diesel leaving that store like our tail was on fire and our ass was a-catchin'. No one said a word until we reached the turn-off for Snowshoe.

"Whatcha say we never stop there again, huh?" Belle asked.

"No argument here," replied Ramirez, making the sign of the cross and kissing a crucifix I'd never seen before. I just nodded along with him. No damned argument at all!

"I'm willing to drive around, even if it means an extra day." I finally managed.

"Yeah, worth looking at a map, anyhow." Ramirez agreed. It was Belle's turn to just nod, still a little pale.

209

Chapter 22 – Snowshoe

It was a hard pull up the mountain, and the falling temperature made me glad we didn't have the horses. The colder it got, the more I began to wonder if we had made a good choice for our hunting ground. As a general rule, Murdochs seemed to avoid the cold. We pulled into the resort, and I was almost sure this wouldn't work. There was no one in sight.

The sheer number of hotels and condominiums in this place should have had us overrun with Murdochs, but we didn't see any on the street. I had never been to Snowshoe. This place must have been incredible back in the days before The Fall. I'd bet thousands of people could vacation there at once. It seemed like we saw a new restaurant or store around every turn, and the ski lifts were huge. It reminded me of the pictures I'd seen of one of those big resorts in the Rockies.

We made a pass through the resort and back around to a big parking area for the Snowshoe Mountain Lodge at the "Top of the World". You could almost believe you were on the top looking at the view. Unfortunately, we had business, and it was time to get to work. We decided to drop the trailer and set it up in the parking area. From there, I could make my rounds through the resort and try to drum up some business.

During the four days before leaving to come to Snowshoe, we had modified more than just the tongue of the trailer. We had removed the plastic vent covers in the roof and replaced them with steel grates. We also needed a door for our improvised trap, and since we wanted to be able to use the trailer later, we left the rear ramp alone. I built a cage door that would open up hanging from the inside of the roof. We could prop it up and allow it to swing down into latches on either side. We could then close the ramp with the gate down and latched. Nice, simple, and safe; just the way I like it.

While I double-checked the ignition and battery connections on the Lady, Ramirez propped the gate up with a pole we'd brought along for the purpose. He then tied a long rope to the pole's lower end. With the gate ready, he opened a couple cans of potted meat to place in the trailer for bait. The trap was set. All he had left was to take the other end of the rope and find some cover. Well, that and we need some Murdochs.

Everything checked out, so Belle and I jumped into the Lady and headed back down the main road. I used the exhaust cutout to increase the noise made by our dear Lady, and we started down the road playing Jimmy Buffet's 'Songs You Know By Heart'. Why Jimmy Buffet, you ask? Because I like Jimmy Buffet, that's why. It was either that or Old Crow Medicine Show, and after our encounter at the country store, I was in the mood for something a bit more upbeat. Before long Belle & I were singing along to Margaritaville. It just seemed like a tourist resort sorta song. Besides, I like listening to Belle sing, and she enjoys laughing while I dance & drive.

Now, there is a completely unsubstantiated rumor that we may have been having such a good time that I inadvertently ran over the first Murdoch we found. But if we did, that would totally have not been my fault as the little bastard just ran out in front of us. Or he would have if that had actually happened. I admit to nothing.

After cleaning the blood off the windshield, did I say blood, I meant mud. Anyhow, after cleaning the windshield, we started back down the main drag. There only seemed to be one or two Murdochs around, so we even stopped and blew the horn a few times. I felt like we were in the Mommy parade trying to get Junior to stop staring at the girls and get his ass in the truck. Nope, it didn't work.

If this town had a horde of Murdochs they were stubbornly staying out of sight. Belle theorized that if that alleged incident had actually occurred, perhaps they were all too smart to show themselves. Then we just laughed because everyone knows Murdochs aren't smart. Otherwise, they wouldn't run out in front of big, loud trucks, right? Supposedly run out in front of them, I mean.

I will note here that Belle skipped the song 'Why Don't We Get Drunk'. An "accident" she didn't bother to correct. That's all I'm gonna say about that.

We made it back to Ramirez during 'Cheeseburger In Paradise' and we all decided that was a good enough reason to take a break for lunch. As we ate, I explained my idea about the elevation and wondered aloud if the Murdochs may have headed down the mountain to find warmer temps and more food. After all, it had been a year since The Fall. We decided to take a stroll up through the shops and see what there was to see. It also seemed like a good time to shop for winter wear or other dry goods these fine establishments might have to offer.

We were half dancing through the streets singing 'Volcano' when the Murdoch made a run for us. Luckily, Ramirez is a Ranger and wasn't about to miss such a golden opportunity for target practice. You can imagine everyone's surprise when he missed. The Murdoch had been a young girl around 10 or 12 and did a complete backflip when the stock of my M1 hit her in the chest. Ramirez quickly recovered, but instead of shooting her, he rolled her onto her stomach and pulled out zip ties to cuff her hands. I pulled off my t-shirt, and he used that as a gag so she couldn't bite anyone. Unlike the zombie movies, getting bit won't turn you into a Murdoch. It's an engineered virus that the lucky few like us are immune to. If we weren't, we'd be Murdochs already. No biting is required, but that biting shit hurts!

After restraining our new pet, we settled down and became a bit more serious about watching our surroundings. Rather than dragging her around with us, we tied her to a light pole. We continued up the avenue and did a little shopping, finding clothes for everyone, with a lot of help from Belle. She seemed to have a much better idea about sizes, although Ramirez knew them for Con and guessed for Ben. Mom, Amy, and Jules would just have to fight it out for the rest.

Most everything there was for downhill sports. One shop did have some cross-country skis though. Ramirez thought we might need them, so they joined the pile. Other things like goggles, gloves, and even energy bars were no-brainers. And then we walked into the first bar. Now, I'm not a big drinker, but I have been known to partake on occasion, for medicinal purposes, you understand. Apparently, a resort bar is an excellent place to sample the finer drinks you may have seen. We took a small sample and Ramirez helped us find a nearby storeroom to stockpile some for a future supply run. He insisted we leave some of the cheap stuff out on the shelves. That way it wouldn't be so obvious that some looter would look for the missing booze.

Our shopping done and no other Murdoch encounters, we had to conclude the trip up to Snowshoe wasn't going to produce the horde we wanted. After an awkward walk back to the truck, we loaded everything and hooked the trailer back to the Lady. Our new pet did at least verify that potted meat was good bait as she nearly sprinted into the trailer trying to find one of the cans.

With Mary Murdoch all packed up and ready for transport, Ramirez pulled out the maps. We began looking for a likely new hunting ground. To the east was the small town of Cass. It was 2,000 feet lower in elevation and seemed like a good place to start. Particularly since it was the next place down the highway, logistics, ya know.

We all piled back into the Lady and headed across the Top of the World and back down to Highway 66. Forty minutes later, we were pulling into Cass. The town had that old company town look, complete with the Cass Company Store, for the scenic railroad down by the tracks. Before The Fall, I wouldn't have expected a big population, but having just driven into town, we had already seen three small groups of Murdochs. With a little noise and bait, I was betting we would find a whole lot more.

We pulled into the railroad parking lot and turned around to be facing out towards home. With several sightings already, Ramirez decided we would change our tactics a bit. Belle was overwatch while I helped Ramirez set the trap.

One of the biggest changes was leaving the trailer hooked up. We set the cage door and ran the rope back to Belle, up on the Lady's roof. Our bait would be a little different, too. We tied one ankle of our pet to a wall hook. She didn't seem too fond of restraint. She really hated it when we opened another can of potted meat and set it just out of reach. I held her arms while Ramirez cut the zip ties and pulled her gag. She began to scream bloody murder as we turned to run.

"The door!" I yelled coming to a stop. "Belle's got the rope," Ramirez replied. "No, not the gate. The door. We can't close the door for the trailer."

"Well, shit!" I ran and grabbed a second rope out of the truck and began tying it to the latches on the trailer ramp door. When I had it tied to both corners and centered to pull up evenly, I laid it loosely to one side just under the lip of the ramp. Ramirez caught on and draped it up the side and onto the roof. From there we fed it back across the trailer to the Lady. No sooner had we tossed the rope up than Belle yelled, "Here they come!"

We had definitely found the horde. The Murdochs seemed to flood out of every corner. There must have been hundreds of them. We both sprinted for the truck. I hit the driver's seat and immediately fired The Lady up. I had barely locked the doors when we heard them reach the trailer.

Ramirez was up through the hatch and climbing onto the roof as I turned to put the truck in gear. The Murdochs were swarming around the truck like rioters at an animal rights protest. I angled the blade and prepared to get underway. This time, I switched her over to rich and let the smoke boil out from underneath. At least a few Murdochs seemed to shy away from the smoke. I heard the gate slam and Ramirez yell, "Go Go Go!"

The Lady started to roll as I heard Belle open up with her

M4. In the mirror, I could see Ramirez straining with the rope for the door. I wondered why Belle wasn't helping him until I saw the first Murdoch fall from the roof as her rifle barked again.

Then I noticed the Murdochs climbing up the cab all around me. They struggled at first because we were moving and gaining speed, but once they had a good grip ,they seemed committed. I looked over my shoulder at the roof hatch, the very open roof hatch. This was not good.

At first, the Lady merely pushed the Murdochs aside. As we gained speed, I felt a few go under. I thought of the low-riding trailer behind us and dropped the blade down almost to snowplow level. That was when the blood began to spray across the windshield. It wasn't much each time, but was quickly adding up. I didn't dare use the wipers for fear of smearing it, and blinding myself.

All the while, there were Murdochs climbing towards the hatch. A few became distracted trying to get through the locked doors, but at least two kept climbing. The shots continued from the roof as well. At least Belle was still up there able to shoot.

I pulled the 1911 from my holster and laid it on the console beside me. This was getting ugly fast. A real soup sandwich, as Mom would say. Just as the first Murdoch found the hatch, I heard a scream of pain from Belle. That was abso-fucking-lutely it, I had had enough of this shit! Looking in the mirror, I couldn't see the horde any longer. I took my foot off the gas and eased on the brake. I would have stood on it if Belle and Ramirez hadn't been on the roof.

As we came to a stop, I rolled down the window and put the

muzzle of the .45 to the forehead of the Murdoch on my driver's step. The report of the 1911 in the cab was deafening. I mean, I couldn't hear a fucking thing! Of course, neither could the Murdoch, as half of his skull was now on the other side of the ditch. His body fell from my step as I popped the air brakes and stepped out.

The Murdochs seemed momentarily confused to see their prey suddenly out in the open. Not one to waste time, I lined up on the one clinging to the rear door and shot him in the chest. Swinging up, I shot a third Murdoch on the roof. That one was turning, and instead of a chest shot, I caught her in the shoulder.

As my feet hit the ground and I was lining up my fourth shot, I heard the trailer door hit the asphalt. Belle let out a scream of rage this time as an obvious fight started on the van's roof. That was all accompanied by nearly continuous bursts from the M4. The song 'Bodies' by Drowning Pool began playing in my mind as Murdochs began to rain down from the van.

A small, quick Murdoch had made it into the cab of the Lady, which infuriated me. How dare that filthy mother fucker disgrace my Lady with his presence in her cab. I reached up and pulled the passenger door open so hard it slammed back into the stops. The Murdoch leapt out past me as I turned to avoid it. The bastard hit the ground in a roll and was already up while I was still lining up for a shot. He lunged forward, hitting me with both hands. The impact pushed me back, trapping the pistol between us. Rather than fight the impact, I relaxed and allowed him to push me into the truck. The moment of space allowed me to angle the muzzle into him. The first shot took him in his hip and spun the damn thing so hard it hit the ground on the other side of the ditch. The second shot took it in the chest, and my rage-induced, totally unnecessary third shot was into the head of its prone body.

I turned back to see Ramirez standing on top of the truck van with Belle's M4. When he looked over and saw that I was alone, he began to bark orders.

"Check the gate then bring me my med bag. She'll be fine but I need to mop her up."

I jogged back to the trailer and cautiously looked inside. The trailer was absolutely packed with Murdochs. I was so startled by the sheer number, I took several involuntary steps back. Seeing that both latches were engaged, I hurriedly raised the ramp and locked it in place, just to be sure they stayed put. With that done, I sprinted for the cab and the med bag.

I tossed the bag up first. When I finally got up there, Ramirez had the med bag open and was kneeling over Belle. There was blood everywhere, but she was still conscious and holding her leg.

"Good, come over here and give me a hand," Ramirez said when he saw me standing there.

"Use that squeeze bottle to clean the blood away while I stitch her up. Belle, relax the pressure a little. You're holding it too tight."

"It fucking hurts!" she almost managed not to yell.

"Yes, and this is going to hurt more, but will take longer if you don't let up."

I used a squirt bottle to wash the cut, then Ramirez used another to apply antiseptic. All to the dulcet tones of Belle's screams. Then he began stitching, working so quickly that it was almost hard to keep up with him. Halfway through, he told Belle to let go, and she immediately reached over and grabbed my ankle. At this point, I realized I may have underestimated Belle's strength in the past. Holy hell, that hurt! I think some of it was on purpose because when I looked back, her face was a cross between a pained grimace and a sadistic grin. Misery loves company and she was damned sure going to have company. I reached down and gave her my hand so I would at least still be able to walk when we finished.

Luckily, Ramirez finished stitching quickly and before long he was wiping the area down with an antiseptic wipe. He wrapped the stitches in gauze and then taped up her entire calf, which apparently Belle decided meant I needed to be in more pain.

"Sorry, Belle, but I know you're not going to stay off this and I don't want you tearing those out if we can avoid it. Here, take these four ibuprofen and stop trying to maim JC. Then he can get you some water to swallow them."

She released me, and I gratefully dropped back down to the cab to get a canteen. When I got back up on the roof, she was sitting up and staring around at Murdochs. Her gaze said quite clearly that she would like nothing better than to bring them all back to life so she could kill them again. I reached down and helped her slowly to her feet, handing her the canteen once she was up.

Chapter 23 – Homeward Bound

We turned onto Highway 1 and headed southwest because none of us wanted to drive back past that old country store. The Lady had run flawlessly since our encounter at the store, and I was at a loss for what could have kept it from starting. Every time I thought about it too long, that tall pale figure seemed to stare through the distance with those empty eyes. We considered going down to Stilwell, the town welcoming traders, but didn't want to have to explain our cargo. We doubted they would let us into their town with a trailer load of Murdochs, not that we would blame them. Come to think of it, I wasn't even sure how many Murdochs were in the trailer.

The day was getting late though, and we needed to stop while we still had light. We were all tired, and the stiff suspension of the truck made sure Belle's leg felt every pebble we bounced over on the road. A fact she was kind enough to share with me on multiple occasions. These were usually accompanied by a slap to the back of my head and questions about my parentage. Was I trying to hit every damned bump? No, no, I was not. Especially since I'm pretty sure she wound up hurting me more than they hurt her.

We were driving through a wide mountain valley full of farmland when we came to a spot with large fields on both sides of the road. That was it; I made a command decision and just stopped in the middle of the damn road. The moon was nearly full, and the sky was clear, so the night watch would have good sightlines at least a couple hundred yards in every direction. Ramirez dug a Percocet out of his bag and gave it to Belle. After she was out cold, he confessed he would rather pull double watch duty than continue to listen to her bitch, I couldn't help but agree.

What should have been a quiet, peaceful night had a constant background of moans and groans from our trailer. When you combined that with the occasional rifle shot by the watch, it was difficult to get much sleep. Our Murdochs seemed to attract others. One or two at a time, and it made the watch exhausting as you had to constantly keep an eye out for the next Murdoch. You just knew one would pop up at any minute. By morning, Belle was the only one who got any rest.

We didn't waste much time getting started and after a quick bathroom break, we were back, or is that still, on the road for home? We drove for nearly 15 minutes before having to stop and cut a tree out of the road. It was shaping up to be a long day.

When we finally got to Highway 219, there was a truck with a flatbed trailer and a group of men in the back. They were blocking the road, and Ramirez was in a pretty foul temper. He opened the roof hatch and manned the .50 as we slowed to a stop. I angled the truck so that he would have the best line of fire if they tried to flank us. I heard a muttered thanks filter down from the hatch.

The sight of our Lady seemed to have the men rethinking their roadblock, and you could see them trying to decide if the potential loot was worth the risk. Ramirez was apparently not in the mood to wait for their decision. There was a short burst from the .50 that shattered the silence and all conversation on their truck.

"I'm going to make this real simple for you boys," yelled Ramirez. "I've had a long night and I want to get home, so, you can move that piece of shit out of our way, or I can kill you all right here and now. We'll loot your bodies, dump them in the ditch, and my associates will take your truck. If you try to follow us as Plan B, it will simply ensure that anyone you might have waiting for you back home will never find the bodies. Now, what'll it be?"

A smarmy-looking fellow with a weasel look to him got out of the passenger seat and started walking towards the Lady.

"Now just hold on there, friend."

The sudden burst of .50 caliber fire that disintegrated the weasel's chest sent a ripple of shock through both trucks.

"This is not a negotiation and the next one who tries to weasel his way closer to our truck is going to seal the fate for you all," Ramirez called in a flat tone.

Despite the murmurs from the back of the truck, it started up and backed into the church parking lot beside the intersection. One of the men hopped out, and with his hands raised, asked if he could move the body. Ramirez agreed, and the man pulled the body back towards their truck. In the meantime, an argument had broken out in the group, and several of the men began shouting. I made out at least one "can't let them get away with this" among all the yelling.

"Let's go." Ramirez called down through the hatch.

As we began moving, I kept an eye on our mirrors. The driver of the truck stepped out, and several other men broke away from the group. They began walking toward the church while the remaining idiots got back in the truck and started their pursuit.

"Here they come!" I yelled up to Ramirez. His only response was to reach down and grab his M4, then climb out onto the roof of the van. There was no way for us to outrun them, so I didn't even try. I just found a nice even speed that would provide a smooth platform for shooting. As soon as the truck began to catch up, I heard the crack of the M4.

Rather than start with the driver and stop the pursuit, Ramirez seemed offended by their feeble attempt at payback. With the first shot, a man toppled from the back and onto the pavement. I heard the truck begin to accelerate, and several men returned fire. Although that may have rattled someone else, Ramirez was a Ranger and veteran of several "conflicts". He simply responded by increasing his rate of fire. He fired three more times, a new body falling overboard each time before I saw the truck slow to a stop.

"Pull around that next turn and stop," he yelled down.

Feeling a little uneasy about it, I did as he said and waited. Sure enough, the truck came speeding around the turn. This time, Ramirez shot the driver first, causing the vehicle to shoot off into the steep rocky bank. The truck ran up the bank and rolled back down onto its top onto the road. I heard Ramirez climb down and watched as he walked towards the wreck. He never asked for help, but I pulled the air brakes and grabbed my rifle. Rather than try to catch up, I climbed onto the roof, taking an overwatch position. I had a clear view of the wreck and could turn around to watch our back as needed.

The calm Ramirez showed was unnerving as he walked toward the moaning men in the wrecked truck. The noise was agitating the Murdochs, who also began to moan. None of it seemed to faze him as he continued walking toward the truck, weapon raised. When he got there, he didn't say anything. He just shot them one by one.

After a few minutes, he walked back carrying a coat like a satchel, full of guns. I continued to keep watch while he went back and retrieved two boxes. One marked Spam and the other Little Debbie.

"The spoils of war," he said as he reached the truck.

Our grim task complete, we got back into the Lady and headed on up the highway.

"Why didn't you look through the rest of their cargo?" I asked.

"Figured the smart ones at the church might need it. I just couldn't pass up the Swiss rolls, and our cargo in the back probably needs the Spam."

"Good call," I said, "I hadn't thought about our Murdochs. I bet they are hungry."

I climbed up on the roof of the trailer, and Ramirez started throwing up cans of Spam. I would open them and set them by the roof vents. Luckily the bars were just wide enough to fit a can through. Once I had about half the box open, I started shoving them through the grates. It caused a pretty big ruckus, but they were so tightly packed in there I figured fights couldn't get too bad, or at least I hoped they couldn't.

We decided to save the rest for later and found a hole in the Lady's van to shove it into. The Little Debbie box we tucked gingerly into the rear floor of the cab. I was delighted to see a box of oatmeal pies next to the Swiss Rolls that Ramirez hadn't mentioned earlier. That was a good haul, indeed!

Each of us, with a Debbie cake in hand, climbed back inside. I got our Lady headed back up the road.

"Why did you kill them all? I mean, I'm not defending them, but after their truck wrecked, they couldn't hurt us?" said Belle. Ramirez and I both jumped, neither of us had realized she was awake.

"You heard them. They all would have died from their injuries. There's no hospital to take them to and I certainly wasn't spending our medical supplies on that scum. Belle, they stopped us to rob us and possibly worse, especially for you.

I gave them a chance, and the leader thought he could outmaneuver me. Then I gave them another chance, and only a few of them took it. I gave them three more chances by killing men in the back to show them each time how vulnerable they were. Their final chance was when I shot a passenger in the cab, leaving the driver so he could choose to live. I don't kill lightly. But when they kept coming after all that, I was done.

They made it clear that we would have to kill them all before they would stop. That is why I did what I did. I did it so that you and JC wouldn't have to. I did it so that I could keep us all safe. Those are the rules of this new world. I don't like them, but they're not new to me. We are the only ones who will look out for each other. The old days of law and order, of civilization and the good ole USA, are long gone. At least for now. The sooner you accept that, the longer you're going to live, and hopefully live free."

Ramirez turned back around, and we all rode in silence. It was a grim reminder of how brutal and how changed this new world had become. There was no glamour in our post-apocalyptic survival. No TV prizes or islands to win. No timeout or do-over. No extra life.

Chapter 24 – First in Flight

We pulled back into camp around lunchtime that afternoon. It was hard to believe we had only been gone 2 days. I felt like it had been a week. All our time since The Fall seemed to stretch out. The days of easy living were gone, and it made me long for our past. The incredible wealth and luxury we had enjoyed, even after the SSA took control, seemed like a fantasy now. I knew the biggest irony was how much better off we were than most survivors. The last year had brought famine to huge numbers of people, who only knew how to get food from a supermarket. Many of those who had survived this long had done so by looting early and becoming raiders or worse. The next few years would continue to bring vast changes to what remained of our country. Stored supplies would run out, and only those who could farm, gather, hunt, or steal from those who did would remain.

Jules, Ben, and Con ran out to meet us and see how our trip went. They all gave Belle tons of sympathy and helped her into the camper. The boys, fascinated by the sounds of the Murdochs, seemed drawn by the sound creeping slowly closer to the trailer. Everyone else stepped farther away, repelled by the stench that was emanating from it. Ramirez tried to hide his Little Debbie box. However, that particular bit of loot seemed to draw every eye in camp as though equipped with a homing beacon, and everyone had a receiver. Two boxes of the precious resource were gone not 5 minutes after Con's keen eye noticed the hoard.

Mom, it turned out, was back on one of the ridges

overlooking the farm conducting more surveillance and Amy was grooming the horses. Jules had been helping, but couldn't resist abandoning the task when she heard the Lady's approach. Amy came over just in time to grab the last Swiss Roll from the open carton and examine the box with a hungry expression.

"I think you'd better hide that behind a locked door with at least one 24-hour guard." I commented to Ramirez.

"No doubt! These vultures are almost as bad as the ones we ran into on the road."

He disappeared so quietly it surprised me. When I turned back to ask him another question, he was gone. I sure was glad that man was on our side. That thought brought me to our opposition on the farm, and it gave me a chill to think that they had an operator down there that may be as good or better. He would have to be our primary target.

Jules had been busy during our short time away. With a little help, she had pulled out the electric fence and solar charger to set up a nice paddock for the horses. She said that she and the boys had spent hours clearing out small brush piles and filling in the few stump holes they found. They had also used a tarp to create a makeshift shelter. I was glad to see that they tied it tight and even had ropes across the top to keep it from flapping. I was sure you'd hear it for miles if it started popping up and down in the wind.

Con had apparently been busy on the laptop, too. He had used the elevation lidar to map out all the old roads and trails in the area. Then he combined it with the vegetation layers to look for potential sniper hides we could use. He found a few odd roads and mounds that he thought might be from an old mine. That could have intriguing possibilities, but it didn't seem all that unusual in the mountains of West Virginia. Finally, he added the nationality of the opposing force to increase the accuracy of the predictive model.

Looking as though he might actually pass out from the excitement, Con showed us his newest obsession. It was a small, fixed-wing drone that Mom had pulled from a secret hidey hole somewhere. Con had been practicing with the software and was very confident that he could use the drone for recon. He said it had both visible and infrared spectrum cameras and would give us a huge advantage over the troops on the farm. Ramirez tamped down his excitement a bit by pointing out that, as they were PLAGF troops, it was likely that they had drones of their own. Con said that Mom had planned their first flight for that night. It would be a high-altitude flight to get an overview and search for observation posts and devices. He hadn't considered that that may include other drones.

Mom returned just before sunset, in time to grab a hot meal. She seemed impressed with the number of Murdochs we managed to gather, but a little concerned too. It would mean more danger for us as well as the occupying force. I pointed out that we could thin the herd a bit before release. In the end, we decided to just stick with what we had. The PLAGF troops were a serious threat, and we could use all the help we could get, even if it was a double-edged sword. Perhaps the high number would allow the Murdochs to make a few kills before we even entered the fight.

As night fell, Con got his wish. Mom took him out to launch the drone. They immediately came back into the trailer and Mom sat down with the controls. It wasn't nearly as loud as the hovering helicopter-style drones I had seen. By the time the controls said it was at 300 feet, I couldn't hear it at all. Mom continued to fly it higher as Con watched intently. She finally leveled off around 1,200 feet, saying that the air was becoming more unstable and she didn't want to risk going higher. We watched her designate a grid pattern that stretched across our camp and the farm below. She said she had set it to 80% of the drone's range. We would get great coverage, but were less likely to lose it on our first flight.

Once Mom had the flight path designated, she brought up a program called Raptor. It only had two buttons: Initiate and Cancel. Mom clicked Initiate. The screen went black, then a light gray frame appeared. When I looked closer, I saw the screen wasn't exactly black, but more of a gray-scale. Suddenly, I realized I was looking at the camera view from the drone. In the dark of night, there was very little to see until Mom hit the I-key. The screen suddenly changed to shades of navy blue with occasional orange or yellow dots.

"Infrared?" I asked.

"Yes, the cameras are actually capturing other spectrums as well. It is a very sophisticated drone, despite its small size".

Suddenly, the frame on the screen went from gray to red and tightened down to a small box moving quickly across the screen. Text appeared at the bottom of the screen, but only said "Calculating…". After about 15 seconds, the text changed to "Single Soldier 1 – 300 meters 60km/hr Bearing: East".

"Well, shit. That's not good. They have a drone and likely know we're here. We have to assume they have detected our recon. The only good news is that they are flying low too, and our drone is above theirs."

"They know we're here?" Jules nearly shouted.

"Yes, dear, almost certainly, and you're still alive. So calm down. We look like refugees, and the improvements you've made, like the paddock, just reinforce that idea. We don't appear to be much of a threat yet. It doesn't change anything other than our approach. If Miles told them anything, we would not fit his description. After all, he certainly didn't expect all this. He would expect a single truck with a trailer. Speaking of, JC, please throw a tarp over that .50. They may have already seen it, but just in case they haven't, it's worth hiding. Don't rush, just do it like you're performing any nightly routine."

"What about the heat from the Murdochs in the trailer?" I asked.

Mom laughed a little at that. "Ya know, I bet that will confuse them. They probably have IR so they'll see the glow, but it won't make much sense. It's just a trailer emitting a lot of heat. They may think it's sleeping quarters with a stove inside or maybe more farm animals like pigs."

"Mom, they'll know how many we have, and we can't sneak up on them. What are we going to do?" Jules asked

"Well, July, the first thing we're not going to do is panic. Next, we will play up the refugee angle. Tomorrow, I want you kids to act like kids and play with Ben. Maybe go riding, the horses need exercise, anyhow. No movies or anything that would keep you inside unless it's raining. Why don't you, Ben, Ramirez, and Amy go riding. You can take the road past the farm and do what you can to look like a family. It should help set their minds at ease, and Ramirez can get a second look to see if he notices any changes."

The computer screen flashed once, and the message Raptor Landing scrolled across the bottom of the screen. Mom walked back to where she had launched the drone and waited. It seemed to come out of nowhere, but she made it look easy, snagging it out of mid-air. She then walked quickly back into the camper, motioning for Con to stay inside. Once inside, she pulled the battery for charging and stowed the drone. Then she walked back to the laptop.

Con was already manipulating the controls and seemed to know what she would want. The screen turned black and displayed "Processing" with the hated flippin' hourglass icon. Approximately 15 minutes later, the laptop beeped and Con's gray-scale lidar hillshade filled the screen. Other items began to fill in across the image. Buildings appeared and red dots appeared scattered around and in the buildings. Each dot had a number and a light pink line stringing out of it. It appeared to represent people and the paths they had taken during the flight. The outlines of two vehicles appeared; a van by the house and a pickup by the barn.

When it was complete, Mom and Ramirez both seemed lost in thought.

"Not much different than what we had on the map, except for that one." Mom pointed to a red dot near the back of the barn, close to a side door. It was smaller than the other 2 red dots marked equine.

There were four red dots outside, and what appeared to be seven pink dots, with 6 in the house and one in the barn.

"The pink dots are estimates based on heat signatures and variations observed during flight," Mom explained. "They are not exact, but the estimates are usually very close. Close enough that I'd bet they're dead on. With ten soldiers in a squad, this looks accurate to me. Ramirez?"

"You're thinking the eleventh is your guy?"

"It would make sense and explain the sentry at the back of the barn."

"Guarding a prisoner."

"I certainly hope so. Miles is a good man and a fellow Marine. He retired a few years back and wanted to move close to his grandkids in Virginia. The farm seemed like a good option for both of us. He was only an hour from them and visited several times a week before The Fall. I trust him, and he's done a great job getting the farm to stay in the black. Not an easy task in West Virginia, but he managed it.

Miles worked a deal with one of the restaurants on Snowshoe as a beef supplier. He formed a Co-op with several local farmers, and we've all prospered. I want to get him back alive. As I said before, he's a good man and my friend."

"Yes, Ma'am. We will make that happen." Ramirez said, with a confidence I didn't feel. The reality of what we were facing seemed to grow as I looked at the map. I think it was the fact they have a drone too that really made it hit home. We had been facing amateurs who were still playing apocalypse games and trying to be bad men. These men were professionals. I was looking at the group of good people surrounding me, and Belle's injuries, and I just didn't want any more of us getting hurt.

"Snap out of it, JC," Mom called. When I looked up, she was staring straight at me. "We're all going to be fine as long as you do your job. No mistakes. No heroics. Just good soldiering. Yes?"

"Yes, Ma'am." I replied. She stared a minute longer, then just said "Good", and let it go.

Chapter 25 – Oscar Mike – 06:00

Jules and Mom were our Alpha team and had the joy of walking the 3 miles around the ridge. Once they found the correct drainage, they began the long slow trip down towards the farm. The goal was to come down near the valley and then climb onto a small spur ridge that ran from the back of the barn at a diagonal. They almost made it on the first try, only having to spend a half hour adjusting to find the small gap in the trees Con found with the drone.

Twice on the way down they had to stop and listen after something snapped a branch or pushed through a bush. Both times it had been deer, and both times Jules nearly threw up afterward. This was one reason Mom wanted Jules with her. No way was her baby going to be out of her sight on this mission. Once they were in place, it was time to wait.

We chose 10:00 as our attack time. Attacking at night would give the advantage to the PLAGF, who almost certainly had night optics. Shift change was often a good time to get everyone out in the open. Our opposition was smart enough to realize that and only changed one man at a time. Just prior to shift change seems good as the sentries would be tired. Unfortunately, these troops were well-disciplined. That probably had a lot to do with the Special Warfare officer in charge. They actually seemed more alert at all the times typical sentries would allow their minds to wander. Therefore, we chose the middle of their morning shift, in the middle of the doldrums.

Jules and Mom had 2 jobs. The first was to lob bait into the camp. They would do this with an impromptu slingshot made from rubber hardware tie-downs and a small plastic bucket. The tie-downs would be secured to two trees with large zip ties. Then Mom could launch while Jules kept watch. The bait was our favored potted meat wrapped in leaves to help with surface tension, then wrapped in honeysuckle vines. It took several attempts for us to get the right layering, but the end result was a nice payload that sprayed apart at impact.

The troops would probably figure it out, but that doesn't really matter when a horde of Murdochs are charging your position. It's a distraction, and you know it's a distraction. That doesn't change the fact that you have a horde of strong and fast zombie-like creatures sprinting towards you. They go down but it's like shooting a hyped-up druggie, you gotta hit 'em somewhere critical or they just keep coming. Hit one in the arm and it'll ignore it, you're screwed.

While they waited, Mom secured the slingshot to the trees and conducted a few test pulls. Everything seemed good, so they loaded the first 3 meatballs (get it, meatballs… never mind). Fully loaded, they stood ready to commence bombardment. Jules was a nervous wreck and trying to hide it.

"We good to go?" Jules whispered. Mom looked over with a raised eyebrow and a disapproving look, followed by a nod. Jules mouthed "Sorry" and went back to nervously glancing back and forth. She felt Mom's hand on her shoulder and looked back. Raised eyebrows, asking "Are you OK?" Jules nodded and took a slow, deep breath like Mom had taught us to do when we were nervous. Mom's hand remained for a few minutes longer as she waited for Jules' breathing to settle into a slower rhythm.

At 10:00, the first volley of bait flew into the farm below. Jules abandoned her watch and reloaded the slingshot as soon as Mom had it pulled back again. Mom adjusted aim and released again. The third and final volley flew to yet another area of the farm's yard. Two volleys aimed toward sentry locations, with the third toward the main house. Mostly, they landed scattered throughout the yard in front of the house. Not ideal, but it would have to do.

As soon as the third volley released, Mom and Jules were on the move. Rather than moving up the ridge to gain distance, Jules followed Mom down the ridge. They headed toward the valley floor but away from the barn at nearly a 45-degree angle. Hopefully, the launch was too quick to track, but they were taking no chances. The shouts below left no doubt that the soldiers found the bait. Sure was nice of those gentlemen to confirm the bait was in place for the next step in our plan. Not to mention those who kindly picked it up and spread the scent to themselves.

"Down." Mom commanded, and they both dropped.

The crack of gunfire pierced the quiet morning as shots whistled through the air above their heads. When Jules looked up, Mom had disappeared. She was there one second and gone the next. Rather than whine about it, Jules stomped down her fear and started to crawl downhill as quietly as possible. She made it about 100 feet before she heard the quiet steps behind her. She stiffened expecting a shot in the back. Instead, she heard a short, muffled intake of breath followed by the sound of something heavy being lowered to the ground.

"It's ok, sweetheart, I've got him." She heard Mom's reassuring voice coming from the figure looming over her.

Jules heard almost nothing as Mom leaned down and began quickly patting down the sentry. She saw her pull a few things off the body and then wipe a knife clean on the sentry's jacket before sliding it back into a sheath. Without a word, Mom walked down to Jules and motioned for her to follow, after a quick once-over, of course.

Jules looked over as she heard Mom in a deep voice say, "Zhen bang" (super!) and saw the throat mike from the soldier's radio she had pushed against her neck. Mom just nodded and pointed downhill. They continued, moving carefully to stay quiet and avoid tripping.

As they rounded the end of the slope, the farm came into sight. And a beautiful sight it was, watching the Murdochs sprinting through the pasture towards the PLAGF troops. Most of the troops were firing in short bursts. One soldier seemed to have completely panicked at the sight and was cycling through rounds as fast as his QBZ-95 would spit them out. He hit several Murdochs, but the continuous fire only seemed to draw more to him. It was hard not to watch as the flood of Murdochs descended on him like a pack of wolves. The other troops were too busy trying to survive to worry about that idiot.

As Jules and Mom approached the barn, they saw the rifle muzzle barely poking through the crack in the open loft doors. The wood above the gun suddenly splintered, and the muzzle dropped. The echoing report of the Dragunov crossed the valley a split second later, score one for Belle. The report of that heavy rifle seemed to momentarily stun the sentries. That moment of distraction cost the sentry closest to the river, as the Murdochs never even flinched. They just increased their speed when they sensed distracted prey. The sentry returned to firing at the mob, only to find 10 Murdochs nearly on top of him.

The PLAGF radio Mom had taken from the body of the sentry she killed suddenly came alive with shouted orders. Things were not going as planned for the defending force.

Mom motioned for Jules to follow her around the side of the barn. They approached the side door and stacked up. Mom moved through the door and around the corner, quickly scanning as she swept her rifle along the stalls. She moved left towards the front while Jules turned right to cover the rear of the barn. A quick sweep of the lower level revealed a thoroughly pissed-off and dehydrated marine tied up and lying in the hay of a horse stall. Mom moved in and quietly cut the bonds, dropped a pistol into his hands, and then left the stall.

While Jules watched the doors, Mom climbed the ladder into the hay loft. It was full of hay and left little room to hide, but she hadn't lived this long being careless. She moved cautiously through the loft towards the big doors where the sniper's rifle lay, only there was no sniper there, just a small pool of blood. A board creaked under her foot and she immediately dropped to the floor.

The move saved her life as a QBZ-95 opened up on full auto through the hay bales to her right. Not waiting for the sniper to finish, she fired six quick shots. Each shot was aimed at a different spot around the area where the 6mm rounds were splitting the hay. The firing stopped. Mom couldn't tell if she had hit the sniper or he just stopped shooting.

As she began inching toward the front of the barn on her back, the hay bales seemed to explode toward her in a wall of tumbling hay. She desperately flipped her own rifle selector to auto and squeezed the trigger. When her rifle ran dry, she lay buried under a mound of hay bales, struggling to get free. She heard a dry chuckle and the sound of someone reloading a rifle. Her last thought before the shot came was that she hoped Miles would protect her baby.

The sound of 3 rounds fired in the small loft was deafening despite the dampening effects of all the hay. The shots were well-placed, hitting the combat vest dead center and traveling up with the recoil. The final shot hit the neck, spraying blood across the hay. Jules stood shaking at the top of the ladder, still pointing her rifle at the sniper's back as he crumpled to the loft floor.

Mom finally managed to shove the remaining bales off her and sat up to see her daughter standing there, rifle trained on the dead soldier. The daughter she had kept with her to protect her had just saved her life. Mom jumped to her feet and enveloped Jules in a hug.

"Oh, baby, you saved me! Thank you, sweetheart, you were brilliant! Now, we're both OK, so I need your help. Please go check on Miles. I'm worried about him."

Jules nodded and slowly climbed back down the ladder in shock. Mom rushed over to the sniper to make sure he was dead. Once confirmed, she performed a cursory search, and then followed Jules down to check on Miles.

"Knew you would come Major, I do greatly appreciate the

rescue," Miles said as soon as he saw her.

"We're not done yet, Miles. Are you mobile?"

"Oorah. I played old and dumb. Figured I'd wait for the opportunity to issue a little payback. I'm ready to bag some bandits, ma'am."

"Oorah, get your ass ready then, Marine. We got work to do. Brought a bang bang down for you. He wasn't usin' it any longer." Mom threw Miles the rifle and a canteen, then held her hand out for her pistol.

Miles was up and had been stretching while they talked.

"This is my daughter, Jules," Mom said by way of introduction.

"Good to meet you, Jules, I'm Miles."

Without any further chatter, they eased back out the side door and headed towards the front of the barn. They wanted to be sure Belle could see them. They didn't want her to mistake them for the Chinese soldiers. Without a word, they had instinctively taken a position with Mom in front and Miles behind. As they approached the corner, Miles came up even with the other two so they could communicate more easily.

The yard and front pastures were a mess of Murdochs with one remaining sentry fighting for his life. Reinforcements had tried to join him, but Belle had picked two off, leaving only one pinned down by the truck. Mom had watched as the second of the reinforcements caught a bullet in the shoulder. With the reinforcements dead or pinned down, it took less than a minute for the last sentry to be overrun. Four Murdochs dove into this foxhole and began tearing him limb from limb. The screams seemed to rouse Jules from her stupor, and she raised her rifle. Mom's hand shot up to the barrel and eased it back down.

"Glad you're back with me, baby. Now, let's find a better position before we start giving those Murdochs another target."

Jules just looked Mom in the eyes and nodded.

"We'll circle back up the hill behind the barn. That should let us cover the back of the house and ease down slowly. Do not fire unless I tell you to or there is imminent danger. Understand?"

"Understood," both Miles and Jules said at the same time.

Chapter 26 –War Damn Eagle – 06:00 meanwhile...

"Precious." Belle said affectionately as she petted the Dragunov.

"What was that?" I asked

"Oh, just admiring the Precious."

"So, you're Gollum now?"

That elicited a rather rude gesture.

"Belle, I can't believe you. That was completely uncalled for." I replied in mock condemnation.

"Precious wants to plays with me. Precious wants us to plays with the mens downs in the valleys's" Belle said in her best Gollum voice. "OK, I'll be leaving now. You and your Precious have fun. Just remember which mens you supposed to plays withs."

"Oh, Precious knows. Precious always knows."

I walked away mildly concerned, looking over my shoulder. One last worried glance over my shoulder elicited a small giggle from Belle. What a goofball, she seemed to be saying. That quickly transitioned into a sense of unease as their thoughts turned to what was in store for them in the upcoming attack.

Belle and Amy had been working together ever since Mom assigned them as a sniper team, so about a day. Belle's injuries would prevent her from being in the attacking ground force. Since she was one of the better shots, she could still be a valuable asset as overwatch. Mom and Ramirez had both offered Belle and Amy advice, doing their best to teach Amy the ins and outs of the spotting scope and her role as spotter.

After that, Amy and Belle spent hours calling targets. They confirmed ranges, elevation changes, wind direction, wind speed and looked for indicators of different wind currents across distances down range. This fun exercise quickly became a grueling process. The two professionals aided this by alternately stopping in to evaluate their progress. They would provide unvarnished feedback and assign new tasks to practice. The worst part was that they were not allowed to shoot due to limited ammo and the noise that would travel to the valley below.

Both the best and worst parts of the assignment were their relative safety from the action down on the valley floor. If things really went sideways it was their job to grab everything they could and take Ben and Con to find a safe home. Belle and Amy both alternated between concern for those heading into action, guilt for not going with them, and relief that they would not be directly in the line of fire. The relief was always followed by more guilt.

Belle and Amy saddled up on Dakota and Gin and were ready to ride out to their perch after first light the morning of the attack. The PLAGF drone seemed to mostly fly at night. The assumption was that this allowed them to maximize flight time and use the thermal camera to the greatest effect. The sniper team didn't want to be in position until after the drone was on the ground. Besides, two people riding out at night was suspicious but leaving in the morning was pretty normal behavior. Leaving early in the morning with rifles could easily be a hunting trip if the soldiers spotted them.

After their earlier banter, it was time to get on with the day. Belle slid her precious into the scabbard and asked me to help her get into the saddle. Her leg was still sore and Ramirez had warned her about tearing the stitches, particularly with medical supplies being so limited. Once she was seated and ready, I looked up at her.

"Be careful out there, War Eagle."

"OMG, I mentioned liking Auburn once when we were in Middle School, MIDDLE SCHOOL and you're STILL calling me that!" said an exasperated Belle.

"Well, I guess it is better than the tide but..." I trailed off. My heart wasn't in the taunting game as I told her goodbye. "Just be careful and if you have a minute up there on your perch, watch our back. OK?"

"Yeah, I got you and I will bring the true wrath of the Dragunov War Eagle down on anyone who dares mess with my people. Ain't nobody fuckin' with my family." Belle stated with conviction.

"Well then, let's get this show on the road. Ramirez, you ready to rock'n'roll?"

Belle heard Ramirez call back from the other side of the Murdoch trailer. They hooked it back up to the Lady a few minutes before and now he was waiting for me.

Belle and Amy turned their mounts and began walking out of camp toward the ridge. It was a short ride, but the horses were the best way to get Belle there. It also kept up the illusion of a morning outing. They had even brought a picnic basket; well, it was really a cooler. It was good cover if the drone stayed up longer than expected. Besides, they might get hungry, and Belle had taken advantage of the cooler, loading plenty of food and coffee. She'd even found and subsequently acquired a couple Little Debbie cakes, unbeknownst to Ramirez.

By 08:00 Belle and Amy finished settling into their perch while happily munching a Swiss Roll apiece. They spent the next hour improving their concealment. The sniper hide was really just a dense laurel hell on top of a rock outcrop. They cut some of the lower limbs out of the bushes and brushed the leaves away. That way they would make less noise if they moved around. The girls were counting on the horses to help watch their back and they needed to be quiet enough to hear them. Once they cleared brush and debris away, they rolled out a couple foam bedrolls. No reason to rough it when you were bringing supplies in on horseback, after all.

The next hour passed quicker than expected as they watched the camp below. Amy gave Belle ranges for each sentry they could see and then began scanning for other bandits. In the meantime, Belle was watching the wind and dialing in her scope. She found several trees slightly higher than the general canopy that acted as good windsocks. Once she felt good about her settings, she too scanned for enemies, with the occasional almost OCD checks of her gun, her scope, and the wind.

Belle wasn't sure how long she had been watching me and Ramirez when Amy startled her.

"How are they doing?"

"Holy crap! You startled me. Um, they're good. Looks like they've got the trailer set up and have the release rigged. I just hope it works as well today as it did last night."

"Yeah, no kidding. That going sideways could make this real ugly, but I'm sure they'll get it. The wiring and switches are all real simple and should be more than enough to release the locks. Then it's just on those boys to put their backs into it."

"I sure hope this distraction works," Belle mused.

"Yeah, I don't want to lose them either. I've kinda grown fond of Ramirez over the last few months and JC seems like a good guy."

"The best, we've been friends since before we could walk. I don't know what I would do without him." Belle cleared her throat, "Any more sentries out there?"

"No new players, but the one at the barn has moved farther out toward the woods. I doubt you'll have an angle on him. I also noticed the loft doors seem to be open. I don't think they were like that in the drone footage."

"No, they weren't. Good catch. We must have them worried that we're up to something."

Belle began scanning each sentry again, taking her time on the barn doors.

"I don't see anything now. We'll need to watch the barn for a possible sniper position."

"Copy that." Amy replied.

From their position on the ridge, Amy and Belle never heard the bait or even the shouts of the Chinese soldiers, but it was easy to see the change in activity.

"He's gone!" Amy almost shouted.

"Who?"

"Sorry, the barn sentry. I could just make him out at the edge of the trees until everyone got excited and now, he's gone. Do you think he heard them?"

"Nothing we can do about it if he did, but I hope not. Ms. McKinney will have to take care of him. Don't worry, that woman is a certified badass! Well, the shit has officially hit the fan. Here come our Murdochs!"

Belle watched as the sentries began firing on the horde of Murdochs coming their way. The noise seemed to enrage the Murdochs, and they increased their pace from a fast walk, to a jog, and then an outright sprint. Hell, it was intimidating from up on the ridge. Belle couldn't imagine what it would be like from a foxhole down there in front of them.

The sentries started with slow, methodical shots that quickly turned into bursts of fire as the Murdochs closed. The sentry in the closest foxhole to the Murdochs seemed to be understandably panicked. He was firing more sporadically than the others. That was when Belle heard the crack of the sniper rifle.

She looked back towards the barn, and sure enough, there was the tip of a rifle barely sticking out of the loft doors. The Major would chew her ass if she did that, Belle thought. As the sniper fired, the Murdochs running at the panicked sentry began to fall. Now, we just can't have that, Belle thought and trained her Dragunov on where she estimated the body of the sniper would be lying. One solid hit from her heavy rounds should be more than enough. Amy double-checked the range and wind, calling them out as she did. Belle slowed her breathing and began squeezing the trigger as she exhaled. The rifle jumped as the round exploded out toward the target. She saw the wood blow apart as the round pierced the barn door and drove into what lay behind it. The rifle muzzle peaking through the doors dropped to the loft floor. Belle turned to Amy with a smile.

"Nice shot," Amy said.

"Thanks," Belle said as she moved her sights toward the house, "Now let's see who else might want to come out and play."

Three soldiers came streaming out of the house to cover the retreat of the sentries. The last one out the door was the lucky recipient of Belle's next shot. He lifted off his feet and sailed back through the closing door. The first two soldiers dove to the grass, rolled, and came up sprinting for cover.

The soldier in front was almost to the truck parked in front of the house, so Belle tracked the second soldier. She smoothly followed his progress, leading him along his path as she squeezed the trigger. The heavy 7.62mm round caught him in the shoulder and he cartwheeled in a bizarre ragdoll fashion. It was mesmerizing to watch until he hit the post holding the dinner bell. Belle could hear the distant ringing as the force of his body slammed into the post, causing the bell to swing wildly.

"Well, that was unexpected," Amy said with a morbid little chuckle.

"Why yes, yes, it was." Belle replied, not quite sure how she felt about it. With no time to contemplate what happened, she just started looking for the next target. There was no clear shot on the soldier at the truck, and the Murdochs were making quick work of the last sentry. Belle began scanning the windows of the house, looking for any bandits.

As Belle turned towards Amy, she caught a bright flash that seemed to come from her scope. Blood sprayed across the side of Amy's face, and the Dragunov dropped into the dirt. Amy screamed and began pulling Belle back away from the edge of the rock. Belle's face was covered with blood, and she wasn't responding to Amy's pleading yells.

The Chinese operator smiled as he saw the muzzle of the sniper's rifle fall. He couldn't hear Amy's screams, but he didn't need to hear her to know he had scored on his target. Now they could get back to work without that damned sniper picking off his men.

As the chaos continued below, Amy frantically tore through the first aid kit they brought. She yanked out wads of gauze and clotting trauma pads to press to Belle's head. The blood had drenched both women and Amy just kept repeatedly mumbling "I'm an electrician not a fucking medic! Damn it, Ramirez! Where are you!"

Chapter 27 – Bravo Team – 10:00

Bravo team consisted of me and Ramirez. We were tasked with releasing the Murdochs and the frontal assault element. We had taken one radio and left the other with Con & Ben since we would have the worst sightlines. Con had launched their drone just after 09:30 and had been relaying everyone's progress to Ramirez at ten-minute intervals until the action started. After that, our lack of an earpiece mandated that the updates came only when requested. That would be essential to reduce distractions and prevent the radio from giving away our position.

Ramirez and I had the trailer set up and rigged for the door release. We sat watching and waiting from 30 yards away. As we were about to release the Murdochs, we heard the yelling from the house. It was all the prompting we needed to get our little party started.

The release and rope trick worked like a charm. The Murdochs erupted out of the trailer like, well like they were a bunch of pinned-up and pissed-off zombies, that's what. They actually seemed angry at everything but slightly stunned by the sudden release. It was a bizarre combination of emotions to watch play across the faces of creatures with the general IQ of a Chihuahua.

They didn't stay confused for long, though, as the Chinese soldiers continued to yell. They turned almost as one and tilted their heads back as they sniffed the air. Then it was like somebody triggered a starting pistol because they took off like a shot.

And sure enough, that old George Jones classic began running through my head. I looked at Ramirez and blurted out "Now the race is on, and here comes pride up the backstretch, Heartaches are going to the inside". He just stared at me for a full 10 seconds. I thought for sure I had some serious reprimand coming and was well into my own personal reprimand when he just gave a little chuckle and shook his head.

"Damn kid, we'll make a Ranger out of you yet."

I didn't say a word, just thanked my lucky stars I wasn't getting an ass chewing for my sudden ill-timed fuckery.

As the Murdochs closed in on the soldiers' positions, we moved down into the river bed and began heading downstream towards the house. We crossed to the far bank along the farm fields and stayed as close as we could, still moving slowly downriver. I was glad we were close to that bank when the shooting started. Especially when I started hearing that supersonic whine of bullets as they zipped overhead.

Things got a lot worse when the sniper opened up on our Murdochs. I could feel the report of the big rifle in my chest every time he let loose. It felt like he was coming for me personally.

The one-sided battle above us seemed to continue forever before I heard the distant boom of Belle's Precious. The sniper's firing stopped immediately, and suddenly I could breathe again. Our pace increased, and I realized that Ramirez must have slowed down when the sniper began firing.

We crept slowly up to the edge of the bank to get a better idea of what was happening on the field of battle. With their sniper down, the nearest sentry switched to full auto. He was cycling through ammo so fast that I stood frozen in utter fascination as we watched him rock in one mag after another. Those boys definitely came prepared, and he could cycle rounds like a mother fucker. His aim must have been shit though, because he barely seemed to be slowing any Murdochs down. The Murdochs, on the other hand, must have taken his rapid-fire assault as an insult. Or maybe just heard it as a dinner bell, because they all found a reserve of energy and sprinted even faster for his position.

The forward sentry position turned into a tangle of bodies that erupted into a disturbing scene of carnage. As that tableau unfolded, we heard the front door hit the wall as three soldiers erupted from the house in a sprint to back up their brothers. The last soldier in line never made it through the door. He just seemed to jump backward mid-stride. That thought had no sooner made it through my mind when I heard the report of Belle's Precious again. Go, Belle, go, I thought.

As the remaining two soldiers dove into the grass, Ramirez tapped my shoulder and pointed downstream. We eased back from the bank as the two jumped up to run for cover. As my boots hit the water, I heard another boom from Belle's rifle. One more down, I thought. With all the noise and distraction above, we started to move downstream at a run. We were not wasting any more time getting into this fight.

In what seemed like an eternity and a split second at the same time, we were crawling back to the edge of the bank. We were no more than 200 feet from the house. While we were moving down the river, the Murdochs had been busy. The sentries were all gone, and only one soldier was visible outside. The last of the backup that had sprinted to the rescue, only now he sat pinned down by the truck.

Ramirez eased his rifle into position and took slow, careful aim at the soldier. At the crack of his rifle, the soldier's body slammed back into the truck and slumped to the ground. As he fell, we slid back down the bank.

The soldiers in the house answered Ramirez's shot with searching fire. We just hugged the bank and moved closer to the house. Ramirez's shot had caught the attention of the Murdochs too, but those nice soldiers' return fire helped drag it back solidly to where it belonged.

Just as we slid back into the water, a Murdoch launched itself off the bank towards us. Apparently, not all the Murdochs turned back towards the house. Without thinking, I swung my M1 up and pulled the trigger. The hip shot took the Murdoch full in the chest, and for a split second, he seemed to almost hang in midair. Then he landed almost on top of me and purely by instinct, I lifted the muzzle up to catch him in the chin. The action flipped his head back, the downward pressure causing me to squeeze off another round. This accidental shot blew the top of the Murdoch's forehead clean off. I stood in shock, just before puking on the fallen body. That was just nasty.

After watching the scene unfold, Ramirez looked at me appraisingly and said, "Not sure how much of that was intentional but I'm damn glad you're on my side. Aside from the puke that is." I nodded and replied, "De nada". Although I'm not sure the stunned look on my face and puke dribbling down my chin quite pulled off the cool nonchalance I was going for.

I used my canteen to rinse my mouth out, and we continued to move downstream to flank the house.

To stay close to the bank, we had to swim through a deep pool in the bend of the river. That is not as easy as it sounds when you're trying to keep your rifle dry. To top things off, the bank was very low on the downstream side of the bend where it fanned out into a little floodplain. Light river cane offered some cover, but it presented its own set of problems as they were dense and would shake like signal flags if we moved through them.

Chapter 28 – Assault & Battery

The soldiers had forted up in the house and it was beginning to look like there was a potential for a siege. That was not something we could afford. We didn't have the people for it. It would also mean giving up our Murdoch contingent. If the Chinese soldiers didn't pick them off, we would have to for our own safety. Instead, we went for option B.

When the Murdochs reached the foot of the stairs to the porch, the soldiers increased their fire. We used the time to look for muzzle flashes. While I took aim at a shooter in an open upstairs window, Ramirez flipped his selector to full auto. My M1 barked, and the second-story shooter fell forward into the open window. I fired a second shot into his head as Ramirez opened up on the two downstairs porch windows, shattering glass and splintering wood.

We both dropped down into the water as soon as we stopped firing and moved downstream a good 10-15 feet. The expected answering shots at our abandoned positions served to remind the Murdochs that their targets were inside. We gave them 30 seconds to find the shattered windows, and then we made a break for the house.

Our plan almost worked. As we sprinted for the house it became very apparent that only about half of the Murdochs had found the entrance Ramirez made for them. The rest were milling around in the front yard and saw us as the new objects of their desires. Instead of a leisurely walk through the house behind the Murdochs, cleaning up any stragglers, we were suddenly on the menu too.

All hell broke loose as we sprinted for cover. While Chaos ensued in the house the outside contingent of Murdochs sprinted for us. I dropped to one knee and began firing while Ramirez fired from a standing position just behind me. I shot two Murdochs in the chest before something yanked me backward, and I heard Ramirez yell "Run!"

As I turned to run, I felt a hand grasp my ankle and looked back to see a Murdoch that had leapt forward to prevent my escape. A black hole suddenly appeared on his forehead, and the back of his skull exploded as the boom of a heavy rifle echoed from the trees behind the house. It couldn't be Belle, could it? There was no time to ponder that thought though, as the other Murdochs were closing in on our position.

Miles lowered the QBU-88 sniper rifle briefly to yell to Lindsey and Jules, "Major, we got Bravo heading our way with a group of those damned zombies!"

"Jules, back up Miles while I cover the house. I don't want these bastards sneaking out the back while we fight. Belle can watch the front for us while we regroup."

Jules found a place she could see through the trees and brush just in time to watch me and Ramirez climb up onto the old spring house. I turned and bashed a Murdoch in the head with the butt of my M1 as it tried to follow him up. Miles shot the one beside it through the neck, and Ramirez opened up in a steady stream of 2 round bursts, moving smoothly from one Murdoch to the next. Jules was determined to do her part to protect her brother. She spotted a female Murdoch that had managed to sneak around behind the men. It was scrabbling up the far side of the spring house when

Jules' shot caught it in the temple. Just like shooting clays on the range, she thought.

We were making quick work of the dozen or so Murdochs remaining outside when I noticed one running for the woods. He was making a beeline for what had to be Mom and Jules helping us fend them off. I took a shot but missed, and the clip popped out just as I started to take a second shot. Damn, I thought, I've got the timing of a John Hughes nerd trying to ask out the prom queen! I reached for another stripper clip and watched the Murdoch disappear into the trees. I tried to yell out a warning, but with all the gunfire and screaming, I doubt anyone heard a thing.

While I reloaded, Ramirez continued his game of whack-a-mole, using his M4 as a long-distance mallet. As I turned to find my next target, I realized there were none left. My next thought was of the Murdoch that disappeared into the woods. I slipped from the roof and sprinted for the spot where I saw him enter the woods. As soon as I reached the wood line, I heard a scream from Jules somewhere up the hill.

Adrenaline flooded my system and I sprinted up the hill, ignoring the branches slapping me in the face and snapping against my body. The scream came again, and I pushed harder. I felt a jerk as the M1 tore from my hands as I climbed. I barely noticed it as I surged up the hill for Jules.

When I broke into the small opening, the Murdoch was on top of my sister, lunging at her neck and trying to bite. Jules was holding him back, pushing against his shoulders with both hands. All reason had fled, and I jumped onto them both. Grabbing the Murdoch by the arms, I yanked them backwards and twisted away. The Murdoch let out a roar as I wrenched his shoulders and we tumbled off Jules and down the hill.

My back slammed into a tree trunk, and my legs went numb. The stunned Murdoch was lying on top of me, facing the sky. He seemed to be coming back around faster than the feeling in my legs. My instincts served me well again, and my hand shot down to my side to pull the combat knife strapped to my leg. I fumbled with the retaining snap but managed to yank it out as the Murdoch began to struggle.

I drove it into his side and he roared in pain. The Murdoch twisted, nearly dragging the knife out of my hand as he turned. I barely managed to hang onto it as his left hand shot forward and clamped around my throat like a vise. I immediately began to choke and cough. Pinned beneath him like I was, I didn't have room to knock his hand free.

I was beginning to see stars as he shifted and lowered his head to use his teeth to tear my throat out. His shifting around caused him to relax his grip slightly, and my thinking cleared enough for me to remember the knife in my hand. All I could focus on was his neck as he came down for the killing bite.

I slammed the knife into his throat with everything I had left. Unfortunately, that was barely enough to break the skin and couldn't have penetrated more than an inch. I still had the luck of the Irish, though, and the Murdoch twisted as he pulled away. His own action caused the knife to slice through his carotid artery. I watched through a haze as I gasped for breath. He grabbed his neck with both hands. It seemed like such a normal reaction that it reminded me of how these creatures were not mindless undead rather people driven mad by disease.

The Murdoch fell sideways, down the hill, and off me. I sat up slowly, still somewhat dazed. I wiped my knife on my pants and slid it back into the scabbard. The feeling finally began returning to my legs, and I crawled back up to Jules.

She met me halfway as she was sliding down with her M4 in hand, ready to help me. She gave a startled little scream when she saw me.

"JC! Are you ok? Are you hurt? Damn it, James, answer me!" Jules yelled in a non-stop string.

"I will if you'll shut up long enough." I snapped at her.

"Oh, thank God! It's just, you're covered in blood. You look, I thought, all the blood, it's, it's everywhere."

"Blood?" I stammered. I hadn't noticed any blood.

Jules slid down beside me and started checking me for injuries, obviously no longer taking my word for my uninjured state.

"I can't find anything! Are you sure you're OK?" she asked.

"I'm fine Jules! It must be his. Are you OK? Last I saw, he was trying to rip your throat out."

"I'm fine, JC. Thanks for jumping on top of us, by the way. You knocked the damn breath out of me. If you hadn't pulled him off after you tackled us, I would have been the bloody one. Maybe next time you could grab him without the Superman jump?"

"Such gratitude!" I said with mock indignation.

"Yeah, well… thanks. I guess you did save me. Just try not to incapacitate me next time, will you?"

"Next time? Really, Daphne?"

"Oh shut up, you know what I mean!"

"Yeah, I got you, sis. Just don't want this to become a regular thing."

"No shit! Think about it from the damsel's viewpoint. That shit sucks!"

"Damsel?"

"Oh, shut up."

As we talked, a man walked over to us from the same direction Jules had come. Her lack of reaction seemed to indicate he was on our side. Well, that and the fact that the rifle he held wasn't pointed at us.

"This is Miles. Miles, this is my brother, JC," Jules said as a brief introduction.

"Nice to meet you, son. Now, what do you say we find the rifle I hope you dropped and regroup with your Mom. And where's the rest of your team?"

"Right here," Ramirez said as he slid out of the shadows.

"DAMN!" Miles exclaimed. "You must be another operator. You fucking Special Forces are going to be the death of me one day. My old heart just isn't up to this shit anymore."

"I'm Ramirez, the Ranger Medic. Nice to meet you, Miles."

"Likewise."

"JC, our mission hasn't changed. If you're good to go, we'll head back down and clear the house. Miles, care to join us? We could use a third." Ramirez said.

"Sounds good. Jules, please tell the Major." Miles replied.

It was at that point that Con broke radio silence.

"Dad? She's down. Eagle is down. I don't know what happened, Dad. What do we do? Dad, can you hear me? Eagle is down."

"Con, slow down," Ramirez said in a calm slow voice.

"Dad, they're not in position. What do we do?"

"Con! Deep breath, son. Now, tell me what happened."

"They were there in position, but when I circled back around, they were gone. I found them at least 30 feet back from the outcrop. Dad, I don't know what to do!" Con stammered.

"Con, I need you to listen very carefully. First, tell Ben to go lock everything down. Do it now."

"He heard you. He's working on it now."

"Good, now I want you to check the Remington by the door. Make sure it is loaded and that there is a round in the chamber. Do it now."

A minute, maybe two, passed, but it felt like an eternity. Belle? My desire to grab the radio increased with each passing second.

"OK, Dad we're locked down. The guns are locked and loaded. Ben is keeping a lookout through the window by the door."

"Excellent job, Con. Now, I need you to circle the drone around the farmhouse and let me know where you see signatures. We're in the back son, anyone out front is a hostile."

"What about Eagle, Dad?"

Belle? Belle couldn't be down. I couldn't lose Belle! "They need to check on Eagle!" I managed to force out through the paralysis creeping through my body.

Ramirez cut across me in a strong, but not unsympathetic voice. "No JC! There's no time, and none of us are in a position to help them. I don't want to lose either of them, but they're on their own."

"Con, there is nothing we can do about Eagle. We need to have eyes on. No more questions. Just do it and tell me what you see."

"Yes, sir," Con replied.

The next 15 seconds seemed like an eternity as Con repositioned the drone.

"Dad! I've got two bogies running across the field in front of the house!"

"Damn! Bravo, let's move! Miles, watch our 6."

We half ran, half slid down the hill to the house, with me grabbing my M1 as we slid past. Then Ramirez broke around the corner at the front of the house. He dropped to a knee and began firing. I dropped down beside him into a prone position and sighted in on the lead runner. Mom's training seemed to be screaming in my ear. Slow Down, JC! Line up your target! Now, squeeze the trigger. The M1 jumped in my hands and my target fell.

Just as I lowered my rifle, grinning, the figure popped back up 3 feet away and headed in a different direction, directly for the woods. Damn! Damn! Damn it! Damn! Damn! I missed again! That shit is getting really old! I screamed in my head as I raised the rifle and took aim again. This time, I increased my elevation and lead, slowly squeezing as I eased the sights along in front of him.

Boom! The rifle rocked in my hands again. He dropped again, but this time I stayed focused and searched for him.

"Miles, Jules, clear the house. JC, on me. Let's move!"

I was so focused on the target that it took a second to realize what Ramirez said. A light kick to my shoulder brought me back around.

"Sorry. Moving."

As we began to run, Ramirez said both targets dropped, but that was no guarantee.

Two shots rang out from the house behind us and all I could do was cringe and keep running. Just be OK, sis.

The first downed soldier would never be a problem for us again. Ramirez had hit him once in his hip, once in the flak jacket, and the third in his neck. Despite this, Ramirez swept the rifle away from the body and knelt down to check for a pulse. I continued slowly forward to the spot where I had seen my man drop.

He was gone! Un-fucking believable! I couldn't have missed again. Surely. Just as I was set to lay into myself, Ramirez jogged up and pointed to a dark patch I had missed.

"He's wounded. You watch ahead while I track him. Don't get too focused. Head on a swivel, JC."

"Copy that, on a swivel." I replied.

Chapter 29 – Ops

We had been tracking the last soldier for nearly half an hour, and the adrenaline had long since worn off. Fatigue was hitting me hard, and it saved my life. I was trying to look everywhere and move quietly while Ramirez kept insisting that we move faster. Not sure if you've ever tried that yourself, but it's just not possible for me. I stepped on yet another rock that rolled under my foot, except this time I was too tired to recover. I went down, hard. The impact of my face hitting the ground muffled the sound of the rifle shot for me, so I felt it as much as heard it. The high-pitched whine of the bullet over my head, however, was just as distinct as always. I swear, I nearly shit myself. That had been way too damn close.

I'm not sure how long I had been trying not to fall off the ground when Ramirez grabbed my arm. I jumped and raised my head out of the dirt to look at him. I must have looked absolutely terrified because he used that same tone I save for startled horses.

"He's gone, JC. You're OK. Now I need you to tell me if you're hurt."

I shook my head slowly as I thought about it. I still didn't trust myself to talk.

"Good. Now, I need you to tell me where we are relative to the camp and Eagle's last known position."

I thought hard about what he had asked and began to relax

without noticing. Then it occurred to me that there was absolutely no way he needed that information. I'd never known Ramirez to not have a better idea than I did about where he was. At this thought, I started to grin.

"Nice one. And yes, it worked. Just give me a second and I'll be good to go."

"Knew you would be, kid. That kinda shit will rattle anybody. Let's move."

Ramirez did more than distract me and bring me back. He reminded me that we were moving towards Eagle and the camp. With everyone we had up there, it made sense why he was pushing me to keep moving. Those were our people, and they were relying on us, whether they knew it or not.

It didn't take Ramirez long to find the spot where our man had staged his ambush. I was surprised at first that he merely pointed it out, and we didn't go over to take a closer look. That is, until he pointed out that most people would do just that, making it an excellent place to watch for a second shot at your pursuers. I think it was this, more than anything, that really made it sink in how much training Ramirez had and how little I knew. I may know how to hunt deer, but hunting men was a whole different ballgame. They know how to hunt you back.

We continued our formation with Ramirez taking point and moved slowly up the hill towards our people. My legs were burning, so I was ecstatic when I thought Ramirez was taking a rest break. I had turned to check our back trail, and when my gaze returned forward again, he was gone. I managed to stifle my instincts and not call out for him. Instead, I eased down onto my belly and moved slowly on a diagonal downhill. I had only moved about five feet when I heard the crack of the M4. There came a quiet rustle of leaves and another shot uphill. The quiet rustle came again, and suddenly I found myself looking into Ramirez's eyes.

"Don't get any ideas, sweetheart. This is not a date." Ramirez whispered as a sly grin crept across his face. "Our friend up there was setting up for another ambush, but we've gained on him, and he wasn't ready yet. I doubt I hit him. Still, I thought the least I could do was return the favor. Hopefully, he'll make a few more mistakes now that he's feeling pressured, but don't you count on it. Let's move."

Rather than continue our current line on the soldier's trail, we swept along an arch uphill. We picked up his trail again behind where Ramirez had spotted his attempted ambush. We were moving quickly, and even I was beginning to pick out the trail. Rather than speeding up more, Ramirez began to slow down. I started to ease around him when his hand shot out and stopped me cold. He gripped my wrist so tightly that I winced in pain. I felt him relax his grip and looked over to see him staring down at my feet. It was only then that I saw the thin dark wire only inches from the tip of my boot.

With my heart hammering, I began to move back, only to have Ramirez's grip tighten again. I got the message and stopped. When I did, he let go and held a fist up in a hold sign. Ramirez then began to search the ground and brush in a full circle around us. He went slowly, sector by sector. When he completed the search, he motioned me back the way we had come. I had walked about 50 feet when I realized he was not following and stopped. About a minute later he ghosted up beside me and held out two grenades. Just the sight of those things, and my heart was hammering again.

"Simple and effective. They didn't get us, but it still gave him back his lead. We're done following. Stay on me. Slow & smooth, JC. Keep the noise to a minimum, but first, hold your ears." Ramirez pulled the pin on a grenade and chucked it back in the direction the traps had been set. We both dropped flat and heard the boom of the grenade and the whine of shrapnel.

"A little disinformation never hurts," Ramirez said as he jumped up and started to move.

We turned straight uphill and began to climb. It surprised me to find it easier to keep quiet moving uphill instead of along the slope. My calves, on the other hand, felt like hot Jell-O in the Mojave. We topped out on the ridge, and to my immense relief, Ramirez stopped to let me catch my breath. I was sucking air so hard, a golf ball through a garden hose would have been a piece of cake. Meanwhile, that damned Ranger wasn't even breathing hard!

I heard Ramirez quietly ask Con for an update, but the volume was so low I couldn't hear the reply. He simply gave me a thumbs-up and a questioning look. When the desire to puke up last week's dinner passed, I rose and managed my own thumbs-up. We began to move down the ridge towards Eagle's last known location and the camp.

As we topped out on a small knob above the camp, I realized we had already passed Eagle and were heading directly towards the camp. This suddenly made sense to me when I remembered the PLAGF drone that we had seen. Of course, he knew where our base camp was, they had just thought we were harmless. Now, knowing better, he was making a beeline for the source of his problems. Too bad for him the source of his problems was on his ass!

Ramirez stepped up the pace, and we double-timed it down the ridge towards Ben and Con. Hopefully, Belle and Amy were there by now, too. I was doing everything I could to keep up and had long passed any effort to be quiet. Apparently, Ramirez wasn't worried about noise as much as he was about getting to his son quickly.

I thought Ramirez had a change of heart when he slowed near the top of a small knoll. That is until he turned slowly to me and whispered in my ear, "JC, you better get your shit together and start moving like pond water. This shit is about to get kinetic and if you cause us to go tango uniform I will be the mother fucker who haunts your dreams. You copy?"

Somehow, that statement whispered in your ear by a Ranger is enough to dump your body's remaining adrenaline into your system all at once. I sucked in my breath as my shaking legs were suddenly more from fear of my companion than exertion. At that moment, I was truly more afraid of Ramirez than any Chinese soldier, regardless of how high-speed he may be.

Ramirez watched me collect myself and nodded in approval. Then he motioned me forward, slow and smooth. We crept up across the knoll and found a vantage where we could see most of the camp.

"I need you to stay here and watch the door on that camper. No one gets in. The boys know to stay clear of the door. You shoot anything that steps in front of it. Copy?" Ramirez ordered.

"I copy. You?"

"I'm going to swing back around where our guest should be coming up. If I don't cut his trail, I'll find a spot on the other side, and we'll wait. I think we've beat him here, but that's hard to know. Stay frosty. I will not come back this way. Keep alert for anyone approaching because it won't be me. We do still have Eagle out here somewhere, so identify your target."

"Copy."

I swear that man practically disappeared as I watched him go. One minute he was creeping away, and the next I couldn't see or hear him anywhere. Like a damned ghost. A chill ran up my spine as I thought about it. Definitely don't want him hunting me. Hell, he may be haunting my nightmares no matter how this turns out.

As I sat watching, I began to worry about Belle and Amy. I couldn't help wondering what had happened and who was hurt. I couldn't bring myself to admit that it had to be Belle. Only a stray shot would have hit the spotter, and at that distance, there weren't likely to be any stray shots.

Suddenly, something moved to my left, but that couldn't be the bandit. He was coming up from the right. The motion was so quick I couldn't make out who it was, if it even was a who. A Who? What am I, Horton? Not now, brain! Maybe a deer or turkey? Maybe Ramirez? No, he said he would set up on the other side.

I looked away and then looked back, taking the area one section at a time. I tried to keep aware of my peripheral vision for movement while I scanned each block for details that didn't belong. I got to the Lady and stopped. At the rear, that shadow was wrong. I don't know how many times I've sat staring at that beast back home, and that shadow was just-- wrong.

I sighted in on the shadow and began to slow my breathing and count backward. With each count, I slowed my breathing more and relaxed while tightening my finger on the trigger. The shadow twitched, and I squeezed the trigger.

Now this is a bad time to realize that you, in fact, did not completely identify your target. Not to mention that you just told yourself that the bandit you're after should not be there. The only reason I didn't have a coronary at this realization was the roar from the black bear I had just shot in the shoulder. I lay there immobile somewhere between; holy shit I just fucked up and shot a damn bear while we're trying to evade & kill a PLAGF special forces operative AND oh, thank God, that's not one of our people.

Somewhere within this momentary mind-funk paralysis, came the realization that someone was standing behind me. Well, that is not good. I started to roll to my left when my spine felt like someone drove a knife through it and down into my kidney. Before I could process that this ball of awful in my back was the soldier's knee, I felt the knife pressing against my throat. My brain immediately went to, well your dumb ass isn't dead yet, so that's good, but... that's probably gonna happen real soon, so maybe not that good.

"Where is the other one?" the soldier spoke softly with a Boston accent. No shit, an honest to God Boston accent. That fact alone seemed to overwhelm my brain, and I just sat there completely dumbfounded. Obviously, he did not appreciate my lack of response, as the knee briefly left my back, only to slam back down, breaking at least one rib. I screamed in pain. That didn't seem to be the answer he wanted either, as I suddenly found a hand clasped tightly over my mouth. I nearly passed out trying to suck air through the tiny bit of my nose that wasn't blocked by a finger that smelled like curry and a three-day-old cat that's been left in the sun too long.

"I'm going to remove my hand, and you are going to tell me where he is. Nod if you understand."

I nodded. Well, I tried to nod. That's actually really difficult when someone has your head wrenched back with their nasty hand clamped over your mouth. He moved his hand and said, "Well?"

Now, as you may have noticed, my brain has a mind of its own and doesn't always follow the direction I point it. My reply?

"Well, now that's a deep subject."

He grunted, this high-speed professional operator actually grunted, in frustration at my tom fuckery, I guess it had been a rough day for him too. I felt his knee lift from my back and braced for what I knew was going to be excruciating pain. I held my breath waiting for the next blow.

It didn't come. The knife dropped to the ground by my cheek as all his weight lifted away. I managed to roll over onto my left side and looked up to see a shadowed face looming above me. My attacker seemed to hang suspended a foot off the ground. The wraith holding him had one hand clasped over his chin and mouth while the other seemed to be holding something that was sticking out of the back of his neck.

I heard a noise behind me and turned to see Ramirez standing on the other side of the clearing gaping at me, or what was above me. His mouth hung open as he stared in obvious shock. For my part, my brain refused to acknowledge the fact that it was not Ramirez holding my attacker. I sat there in dumbfounded shock and wonder, contemplating how the hell he could be in two places at once. I simply couldn't make it work.

The foot near my head twitched, jerking my attention back towards the tableau of wraith and villain. My attacker seemed to sigh as his body finally relaxed. I watched mesmerized as the wraith slid the combat knife from his skull while practically throwing his body to the side. My gaze locked onto the blood dripping from the knife, and I watched each drop slither down the blade and jump to the ground.

I have no idea how long it took before I heard my name. The sound was familiar, but it just didn't make sense. The wraith seemed to have suddenly appeared over me, and when I saw it, I tried to scramble backwards.

It was at this point that I remembered each and every blow I had taken from that bastard lying barely five feet away. I screamed in a combination of fear and agony as I tried to get away. I felt unseen hands grab me from behind, and I screamed even louder.

This time, the name registered. I saw Ramirez leaning down over my head.

"JC, I need you to stop moving! You're safe now! Please JC! You've got to hold still before you make it worse." Ramirez's tone seemed to almost transition from command to plea as he spoke.

"James?" I heard my mother ask. My confusion deepened at that, and my head whipped around looking for her. What the absolute fuck was going on? Where did that come from?

"James?" her voice came again as the wraith grabbed my hand. I screamed again, pushing back into Ramirez.

"EASY JC! It's O.K. No one is going to hurt you anymore." Ramirez said.

I heard a short, choked sob and looked back at the wraith. That had come from the wraith. The sob. What the... "Mom?" I croaked.

"Yes, James. It's me, baby. I'm not going to hurt you." The wraith replied.

As my body relaxed I felt one last shooting pain through my back and passed out.

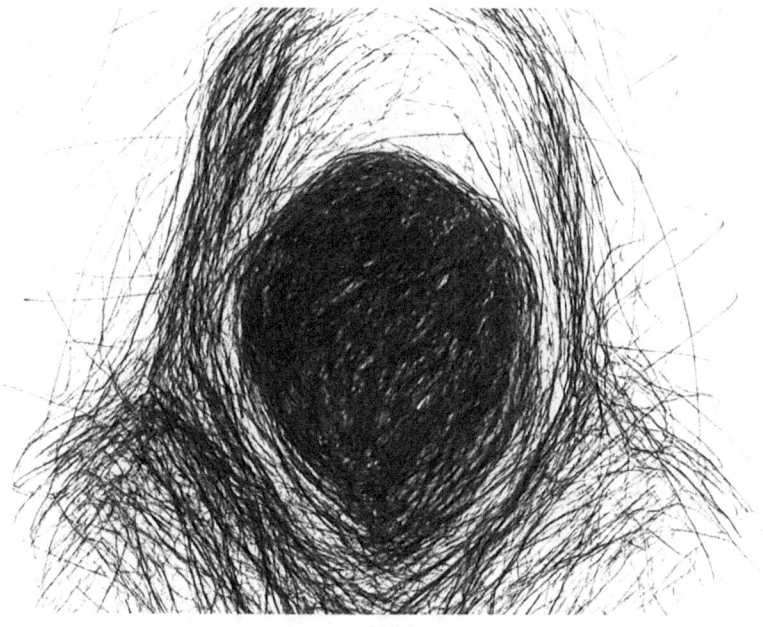

Chapter 30 – Recovery

When I woke up, I was lying in bed. At least, I was pretty sure it was a bed since it was soft and I was staring up at a white ceiling. It had to be the ceiling of a house or building because our trailer had that thick plastic paneling for a ceiling, and this was shiplap. You know, that old farmhouse-style stuff. Well, that was good, my memory seemed to be working, so no serious head injuries. Bonus!

At that point, it occurred to me I couldn't move. Even my head seemed to feel restrained. Restrained? Well, okay, that's not quite the same as can't move, then. I tried to speak, and heard a sort of mumbled grunt. It seemed to work, though, as I suddenly saw a haggard-looking Ramirez lean over me.

"Good. You're awake. Before we remove any restraints, I need to run a few tests. I'm going to hold your hand, don't worry we're not dating now, either; I need you to squeeze my fingers."

The joke was a little strained, but I appreciated the attempt. I felt him put his hand in my right hand and squeezed his fingers.

"Good!" he said, and I thought I heard relief in there. Honestly, that worried me more than I care to admit.

"Now the left. Good. Now I want you to wiggle your toes. First your right, then your left. Very good!" I definitely heard relief that time. What the hell happened to me?

"JC, I'm going to remove your neck brace and I want you

to slowly, so very slowly, move your head. You will be sore, and that's okay. If you feel any sharp pain or numbness, I want you to stop immediately. Squeeze my fingers if you understand." I squeezed. I'm not sure how long I'd been out, but when he removed that neck brace, I nearly gagged. That thing had some serious funk going on.

"Yeah, I know. We don't have air conditioning and keeping you two clean has been a job in itself." Ramirez said when he saw my reaction. "OK, go ahead." Sore was an understatement, and I had very limited movement. Everything felt tight as a bowstring. The lack of sharp pain sent relief flooding through me. It must have shown, because I heard a sigh from Ramirez.

Ramirez confirmed I was in a house. It had to be the farmhouse. There was a sheet hanging down the length of the room that looked like someone hung it as a temporary measure to block my view. Ramirez couldn't help but notice me staring at the sheet and said, "Don't worry about that for now. I'll explain everything. Right now I need you to help me check your progress. I don't exactly have an x-ray or MRI that we can use"

I nodded, ooh that was cool, and looked back at him. I saw Ramirez smile for the first time as he watched me. Then he leaned down toward my chest.

"I'm going to release the rest of your restraints. Just like your neck, you will need to move your arms and legs slowly and stop if you feel any sharp pain. You have several broken ribs and very little of your body is bruise-free. I don't recommend trying to move anything other than your limbs or head. You are absolutely forbidden to try to get up from this bed or even sit up. If you try, I will restrain you again. Understand?"

I merely nodded as my throat still felt raw. As the restraints fell away I began to move my arms and felt like I was in a pool trying to lift a 50-pound bag of feed with each hand. Everything was so heavy and my movements were so slow. Just as I was about to try to gesture for a glass, Ramirez turned back to me with a small glass of water and a straw. "Take it slow JC," he said.

I immediately took a long slow sip and sighed with relief as the water soaked into my desiccated throat. "Thanks," I managed to croak.

"You're welcome." Ramirez broke into a big smile as he replied. "I'm going to let your Mom in for a few minutes, but then I want you to take a nap. Understood?" I nodded, exhausted by the effort of drinking a few ounces of water.

Mom seemed almost tentative as she came in, as though she didn't want to startle me. I smiled, delighted to see her, and watched her expression change to mirror my own. "After what happened… I just wasn't sure." She said quietly as she leaned down to kiss my cheek. I wanted to hug her, but couldn't seem to muster the strength to manage it. As she leaned back, I saw tears slowly sliding down her cheek. In true Mom fashion, she didn't bother wiping them away, just sat and smiled. "I'm so proud of you, James. I couldn't have asked for anything more from you or July, who is fine by the way."

"Belle?" I asked.

"Other side of the sheet. She's doing better, but she, like you, needs her rest." She replied with a smile that seemed a little…off. I didn't comment further, but the evasive answer bothered me. Luckily, I was too tired to dwell on it and fell back asleep before Mom even left the room.

It was dark when I woke and Belle's steady breathing in the bed next to mine put me right back to sleep. Steady breathing was good, right? I couldn't quite remember. I was so tired.

So, here's what they would tell me about Belle the next day when I refused to accept vague assurances that she was fine. The Chinese officer shot Belle in the head. He must have either shot at the muzzle flash or somehow seen the scope because he missed. Well, kinda. Amy thought Belle had turned to ask her something just before the shot. The turn must have moved her to the side and saved her life. The bullet actually creased her skull, which Ramirez said is an awfully good thing. Without a hospital for surgery, the pressure in her head could have caused brain damage. The small crease actually allowed fluid to escape. He was unable to find any bone fragments and could only hope that the blood and spinal fluids flushed out any remaining fragments. With luck and some divine providence, those two actions will hopefully have prevented any permanent brain damage. That thought terrified me. I can't stand the thought of a Belle who just isn't Belle anymore. Now we began our wait for her to heal while Ramirez kept her loaded up on antibiotics (assuming we didn't run out).

It was a week before Ramirez would let me out of bed. I was so tired of his reflex tests and physical therapy, I could scream. Have I mentioned that Ramirez is a seriously scary badass when he wants to be? Which was pretty much any time I started to protest too much. Once, he even went so far as slamming a combat knife into the wall by my head when I wouldn't stop asking about Belle. I think I peed a little.

Walking suuuucked. Everything hurt. You would think over a week in bed would have healed most of the ass beating I took. Apparently, I had broken ribs and most likely a bruised spine, I didn't even think that was possible. Those 2 things do not just suddenly get better after a week. Trust me on this. It was great to be able to use the bathroom all by myself again, but I still spent most of my time in bed next to Belle. Because of that, I was there when she woke up. OK, so maybe I was staring a bit and actually watched her eyes flutter open. And maybe I was actually sitting on her bed again, despite all Ramirez's threats to bar me from the room. And yes, damn it, I was holding her hand! Are you happy?

Belle just smiled and mumbled something about Nightingale. I'll take it. Anything close to a smart-ass comment seemed like my Belle was still in there! Our Belle, I meant our Belle, was still in there.

The story continues…

A Note From The Author

Leaving my independence behind: I've partnered with Sthenotype. In a different approach from the norm, Sthenotype is working with me to relaunch my previously published works. Look for special editions with new covers and a lot of extras to replace the current versions, starting here with 2078 - The Fall.

Don't worry if you've read them already, the stories will stay the same (although the editing will improve).

Thanks for taking the time to check out my books.

.

About The Author

J Spencer is a wildland firefighter, forest manager, farm hand, and volunteer firefighter with a writing habit. As a young reader, J was a fan of Louis L'Amour and John McDonald novels, but his dreams of writing always seemed far from his reach. That changed with inspiration from Craig Alanson, which led to the creation of this novel.

The journey to becoming an author opened a doorway to another world. A world that he had only scratched the surface of as an avid reader.

"My goal is to write fun books that are easy to read and escape the headaches of daily life. In other words, I'm trying to write the same type of books I enjoy reading. I hope you enjoy reading my books as much as I enjoy writing them! All I really want is to tell a good story.

Thank you for reading my story!" J. Spencer